Redemption

an *AROTAS* novel

ALSO BY AMY MILES

The Arotas Trilogy
Forbidden
Reckoning

The Rising Trilogy
Defiance Rising

Amy Miles

Redemption

an AROTAS novel

For my mom.

Prologue

A dark shadow of a man perches high above the streets of London, his gaze focused intently on the front doors of the Fortune Theatre. The deserted path below is lit with a golden glow, the light spilling out from the closed glass doors. A marquee above the theatre's awning announces another nightly performance of *A Woman in Black* is under way.

He shifts not out of discomfort or necessity but out of sheer eagerness.

This is the first attack. The first of many to come.

His fingers curl around the rooftop ledge as he leans forward, checking once more to make sure the bodies have been positioned perfectly. A single drop of saliva drips from the corner of his mouth, evidence of his rising excitement.

The victim's eyes stare up at him, glazed and vacant. The flesh of their throats has been sliced open, carved from ear to ear. Not a single drop of blood will be found along the wounds or the pavement below. He made sure of that.

Clean cuts, he smiles, stroking the sharpened blade at his side.

The three college-aged girls below never saw their attacker. He had kept to the shadows, stalking them as they rushed to meet up with a group of friends. Only the blonde sensed his presence. She had cast several cautious glances back over her shoulder, her brown eyes widening with alarm when she saw him swoop down upon her. Her gurgled screams were masked by the honking of taxis as they raced down the streets. The other two didn't have a chance to put up a fight.

A slow grin stretches across his face as he imagines the frustration of the waiting party. How long did they linger before they took their seats? Were angry texts later followed by frantic pleas to respond?

He had watched a group of girls emerge during intermission, searching both sides of the street. They seemed agitated to be sure but not nearly enough. That is why he chose this location for the big reveal. Soon the theatre doors will open and the real show will begin.

The victims' arms are spread wide, hands clutching hands as they stretch across the narrow paved street. Long blonde hair is knotted into ginger curls and then into shiny brunette strands, adjoining the three girls in death.

Their abdomens have been torn open, as if mauled by a bear right in the heart of London. He flexes his fingers, noting the scent of blood that still clings to his claws. This final wound had been an afterthought, a nice touch for the front page of the Sun newspaper tomorrow morning.

He looks down Russell Street, toward the hustle and bustle of Covent Garden. At this time of night, it is usually packed with shoppers, tourists and street performers. The screams should draw a nice crowd.

Looking back down at the girls, he smiles at his handiwork. Their skin is abnormally pale, their veins absent from sight. Investigators will not find a single drop of blood in their bodies, nor fingerprints to tie anyone to the crime. The only clue will be the bite marks along the girls' forearms and wrists.

The creak of opening doors draws his attention. He crouches low, eager for the show to begin.

The first to emerge is an older couple, the woman draped in furs and jewels. Her salt and pepper hair is elegantly coifed at the back of her head. She is on the arm of a man who wears a fitted suit, his shoes shined and his steps careful. Neither of them peers into the darkness of the street as they pass.

The murderer frowns, annoyed that his masterpiece has gone unnoticed under the veil of night. The streetlamp flickered and died nearly an hour before, leaving much of the road cast in shadow, but youthful eyes will easily be able to see the hand that stretches toward the gutter.

A pair of younger couples emerge next, the women clutching their chests as they discuss the final scene of the play. The tall man on the left notices the lifeless hand first, his muddy brown eyes widening in shock behind gold-rimmed glasses.

He yanks his wife back, wrapping his arm around her shoulders to draw her away. Her screams beckon a flood of people from within the theatre. Mouths gape wide as pallid faces stare in horror at the macabre scene before them.

The shadowy monster rubs his hands together, grinning. He rises up slightly as the group of girls he has been waiting for emerge. They rise onto their toes, craning to see over the crowd. As murmurs float through the cluster of theatregoers, one girl's shriek pierces the night.

She struggles through the crowd, her petite hands trembling as she tries to push people aside. Her hands cover her lips as she stares down at the beautiful brunette sprawled at her feet. Their likeness is uncanny.

Her friends cluster around, trying to console her, as she doubles over and yanks on her hair. Her screams turn to mournful wails as she sinks to the ground, arms outstretched toward her sister.

The concealed man closes his eyes, relishing the sounds of pounding footsteps drawing near. The scent of blood lingers in his nostrils. He breathes deep, savoring the heady scent of death. He licks his lips, capturing a lingering droplet of blood from the corner of his mouth as people speak frantically into mobile phones, some calling for help, others dialing family and friends to give a first-hand account of the gruesome scene.

A cry of protest rises as camera flashes light up the crime scene. Employees of the Fortune Theatre push their way through the crowd, doing their best to keep people back off the street.

The killer rises fluidly from his crouched position. He tilts his head, listening to the squealing tires and blaring sirens that converge on his location. The crowds below swells, creating a writhing circle around the three fallen girls.

Opening his eyes, Lucien Enescue takes a slow, deep breath. His eagerness has blended into long awaited satisfaction. Too long has he lived in secret, forced to hide from the humans…but no longer.

Confusion over the victim's markings will lead to doubt, and hopefully a niggling fear will begin to bloom in the pits of the investigator's stomachs. They will begin to question everything they think they know about this world. And maybe, just maybe, they will allow themselves to consider the impossible: that monsters really do exist.

Tonight, they will begin to fear the unknown, that which lurks in the shadows. Tonight, the existence of immortals becomes a reality.

<u>One</u>

Smoke hovers over the courtyard below, the moans of the dying rising from its depths. The heavy stench of death clings to the nighttime air. Nicolae Dalma wipes sweat from his brow, groaning at the effort that it takes to lift his arm. His vivid green eyes take in the scene below him. He is exhausted, more so than he has ever been before.

Victory is theirs. Bran castle has been overthrown.

He looks out over the broken bodies and rubble strewn about the castle grounds with mixed emotions. From atop the stone staircase landing, he ponders how this sweet triumph has come at a high price. Countless immortals have fallen, and although he is grateful for their exit from the world, he knows this night will anger those who remain.

This battle may be over, but the war rages on.

His own men, loyal hunters, have fallen as well. Their bodies will be buried in the earth with a monument erected in their memory, but that will not be enough recognition for the service they gave here.

People said it was impossible to take down the mighty Vladimir Enescue. His reign of tyranny lasted through many generations, but tonight all of that has come to an end. Roseline went after him and, judging by the look in her eye, Vladimir won't live to see another sunrise.

Nicolae looks toward the right, to the far end of the courtyard, and dips his head in gratitude to Fane Dalca. The immortal's long blond hair falls over his shoulders in sweaty locks. Without his help, this victory would never have come. Although they only spent a couple of weeks together while in London, Nicolae has grown to deeply respect Fane and is proud to have fought side by side with him.

His thoughts turn back to Sadie, locked away in one of the castle towers. He prays that she has remained undiscovered, left to rest. His jaw clenches in anger and the muscles of his forearm grow rigid as he forms a fist at his side. Vladimir hurt Sadie, tortured her. Nicolae would like nothing more than to drive an arrow straight through that monster's heart, but he would not take that right away from Roseline.

As he gazes up at the tower, he sees movement along the rooftop. "Roseline," he calls out as Malachi drags her across the open-air balcony. Malachi's grip is fierce on her arm, his eyes wide with terror. Nicolae starts to call again but his mouth falls slack at the sight of the being escaping the shattered window behind them.

The black man is tall, a giant compared to Nicolae's second in command, Grigori. His dark skin is bare to his waist, revealing an intricate pattern of scars across his chest and arms. It is not his enormous size, or the startling scars that makes Nicolae's skin tingle with apprehension, but the two wings that rise from his back.

The feathers, seen just above his shoulders, are deep scarlet, the color of fresh blood. Powerful legs propel him to the edge of the building. The being stops and watches Malachi and Roseline fleeing, but makes no move to pursue.

"Roseline!"

Nicolae's gaze drops to the courtyard below. "Gabriel?"

Gabriel Marston has always been large, his shoulders broad and his muscles strong from hours on the football field, but his transformation into immortality has amplified his natural characteristics. His hair is longer, shaggier than before. An umber robe drapes over him, brushing against the top of his sandaled feet

Nicolae lifts his hand to wave in greeting but whirls around at the sound of Roseline's cry. Her fingers curl around the stone banister, resisting Malachi's grip on her. Nicolae frowns, unease settling heavy in his chest at the desperation on Malachi's face.

Crouching low, Nicolae leaps off the exterior staircase, his knees jarred by the force of his landing in the center of the courtyard below. Fane is already on the move, heading straight for him, his gaze focused intently on Roseline.

Gabriel reaches out his hand toward her, obviously wanting to go to Roseline, but a large hand encircles his arm, holding him back. Nicolae peers through the dispersing smoke, gaping at the being standing behind his friend. The man towers over Gabriel. His wings are the color of pure gold, identical in design to the being overhead.

The being lowers his head and speaks to Gabriel. Nicolae is sure his friend will shove him aside and fight his way toward Roseline, but he doesn't as the second being floats to the ground beside them.

Fane slides to a halt beside Nicolae, his chest rising and falling as he struggles to slow his breathing. Nicolae glances at the immortal from the corner of his eye. "Ever seen one of those things before?"

"Nope," Fane shakes his head. "I'd say they are angels though, but that's only because of the wings."

"Angels really exist?"

Fane shoots him a scathing glance. "I exist. Can we really question their existence too?"

"Good point."

"Where did Gabriel come from? And what the heck is Malachi trying to pull?"

"I don't know," Nicolae mutters, running his hands through his sweaty hair. His black uniform clings tightly to his skin, making him uncomfortable. His crossbow hangs heavily at his side. "I think it's time we find out."

Nodding in agreement, Fane moves forward but stops mid-step as Gabriel turns to look at them. His pained gaze makes Nicolae's mouth go dry. "Take care of her for me," he calls.

Nicolae shares an incredulous look with Fane as Gabriel wraps his arm around the golden being's neck and turns his face away as they lift into the air. The scarred angel rises behind Gabriel, flanking him. "Where is he going?" Fane asks, pointing toward Gabriel.

The angels soar into the sky and are soon lost to the night. When Nicolae's gaze shifts to the balcony above his frown deepens. "Malachi and Roseline are gone."

Fane frowns. "Maybe we should go check on—"

Nicolae's stomach clenches as a mournful howl echoes through the halls of the castle, resounding off the high ceilings and bursting from its corridors. He blinks and nearly misses Fane's desperate dash for the stairs. His friend moves so quickly, Nicolae can hardly see his feet touch the ground.

"Was that Roseline?" Nicolae shouts.

Fane doesn't respond as he leaps from one landing to the next, gracefully springing up to grasp the awning. Nicolae's feet pound against the steps, taking them two at a time. His stomach twists as he reaches the open balcony and races toward the doorway that leads to the great hall.

He leaps over downed hunters and fallen immortals. His footing is precarious on the blood slickened stone and his pace is much slower than Fane's, but he pushes himself to run faster.

Nicolae's chest feels tight as he rounds the second floor staircase and races toward the next landing, the one that leads to the upper room.

Fane leaps through a shattered window and lands just in front of Nicolae. He hardly pauses before bursting forward, taking the stairs three at a time.

Please keep her safe, Nicolae silently begs, unsure of who or what he is pleading with. It doesn't matter. As he runs, all he can focus on is getting to Roseline.

"Nicolae!"

His stride falters at the sound of William's desperate cry. His heart begins to pound in his chest; his breath is all he can hear as Fane disappears from sight at the top of the staircase. Nicolae's stomach clenches as he realizes that he's heading toward Roseline's room, toward Sadie.

"Get in here!" Fane shouts, poking his head back into the hall just as Nicolae breaches the top step.

His legs feel jerky as he moves toward the doorway of Roseline's room. The hair lifts along the nape of his neck as he crosses the threshold to see William rocking beyond the bed.

Nicolae's hands feel clammy as he catches sight of a growing pool of blood just beyond William. Fane stands rigidly to the side, unable to meet Nicolae's gaze.

The sound of his footsteps echoes in his ears as he moves around William and sinks to his knees. He blinks rapidly, struggling to accept the sight before him.

Sadie lies across the floor, her head propped into William's lap at an awkward angle. Her stomach is splayed open revealing muscle tissue, organs and a glimpse of her spinal cord. "Oh, god," he cries, his hands fluttering over his mouth. He swallows rapidly, trying to suppress the bile rising in his throat.

"Help her," Nicolae croaks, turning to look at Fane. "Please!"

"I can't." Fane rubs his hands over his face, shaking his head. "It's too late. She's lost too much blood."

"There has to be a way," Nicolae cries, the pitch of his voice rising. His eyes bulge as he contemplates the alternative. He can't accept it, let alone begin to process the scene before him.

Fane dips low, his gaze direct as he tries to reason with Nicolae. "Most of her stomach is on the floor and the other half has been severed beyond repair. It's not humanly possible."

Nicolae shakes his head, rocking rapidly as he wails. He can't breathe, can't think beyond the acute pain. His entire body trembles as his cry fades out and sobs take their place.

William stares blankly down at his sister, his gaze unfocused. Fane places his hand on Nicolae's shoulder, squeezing it. "You need to say goodbye."

A gargled moan rises from Nicolae's throat as he stares at Fane. How can he say goodbye when he's hardly had a chance to fall in love with her? Has he even told her yet? Said the actual words? Will she die never knowing that she has captured his every waking thought since the first time she rejected him in Chicago?

"No," he croaks, reaching out to take Sadie's hand in his, feeling her rough leather bracelet rub against his arm. Her skin is cool to the touch and unnaturally waxy. He swallows hard, pushing past the fear rising within to stare hard at Fane. "How long?"

Fane's shoulders rise and fall with uncertainty. "A minute. Maybe less. Her heart is barely beating."

"No, no, no," he mutters, wishing more than anything that he could run and hide, only to later crawl out from his hole and find Sadie laughing and joking around with William again. "She deserves better than this."

"I am sorry," Fane says softly. He sinks back onto his heels, giving Nicolae some space.

Anger rips through Nicolae's gut, deep and visceral. It winds through his stomach and into his chest, clenching so tightly he fears he will lose the ability to take another breath.

Slowly, his fractured thoughts begin to clear as he looks at Fane. "Turn her."

Fane's eyes bulge in disbelief. "You can't be serious. Think about what you're asking, Nicolae."

"I am." The grief is too raw, sealing out logic and years of training. None of that matters right now. He closes his eyes and clings to Sadie's lifeless hand, knowing that no matter the cost, he will not let her die like an animal, gutted and left for dead. "Save her."

Fane grips his shoulders, forcing Nicolae to release his grasp on Sadie's hand. "I know it hurts and that you would do anything to save her, but…"

"No," Nicolae holds up his free hand, his voice threatening to give out on him again. "I know what I'm asking for."

William glances between them, his rocking slowing to a halt. "Are you saying there's a chance she can live?"

"Maybe." Fane's expression is troubled as he turns to William.

Nicolae's gaze trails down to the floor, noticing how Sadie's blood has seeped into the cracks of the aged hardwood floor as Fane responds. "It doesn't always work. She has to possess the right bloodline. I'm not even sure she would be strong enough to survive the transformation. She's lost too much blood."

Fane waits for Nicolae to look up from Sadie and acknowledge him. "Sadie might not survive."

"She's dead either way," Nicolae replies, his voice choked with tears.

"But if you could save her, she'd become like you? An immortal?" William gently brushes aside wisps of bloodstained hair from his sister's face.

"Yes," Fane nods stiffly. He looks to Nicolae. "If I do this, and I'm not saying I'm going to, but if it works, I can't guarantee that she will remain pure. She might not be the girl you knew."

Nicolae's eyes darken as his expression grows rigid with determination. "Just do it."

Two

Nicolae paces at Sadie's bedside, his frustration mounting with each tick of the grandfather clock that stands like a sentinel against the wall opposite Roseline's bed. His hairline is damp with sweat, his bare skin still caked with dried blood. His disheveled uniform began to stink a day ago, but he has hardly noticed. He absentmindedly chews on a cracked fingernail only to grimace at the taste of blood and dirt in his mouth. "Why isn't it working?"

"Magic cannot be rushed." Fane blots Sadie's cheeks with a damp cloth, cooling her feverish skin. Although William has grumbled several times about the chill in the air, Fane refused to stoke the fire and risk Sadie's teetering health for William's comfort. Her breathing has slowed so much that he doubts Nicolae can sense its presence. Her chest lies eerily still.

"You said a few hours, a day at the most. It has been nearly two days, Fane. Something should have happened by now."

"She's still alive," Fane reminds him, with forced restraint. "Be thankful."

"You call this alive?" Nicolae stabs a finger at Sadie's still form. The sheets and mattress bear rusty streaks of dried blood, a reminder of just how long Sadie has remained in this catatonic state.

Fane sighs and rises from his position on the floor. His clothes are rumpled, stained from hours spent kneeling at Sadie's bedside. He groans as he reaches toward the ceiling, his neck popping and cracking audibly as he stretches. Nicolae notices that Fane's long hair, previously tied back by a leather thong, has fallen haphazardly about his shoulders, further evidence of the stress burdening the immortal.

He tosses his cloth back into a bowl of pink colored water on the side table as he approaches. "I warned you this might not work. It would appear that her body is fighting the changes. I can't predict what will happen to her, but I do know what will happen to *you* if you keep refusing to eat or sleep. You are human, Nicolae. You can't keep going like this."

"I'm fine." Nicolae's shoulder bumps against Fane as he brushes past, refusing to leave Sadie's side. He caught sight of himself in the mirror and knows how gaunt his cheeks have become, how purple the skin is under his eyes, but it doesn't matter. "I won't leave her. Not again."

"Sadie is strong-willed. If anyone can pull through, it'll be her." Fane crosses the creaky wood floor and dumps the bowl of water out of the window. It splatters against the stone courtyard below. "If I were a betting man, I'd say Sadie will wake before morning."

When Nicolae shivers at the frosty breeze that slips through the window, Fane locks the glass panes, sealing out the blustery night. When he turns back, he finds Nicolae with his head hanging dejectedly. "This isn't your fault, you know? If you'd been here, you might have shared the same fate."

Nicolae's jaw clenches as he vigorously shakes his head. "It was my job to protect her. She needed me and I wasn't there for her."

"I feel the same way about Roseline. For so many years, I've felt like she was my responsibility. Not that she would have ever let me take care of her; she's independent for that." Fane sighs as he leans back against the wall, closing his eyes. "We should have known there was something wrong with Malachi."

"We did." Nicolae frowns. "We knew, but Roseline was too stubborn to listen."

Fane's lips twist into a pained smile. He opens his eyes and stares at the exposed wooden beams that run the length of the ceiling. "She has always been like that. From the first day I met her."

Nicolae sinks down onto the bed beside Sadie, careful not to disturb her. He can't stand to be apart from her, not when death seems to be hanging on her doorstep. He likes to think that, even in this coma-like state, she can hear his voice, sense his presence and maybe it will be enough for her to fight to survive.

When Nicolae clears away the strands of stray hair from her forehead, he tries not to notice the blood that still clings to her hair or the pallor of her skin. "What was Roseline like? In the beginning, I mean."

For a moment, he thinks Fane might ignore his question, but instead Fane moves toward an oversized armchair near the window. The leather creaks as he sinks into it and his face is cast in shadow.

"She was sweet, innocent." A wry smile crosses the immortal's lips. "Her laugh was different then, more like the giggle of a girl with a childhood crush, but there was a buried pain within her as well. Seeing your entire family slaughtered before your eyes changes a person."

Nicolae sinks down next to Sadie, resting his head atop hers.

"Roseline always feared the monster within her, always waiting for the savage desires to overtake her. She was too strong for that, too determined to prove Vladimir wrong." Fane's voice turns harsh as he crosses his arms over his chest, as if trying to repress years of anger.

"I wanted to kill him each time he touched her. I used to dream about it, plan it, but I couldn't risk messing it up. I knew if I did, Vladimir or Lucien would make her suffer for my mistake." He falls silent for a moment, his brow furrowed. "She always tried to hide her wounds from me. I'm not sure if it was her pride or for my own benefit, but I always knew."

Pursing his lips at the raw pain in Fane's tone, Nicolae wishes he'd never asked.

Fane leans his head back against the chair and stares up at the ceiling. "She saved me all those years ago. I was like her in many ways, horrified by what I'd become, desperate to end it all. I was contemplating suicide the day I met her."

"Is that even possible?"

Fane rolls his head to look at Nicolae. "Anything is possible, but would you really want to light yourself on fire?"

"Good point." Nicolae watches the emotions playing across Fane's face. It is strange to see this side of the man he grew up hating. Nicolae had never stopped to consider that the evil Fane lived with would haunt the immortal just as much his own parents death did with him.

His gaze drops to Sadie's still face. "Do you think she will be like Vladimir? If she survives?"

Fane shakes his head. "No, but she will struggle. We all do. Blood calls strongly to us, but we don't have to let it control us. Roseline is the strongest person I know. I can't think of anyone better to show Sadie the right way to live."

"But she's not here," Nicolae protests. He stops and blinks, grimacing as he looks up to meet Fane's hollow gaze. "I'm sorry. I shouldn't have said—"

"No." Fane rises from his chair. "It's the truth. Sadie needs Roseline."

Nicolae watches his friend move toward the door. Fane opens the door, pausing with his back turned toward the room. "Once Sadie is on her feet, we will need to leave. It's not safe here anymore."

"And Roseline?"

Fane shifts so that Nicolae can see his grim profile over his shoulder. "She's a fighter. I know she will last long enough for us to find her again. She has to."

Strong winds tousle Gabriel's hair, biting at his cheeks. Small ice crystals cling to his blond strands, clacking together as he wills the numbness to return. He is adjusting to the cold, just as Elias said he would. Staring out over the thick Siberian forest before him, he can't bring himself to feel anything more than guilt mingled with a heavy dose of remorse.

Why did he leave Roseline behind?

He bows his head, ignoring the whistling winds that whip through the tall mountain pines, as he clamps his eyes shut. He should have gone to her, said something, tried to explain…but he didn't.

Even now, he can't help but wonder if he made the right choice. Elias's argument was annoyingly sound back in the courtyard of Bran castle: leave now and save Roseline later. Of course he had to choose this, but if that's true, why does it feel like he has abandoned her?

Now he is the one who has been abandoned. Elias dropped him off here several hours ago, when the sun was just beginning to rise over the horizon and the cloud cover was sparse. Now the clouds have begun to roll in, thick and heavy with unfallen snow. Seneh is gone too, although Gabriel can't really remember when he left.

He spent most of the afternoon moping, kicking at buried tree roots and staring blankly at the wild landscape surrounding him. Animals scurries from treetop to treetop, no doubt foraging for food.

Frustration soon melts into boredom as the hours pass. He paces back and forth, muttering to himself under the thick canopy. Dry pine needles jut up from the snow at awkward angles, attacking his calves as he sinks into the snow with each step. He can't wait to see Elias or Seneh so he can give them a piece of his mind.

It's not the abandonment that bothers him the most. It's the lack of answers, the secret looks the two angels share when they don't think he's watching. Something is going on. Something that has made both angels flustered enough to leave him here alone, in a strange land, completely unprotected.

Gabriel's shoulders tense at the sound of a footfall behind him. He drops to a crouch, peering into the woods back over his shoulder. The muffled light of the forest plays tricks with his mind as he searches for any hint of a sound or movement of color. He inhales to check for Seneh's scent, but it is not an angel creeping up on him now. It is a human.

He turns his face to the side and sniffs the air again, realizing that he can't even pick up a scent. The forest falls silent around him. His heart beats in his chest as he counts the seconds that pass. Two minutes pass without a single hint as to where the person is located.

Whoever is out there knows how to hide.

His muscles coil as he struggles to decide if he should run or turn and fight. If he runs, his dark robe will easily be seen against the snow. If he fights, he fears how far he will have to take this.

Gabriel has never had to kill before. Although he knows he is capable of it, he doesn't look forward to the time he is forced to. Hopefully today isn't that day.

He begins to grow restless as the forest falls into an eerie hush. Even the woodland animals seem to have disappeared. He knows the human must sense his presence too, otherwise they would have come out by now.

When the footfall finally lands again, he blows out a silent breath of relief, as he spies a hint of brown protruding unnaturally from the side of a tree less than ten feet behind him. With the grace of a mountain lion, Gabriel spins and leaps.

A startled cry rings through his ears as he connects with the concealed figure, knocking them back into a snowdrift. His shoulder slams into a buried tree root before he slumps to the ground. A jagged crack forms along the equator of the aged trunk and with a mighty groan, the tree plummets to the ground. Powdery snow rises in a cloud around the fallen tree.

Gabriel leaps back into a crouch as the hooded figure staggers to their feet. He braces, preparing for the unexpected.

"Для чего Вы делали это?"

"Huh?" Blinking, Gabriel slowly rises as the person draped in heavy furs lowers their hood.

He stares in awe at the beautiful blonde standing before him. Defiant but calm, she gazes back at him with large azure eyes rimmed by long lashes. Her skin is the palest he has ever seen, almost blending in with the snow all around. Gabriel glances at her pink lips, noting that they are slightly parted but still, not trembling from fear or the cold.

"Вы говорите на английском языке?"

Gabriel runs his hands though his snow dampened hair as he watches the girl. She obviously knows these woods, where to step and how to travel with hardly a sound. He is impressed with how well she snuck up on him, but this only makes him wary. If she is here it means there may be more people about.

She's just a girl, a human. It's not like she's dangerous, he tries to argue, but his trepidation remains.

"Who are you?" He asks, ignoring the uncomfortable tightness in his chest.

When she cocks her head to the side, her chin is lost in the folds of animal skins that drape over her shoulders. The wind brutally whips her hair, but she hardly notices. "You English?"

Her speech is broken, but Gabriel nods in understanding. "Who are you?"

"My name Katia. You?" She pokes a sharpened stick toward his chest.

"Gabriel." He steps closer and watches as her eyes narrow, her stance stiffening. Her lips press into a flat line, her jaw set as her fingers curl tightly around her stick. Everything about her stiff stance screams experience and skill. This girl knows how to take care of herself. "Are you lost?"

She shakes her head. A mass of blonde curls dances about her shoulders. Her cheeks have grown rosy now that her face is unprotected by the furry hood. She sizes him up, then lowers her stick and leans against it.

"There," she says. She raises a gloved hand to point toward the tree line at the bottom of the mountain. Gabriel narrows his gaze, trying to spy out a building among the trees but he can't find any trace of one.

"Are you alone?"

Katia's gaze hardens as she raises her spear, ready to attack. Her breath puffs rapidly past her lips, hanging in a fog before her. He can hear her elevated heart rate and smell the rush of adrenaline pumping through her veins. "I fighter."

"No," he holds his hands up to show he is unarmed. He smiles awkwardly, struggling to find a way to reassure her. "No fight."

She shifts in the snow, her fur lined knee-high boots sinking a couple inches. "You alone?"

Gabriel scowls and looks to the gray sky above. Releasing an impatient snort, he nods. "Apparently."

"You come. Eat." She motions for him to follow her as she abruptly turns and heads back the way she came.

Gabriel frowns at this unexpected acceptance. *Is this some sort of a trap?*

"I'm not sure that's such a good idea," he calls.

From nearly fifteen feet ahead she turns and stares pointedly at the sky. "Storm come. Very bad."

"I'll be fine." His voice is lost to the rising winds. With a knowing smile, she turns and plunges down the slope of the mountain, skiing across the snow with impressive ease. It's obvious she has done that before. Numerous times probably. Gabriel grumbles under his breath, searching the blanket of clouds overhead once more before following her lead.

The mountain is steep, no doubt treacherous during the best conditions. He marches behind Katia, amazed at her stamina and sure footing, despite the rapidly dropping temperatures. Her shoulders never hunch against the cold and her pace never slows.

The scent of pine pervades his senses as they move steadily down the mountain. Icicles dangle from the branches, clacking in the rising winds. The terrain is ever shifting as new snow is blown into deep slopes.

The trek back to the small timber cabin takes most of the afternoon and well into the evening. He spies the first signs of the homestead just as the skies begin to darken. A wooden fence marks out a plot of land, which although vacant of animals, shows evidence of hoof prints and chicken scratches in the snow.

A feed trough runs along the northern stretch of fencing, its contents frozen solid. A small barn, barely large enough to hold a tractor, sits beyond the cabin. An outhouse stands to the right of the cabin.

The homestead is quaint but uniquely self-sufficient. Katia catches his curious gaze as she stamps snow from her boots on the wooden plank porch before unlatching the roughly hewn pine door. Heat pours forth from within as she slips inside.

Gabriel closes the door behind himself, careful to make sure the latch falls into place. The winds howl beyond the wooden walls, blustery and fierce. He pauses beside a window for a second to watch the snow tornadoes that carve a path through the pasture.

"Shoes," she says sharply.

He turns to find her stoking the fire, the embers barely glowing red beneath the ash of the previous log. Glancing down, he realizes that the snow has dropped off him in clumps, melting into a puddle on her dirt floor.

"Sorry," he mutters as he slips his feet from his sandals. He looks around for a towel to clean up his mess but quickly realizes that the task would be hopeless as mud clings to the hem of his robe.

Apart from the earthen floor, everything in the cabin appears to be spotless. Metal pots and pans hang from bent nails along the far wall. A small porcelain tub sits on a rickety table, no doubt used as a washbasin. A small shelf, probably carved from the towering Siberian Pines just beyond Katia's homestead holds two metal cups, bowls and plates. A curtain, made from dingy canvas, hangs at the window.

"You've got a nice place here," he says, pulling his robe up over his head. The heat from the new flames is stifling as he removes as many layers as he can while still remaining decent. He can't imagine how unbearable it will be once it's at full burn.

Katia nods as she rises from the stone hearth, a warm blaze spilling forth. Three logs form a tepee over the metal grate. The kindling catches the lower portions of bark. She bends and shakes out of her coat, shrinking nearly half in size as she emerges from the bulky firs. She bustles about the kitchen, clanging pots together.

"Sit," she points toward the small seating area with a spoon as she carries a small pot over to the fire and places it on to heat.

Gabriel follows her direction to a low wooden chair, covered in ratty quilts. A faint musty scent rises from the fabric as he gingerly sinks down, wary of its creaky design. The chair is far from comfortable but judging by the bench across from him, she has offered him the best seat in the place.

Katia moves back to the pot. The contents slosh up the sides as she plops a few root vegetables into the thick soup. Gabriel scrunches up his nose at the hint of decay that greets him when he takes a breath.

Not wanting to appear rude, he looks to his right, glimpsing a small bed behind a draped partition. The curtain is a patchwork of old cloth, more holey than whole. The threadbare quilt that covers the straw bed hardly looks thick enough to keep a person warm through the long winter months.

In a single glance, he takes in the entire cabin. Bedroom sweeps into living room, which flows straight into the kitchen. It would only take him thirty steps to reach from one side to the next.

Craning his head back, Gabriel realizes two lines of rope are strung across the cabin, just below the ceiling. Thermal underwear and other unmentionables drape down, drying in the heat of the fire. He looks away, hoping she didn't notice his gaze.

"You far from home." He can tell it's not a question from the knowing glint in her eye. She stirs the contents of her pot a couple more times before dipping her spoon into the lumpy soup, scooping out a bowlful.

She offers him the bowl, her gaze expectant. Steam rises from the thick broth. He stares at the small potatoes, not quite coated enough to hide the wrinkly black skin. His stomach churns and he holds his breath. He offers Katia a smile, shaking his head as he moves to set the bowl on a side table, realizing too late that there is none.

She smirks down at him, shifting her weight onto her right side as she crosses her arms over her chest. "No like?"

He grimaces, trying to sign a full stomach. "Not hungry."

"Lie." She laughs and grabs the bowl from his hand. She moves over to the bench and sinks back against the wooden frame. Crossing her legs in her lap, she digs into the soup with her fingers, plucking out a bit of the fatty mystery meat. Juice runs down her chin and she swipes it away with her sleeve.

Gabriel rubs the back of his neck and averts his gaze, uncomfortable with the slurping noises she is making. As he looks around the sparse kitchen, he notices that Katia has two of every bowl, cup and plate. "You live here alone?"

"Seneh."

"Excuse me?" His back stiffens as he turns to look at her, shocked that she would know the name of his guardian angel. The gruff, scarred angel doesn't seem the type to mingle with humans much.

"Seneh live here."

Gabriel rises swiftly to his feet and begins pacing. "I don't understand. Is he here now?"

"No."

He glances toward the window, catching tiny glimpses of moonlight through the shifting clouds. The snow has let up slightly, but a great wall of cloud is approaching. Katia was right. This storm is about to get worse. It looks like he's on his own tonight.

He turns back. "Where did he go?"

Her shoulders rise and fall with an indifferent shrug. She slops a bit of stale bread into the dredges of her bowl and pops it into her mouth. "He come and go."

Gabriel grinds his teeth, annoyed at her cryptic answers. Isn't Seneh supposed to be protecting him? And what about Elias? He has vanished again, with zero explanation. Shouldn't Elias be preparing him for his next task?

"Sleep tonight. Back tomorrow." She rises, sets her bowl on a small wooden counter and sinks back down onto the creaky bench.

She watches him closely, eyes wide with unspoken curiosity. He struggles to swallow back his anger. This isn't her fault. "I'm not tired."

"Miss girl." She stares at him, unblinking.

"How did you know?"

She smiles, ignoring his question. "Talk now."

Katia motions for him to return to his seat, so Gabriel relents and moves away from the window. He shuffles his feet, tugging on his ear as he delays speaking.

He doesn't want to talk about Roseline, especially not to a complete stranger. His guilt is still too fresh.

"What's there to tell? She needed me and I left her. End of story."

"She know."

"Knows what?" He can hear the uncertainty in his own voice. *Who is this girl? How does she know so much about him?*

"You love. She know." Her gaze is unflinchingly direct.

Gabriel blows out a breath and leans back into the chair. The pillow behind his head is surprisingly soft and inviting. Even the heat from the flames has begun to die down a bit.

As he stares into the dancing flames, he realizes just how weary he feels. "I sure hope so."

Three

Roseline's arms and shoulders are on fire. It's been hours since she lost feeling in her toes, and her hands have gone numb now as well. Her energy is waning quickly, but she eases her head to one side, gently stretching her aching neck.

She has no idea how long she has been hanging from this wall. Her wrists are manacled in old chains, reaching high above her head. Her ankles are similarly bound, turning her into a human X against this cold, roughly hewn stone wall.

When she first came to, she was dazed and dizzy. As her senses returned to her, she realized the true nature of her captivity. The material that hangs over her body is scratchy against her skin. Holes have been cut for her arms and neck, the edging beginning to fray as she struggles against her chains.

A shiny, black gossamer material was clinging to the metal, binding her. She was confused, but a few tugs on the chains immediately gave her an answer: angel hair. She knew she wasn't getting out of this mess alone.

Now, hours later, she groans in agony. A brilliant white light shines down from above, blinding her from seeing the other walls. The air in the room is close and stifling.

Suddenly, Roseline senses a presence. As she peers into the shadows, she can tell something is lurking there. Its scent is dark and earthy, unlike anything she has ever come across before.

It remains just out of sight, hovering on the edge of the shadow. She thinks she can see a tail swishing back and forth along the ground. Possibly an elongated mouth, similar to an alligators. The clacking of claws against the floor is unmistakable.

"Who are you?"

The creature sways. She searches for a telltale sheen to its eyes, but none appears. There is only darkness. A shiver of apprehension trickles down her spine.

"What do you want from me?" Her chains clink as she tries to crane her neck back to follow the creature as it shifts to her far left.

She feels increasingly vulnerable. She can see nothing more than a hulking form. The creature's moves slowly, sluggish and yet there is something decidedly purposeful about them. As if she is being stalked. Roseline tenses as she realizes that is exactly what is happening. It is toying with her.

"You can't make me talk," she insists, turning her face away.

Raspy laughter rises from the shadows. "And yet you keep doing it."

"Yes, and now you are too." She grins as her head swivels back around. She stares at the creature. "I'm sure Lucien didn't send you to bore me to death."

There is the clatter of metal on metal as a silver tray is pushed out into the light. A wide array of clamps, scalpels, knives and other horrific utensils are spread across the top. Dried blood still clings to several of the sharpened tips.

Roseline rolls her eyes in mock indifference. "Really? Is that all you've got? I've suffered far worse than those."

"Indeed." She can see the massive head bobbing in agreement as it steps into the light, huge and hulking. Its skin is black and leathery and its eyes two lightless voids. The monster's lips peel back into a leer, showing off powerful jaws riddled with teeth. "But you were fully immortal then. I think you will find that your ability to heal has...changed."

The hairs along her forearms rise as it hunches over the table, slowly running its claws over the tools. It hovers over a scalpel, turning its head to grin at her.

She braces herself as the creature whips around and launches the scalpel at her. It plunges deep into the crook of her armpit. Her lips bleed as she bites down against the scream lodged in her throat. She refuses to give this monster the satisfaction.

She bucks against the chains, nostrils flaring as she glares at the beast, defiant. Her skin feels flushed as she tries to ignore the pain. Her pulse thumps wildly in her ears as moisture clings to her eyelashes.

The creature's croaky laughter echoes around her as it rips the scalpel from her arm and stabs it through the palm of her right hand. She is feverish with need, aching to curl her fingers around its jaws and tear it in two.

"See what I mean?" Its dank, moist breath washes over her face as it twists the blade in her hand. She kicks back against the wall, refusing to let so much as a whimper pass her lips. The stench of the creature's breath curdles in her stomach.

She stills her lungs as it leans in close and runs a single claw down her cheek. It tears through her flesh with ease. "I'm really going to enjoy breaking you."

She stares into the soulless eyes of her torturer. "You're lucky I'm in chains."

It chuckles and slams its hand into her stomach, its claws extended. She cries out as it curls its fingers inward, tearing great gashes through her flesh. It retracts its claws and strikes repeatedly.

Her head lolls forward as one jolt of pain melds into the next. She has no idea how long it takes for her to pass out. All she remembers is that the creature never asked her a single question.

A shadow falls over Gabriel's face. His hand strikes out and meets flesh in mid-air. "You left me," Gabriel grumbles sleepily. His head aches, and his back is as stiff as the boards he slept on. He would be hard pressed to imagine a worse night's sleep.

Seneh smiles, releasing his hand. "Not for long. Katia took good care of you."

"She's a stranger. You're lucky I decided to follow her." Gabriel groans as he pushes up onto a chair, his long legs protesting as they bend at the knee.

The fire has burned low and the room is blissfully cool against his skin. Gabriel looks around, noticing Katia's bowl has been washed and replaced on the shelf. The scent of her stew still lingers in the air.

"No," Seneh says, careful to keep his voice low. He looks to the small mound lying atop the bed, still fully clothed. Blonde hair spills over the pillow as a soft snoring rises and falls with her chest. "Family."

"Family?" Gabriel stares hard at his guardian. Only a couple days ago he would have been terrified to be this close to such an imposing man. The fading firelight illuminates his many scars, creating a shine on his shaved head. His lone braid of hair at his back falls over his shoulder, curling near his waist beside the broadsword he always carries.

"Not mine. Yours."

Gabriel props his elbows on his knees, rubbing at the sleep that hides in the corners of his eyes. "This just gets weirder and weirder."

Seneh sinks onto the bench, his large frame making the wood creak loudly. He winces as Katia stirs, holding his breath until she settles back down before speaking again. "Lucien has fathered many children, Gabriel. Did you think you were the only one?"

Gabriel stares at the curtained bedroom in a daze. "You're saying she's my sister?"

"Half. Yes."

"She never told me," Gabriel whispers. A strange fluttering sensation fills his stomach as Katia rolls over, restless but still dreaming.

"That's because she does not know. Her mother was not as lucky as yours was. She lived long enough to give birth but died later that night. Katia grew up an orphan on the streets of Moscow. Elias found her and gave her to me to raise and protect. She has lived out here since she was only twelve years old."

"That's horrible." Gabriel's chest constricts as he considers how many other children grew up with stories much like Katia's.

Seneh shrugs. "It's peaceful. She is safe here."

"But Lucien is dead. He can't hurt her now, so why does she stay?"

"Because this is her home."

Gabriel stares at Seneh in the dim light. The windows have begun to brighten as a new dawn approaches. He can see the smoke that still trickles from the chimney as it drifts past the window.

The storm has blown over, leaving a new, fresh landscape beyond the walls of the tiny cabin. He thinks of what it might be like to live here. No people. No noise. No fear.

Glancing toward Katia, he almost envies her the solitude of the mountains. "Do you visit her often?"

Seneh nods. "When I am able. She is a good girl, kind and generous. You would like her."

"Does she know what you are?" Gabriel looks at him, curious.

"Of course." Seneh turns slightly and ruffles his feathers. "These are not easy to hide, you know."

Gabriel laughs, properly shammed from his lack of forethought. "No. I suppose not."

He falls silent, thinking over what Seneh told him. How many other brothers or sisters might he have out there? Are they like him? Half human? A hybrid?

"Did he kill all of them?" He asks without looking at his guardian. His fingers clench atop his knees as he waits for the answer he fears will come.

Seneh shakes his head slowly. "Some still live. We were not able to save them all."

"What happened?"

The angel's gaze drifts away, his jaw rigid. "Some were hunted and slaughtered in their homes. Others were taken."

"Taken?" Gabriel holds his breath.

Seneh nods. "Humans are not the most patient of beings in the world. Some thought they could speed up the process of discovering the *Arotas*. Those…experiments did not go as planned."

Gabriel closes his eyes, pained at the thought of how many lives have been ruined by the evil schemes of Lucien Enescue. "And the ones who live. Are they like me?"

"No." Seneh shakes his head. The muscles in his bare chest ripple beneath his skin as he leans forward, staring long and hard at Gabriel. "There are none like you."

"Why?" Gabriel stares hard at the angel across from him. "What makes me so different?"

"Roseline," Seneh says simply.

"What's this got to do with her?" Gabriel articulates each word carefully to make sure there is no mistaking his determination to know the truth. The muscles in his jaw flinch as he clenches his teeth and waits.

Seneh sighs. "I've said too much."

"No." Gabriel leans forward and grabs hold of his guardian's arm. "You haven't said enough."

Seneh rises to his full height, but Gabriel doesn't back down. He wants answers. No, he needs them.

"Tell me."

"It is not my place." Seneh's expression is harried as he looks to the door, as if Elias might actually walk through at that exact moment.

Gabriel releases his grip on the granite arm. He sinks heavily into the chair, throwing up his hands in despair. "Wait. That's all I've heard since you guys came into my life."

"I am sorry, young one." Seneh's gaze softens as he looks down at Gabriel.

"Yeah," Gabriel mutters, crossing his arms over his chest as he sighs loudly. "I know."

Warm breath tickles Nicolae's face as he begins to stir. Sleep grips him, beckoning for him to return, but when a finger traces his bottom lip, Nicolae bolts upright. He cries out, pressing back against the wooden headboard as he comes face to face with Sadie.

She smiles, kneeling beside him. "You look like you've seen a ghost."

"Am I?" Nicolae blinks, swallowing roughly. "Seeing a ghost?"

"No," she shakes her head. "I'm real."

He reaches out to touch her, just to make sure he's not still dreaming. Her skin is warm and kissed by the sun. Her lips are rosy and fuller than before, or maybe they were always that beautiful and he just never noticed. Her eyes are bright and wide, staring at him with curiosity.

The slope of her neck seems more graceful, the contour of her arms more refined. His gazes travels lower, pausing at her chest long enough to make her chuckle. He flushes red and continues lower. He involuntarily reaches out to touch her stomach, where her torn shirt hangs open, heavy with dried blood. The skin is smooth, without blemish or scar.

"Like what you see?"

He gulps and meets her gaze, completely amazed by her transformation. "You're stunning."

"It gets even better." With a smirk, she places her hands on the mattress and flips backward. She does a full rotation before landing silently on her feet. The wooden floor moves with her weight, giving without a single sound.

Nicolae leans toward the edge of the bed, staring wide-eyed at her crouched form. She rises slowly, smirking as she places her hands on her hips. "Impressive, huh?"

He nods, mutely. He struggles to comprehend the beautiful creature standing before him. It's almost as if her former beauty was slightly blurred, but now she has come into complete focus.

"How do you feel?"

"Amazing." Her tone is higher, musical like Roseline's. Nicolae feels himself being drawn from the bed to her side.

"And your thirst?" He presses as he rises from the bed.

Her brow pinches into a frown as her hand rises to her throat. "I...I hadn't thought about that."

He hesitantly steps closer. The floor creaks underfoot and he knows Fane will have noticed by now. No doubt he is already on his way. "Do I make you uncomfortable?"

Her eyes narrow as he slowly rolls his neck to the side, exposing bare skin. His heart pounds in his chest, thundering in his ears. If Fane didn't notice their voices before, he is sure to notice the increase in Nicolae's heartbeat now.

"No. Not really." She steps closer, her hand outstretched toward him. She bites her lip, and Nicolae nearly loses it. He groans and grabs her hand, pulling her to him.

She goes willingly, eyes wide with expectation. "I thought I lost you," he breathes. *She's actually here. Alive and healthy and utterly stunning.*

"I know." She leans up on her tiptoes, pressing her hand to his chest. He closes his eyes, fighting against the wild desire that seeks to claim him. He knows this feeling, having spent time with Roseline at the Savoy and Torrent, but this time it's different. With Sadie he can still think, still function. He is not driven by an irrational lust.

She rises to brush his lips with her own. He closes his eyes, aching to feel her touch. He winds his arms around her, fingers splayed against her lower back.

"Get away from her!"

Nicolae cries out as he is launched through the air, toppling over a high-backed Edwardian chair across the room. It splinters beneath him. He groans as he rolls to his side, clutching his back.

Hurried footsteps beat down the hall. When William arrives in the doorway, he sways unsteadily, clinging to the doorframe for support when he spies Sadie crouched on the floor, defending Nicolae from Fane.

"Sadie? Why are you growling at Fane?" William's hand falls free from the door as he stumbles into the room, wide-eyed. "What's going on?"

"She smells danger," Fane replies, sinking low as he stares back at Sadie. "To her, I am a rival. She's just protecting her territory, and by that I mean Nicolae."

Nicolae watches the odd staring match, torn between wanting to leap between them and his undeniable curiosity. He tosses aside the remnants of the chair as he gingerly rises from the floor.

Neither Fane nor Sadie notice him as they weave slightly back and forth like two animals locked in a death match. Nicolae frowns, realizing that is exactly what is happening. Fane is trying to show Sadie that he is the dominate one. "Is this really necessary?"

"She is a killer now, Nicolae. She must learn." Fane's words are clipped, edged with tension.

"By telling her you're the top dog?"

Sadie's lips peel back to reveal a straight row of white teeth, a low growl rises from her throat. Fane's hands clench into fists at his side as he refuses to back down.

William takes a step into the room and both immortals bristle. "I'd stay out of this if I were you," Nicolae calls from across the room, raising his hand in warning.

"You're actually ok with this?" William splutters, his gaze wide with disbelief.

Gritting his teeth, Nicolae forces himself to nod. "The sooner they get this over with, the sooner we can leave."

Casting a doubtful glance at his sister, William nods. "I hope you know what you're doing," he says as he turns to leave the room.

The past few days have been hard on William. Nicolae knows the last thing he wanted was for Sadie to be pulled back into the immortal world, and now she has become one of them. He wonders just how well William will accept Sadie's new life. How easily will he forget how close she came to death if she ever goes for his jugular?

After William disappears back downstairs, Nicolae waits nearly an hour for the staring match to end, pacing the edge of the room. The two immortals hardly notice his presence, too consumed with their battle of wills.

The standoff continues well into the night. Nicolae comes and goes, his growling stomach finally winning over his curiosity. As dawn begins to break over the mountains the next day, he feels a subtle shift in the room.

Sadie finally lowers her eyes. Nicolae breathes a sigh of relief as Fane nods and rises. Sadie follows suit but keeps her gaze fixated on the floor. "She has submitted to my authority," Fane says, pausing beside the chair that Nicolae slumps in. A small smile plays across Fane's face. "That is a good sign."

Four

Lucien's polished black boots glisten under the red lights of the vibrant Amsterdam district. He walks down the narrow street, pausing to admire the 300-year-old gabled buildings with their stunning architecture. "Shame they don't make them like this anymore," he says to no one in particular.

A man lying against a building corner, wrapped in soiled clothes and clutching a bottle tightly in hand, bobs his head in agreement. Lucien stares at him, wondering how much the man can actually see. His nose curls with disgust at the stench wafting from the unclean man and swiftly moves on.

It is nearing the witching hour, and the night is only just beginning to wake in this part of the city. Groups of people converge on the district, hooting and hollering in anticipation of an evening of fun and debauchery. Tourists stumble over their own feet as their cameras flash, attempting to capture the essence of this famous place, but a camera could never do it justice.

It can't express the electric feeling in the air or the scents of hormones that drift on the breeze. The thrumming of so many heartbeats is intoxicating.

Amsterdam is one of Lucien's favorite places to visit.

He passes by crowded pubs, closed street cafes, theatres that closed their doors hours before after a successful weekend showing and overcrowded hotels that lead into the district. Here, where the glass-paned window fronts are open for browsing and anything goes, Lucien finds himself drawn in by the excitement of it all. The thought of what a girl is ready and willing to do for a handful of cash never ceases to amaze and excite him. Of course, none of them ever get to spend it.

But tonight he is not here for the entertainment. He is here for the second phase of his plan.

"You looking for a good time?"

Lucien spins on his heel, eyeing the busty brunette lounging against the aged brick of a three-story establishment. Her accent is thick, but no more so than her make-up. Her red leather mini-skirt cuts so high across her thighs that she leaves nothing to the imagination, and her black halter is nearly non-existent. Fake eyelashes, splashed with glitter, flutter at him as she steps out of the doorway .

Three girls writhe in the window behind her, on poles, chairs and the floor. Lucien reluctantly draws his attention away from them to focus on the girl before him. "That depends."

He casually draws back the front of his unbuttoned suit coat, tucking his right hand into his pocket. His left clutches the top of a silver and black walking cane, hand carved and very expensive. He grins at the rhythmic sway of her hips, her high heels tapping out a steady rhythm as she approaches. "What are you offering?"

She leans in close and whispers in his ear. The scent of cheap alcohol hardly masks the latent drugs that spiral through her veins, and he can see the needle pricks along her inner arm. She stands just over five feet tall, even with a pair of 4-inch stilettos strapped to her feet. He scans her waist, guessing her to weigh no more than one hundred and twenty pounds, most of that spread between hips and bust. Upon closer inspection, he notices small rips in her halter, mended time and time again. The leather skirt shows wear; the zipper is broken and dangling off its threads. A small safety pin is the only thing holding her skirt up.

There is nothing remarkable about her up close, but that doesn't really matter. The newspapers will only care about the placement of her body, not how pretty her face is. He pauses to imagine just how she will look with her intestines wrapped tightly around her neck, dangling from her balcony window over the street.

The bite marks along her forearm and wrist will tie her murder in with the victims he left in front of the Fortune Theatre in London a couple days ago. Her body drained of blood as well. That should be enough to begin to breed the panic he so longs for.

A murderer on the loose, jumping from country to country, creating strange, horrific displays of the victim's bodies. This story should make world news.

He fakes a smile as she pulls away, not the least bit interested in what she's selling, but thinking she has potential. Things are starting to look up.

As he steps over the threshold into the seedy building, a new idea curls his bottom lip with desire. "Why don't you invite a few of your friends to the party as well?"

The instant the door closes behind Fane, Sadie looks up to meet Nicolae's gaze. She runs her hands nervously through her hair, wincing at the blood that still mats her strands together. "I'm sorry if you thought I was going to bite you. I would never—"

"I know." But does he really? That's the question he's been asking himself all night. He thought things had been fine between them, before Fane showed up, but now he's begun to wonder. Was she really trying to kiss him or was she just luring him in?

No. Sadie would never hurt him, but that was the old Sadie. Who knows what this transformation from human to immortal has made her capable of. "That was pretty intense between you two."

She shrugs and climbs onto the bed. She tucks her feet under her backside and pats the mattress beside her. "I got bored, so I gave in."

Nicolae smirks, his shoulders shaking with silent laughter. "Nice to know you're still in there."

She grins and scoots closer as he settles down next to her. He brushes his hand along her forearm, amazed by the silky feel of her skin. Even the fine hairs are softer than before. "What's it like?"

"It's...weird. I know I'm still me, but it's like there is another part of me now. I feel strong, fast. I can see things, hear things that I know should be impossible." Her smile fades into a slight grimace. "It's a lot to take in, to be honest."

His hand flinches in hers and she looks up. "What's wrong?"

"What about me? Has that changed at all?" His voice is low and cautious. Sadie is the only person alive that can hurt him now. A part of him screams to flee from certain heartbreak, but he can't make himself move. He lost his parents and Sorin to the blood feud between hunter and immortal. What if loving Sadie could end all of that? What if, together, they could bridge the gap and show both sides that is it possible to get along?

She reaches up to gently cup his cheek. He closes his eye, sinking into the fiery warmth of her touch. "Nothing has changed between us."

"When I found you lying on the floor..."

Sadie brushes her finger along his stubbled chin, trailing toward his lips to silence him. He realizes how terrible he must look: unshaven and haggard from lack of sleep. He opens his eyes to see her smiling at him. "You saved me. That's all that matters."

He draws back from her touch, fixing his gaze firmly on the floor instead of her. "I couldn't lose you. I'll understand if you can't forgive me for that decision."

"Are you kidding?" Sadie laughs. She leaps off the bed and stands before an oval mirror resting on a wooden stand. She flexes her muscles, twisting this way and that to get a better view before she turns to face him. "I feel amazing."

"But you weren't given a choice—"

Sadie waves off his argument. "Do you know any girl who would be upset over never having to shave her legs again? I mean come on, this is freakin' brilliant!" She lifts her shredded pant leg to reveal smooth, toned calves. She smirks as Nicolae flushes. "Come on, Nicolae. It's a joke. Lighten up!"

He leans back on the bed, propped up on his elbows. "Why aren't you freaking out right now? I expected at least a good slap over it all."

Her grin slowly fades as she drops her pant leg. She sighs and leaps onto the bed beside him, bouncing on her hands and knees. The bed hardly quakes as she lands. "I've spent the past few weeks obsessing over being left out. You know I suck at that."

He nods in complete agreement. Sadie never has been one to think of safety first.

"Well, now's my chance to make a difference." She inches closer to him. "I know Roseline is in trouble. I heard you guys talking about it, and I'm going to help get her back."

"No. No way!" He shakes his head, surging to his feet. He grimaces, rubbing at his neck as he considers what she is suggesting.

"I'm strong now. I can fight."

"Strong?" He turns to face her. "Do you really think that gives you an advantage against another immortal? They have been training for hundreds of years, Sadie."

She slips down off the bed and saunters up to him. His eyes widen as she draws close, pressing her hands to his chest, just over his heart. "You can train me."

"Me?" His voice cracks. He clears his throat and frowns down at her. "I can't just…I'm a hunter. A leader." His voice rises in pitch. "You don't know what you're asking."

"Actually, I do." She leans up into him, pressing her cheek to his neck. He swallows roughly, his hands struggling to find a safe place to rest. He settles on awkwardly grasping her arms. "You know me better than anyone. You know that I'll do something completely reckless if I'm left on my own. Wouldn't it be best for me to know how to defend myself?"

Nicolae groans as his fingers curl around her upper arms. He thrusts her back. "That's blackmail."

She grins and nods. "But it's also the truth."

He sighs heavily, resting his forehead against hers. "Fane won't like this."

Winding her arms around his waist, she smiles mischievously, peering up at him through her bangs. "If he thinks I've submitted to him, he's got another thing coming!"

Roseline is dying. At least she hopes she is.

A bouquet of rotting flesh and spilled blood permeates the air. A heavy dampness clings to her skin, matting her hair against her neck and forehead. The stained sackcloth she wears drapes her emaciated body, soiled by mud and other unmentionable fluids.

Time has no meaning in this pit. There is no light, save from the dwindling candle flickering from a rusted wall sconce beyond the cell bars. The drip of wax against the uneven stone floor in the hallway is the only measure of time.

The near darkness is maddening. The sensation of knives grazing her skin has been nearly constant since Lucien sank his teeth into her neck. Her blood feels like it's simmering in her veins and the gaping wounds in her hands, arms and abdomen keep her in a constant state of agony and weakness.

She is no longer in the torture chamber. Sometime after she passed out she was moved here, to this stinking, damp pit.

Roseline shifts, tucking her legs up into a fetal position as she clamps her eyes shut against the pain gnawing through the lining of her stomach. Her throat is parched, and despite her best efforts, she can no longer deny the scent wafting through the air.

She casts a feral glance at the body lying nearby. Blonde hair. Long legs. A small pink heart tattoo crests just over the waist of grungy low-rise jeans. The girl was probably a college student thumbing her way across Europe. At least, Roseline hopes she was that old.

Even through the halo of hair, Roseline can tell the girl's neck is broken. The blood that runs down the crown of her head has begun to congeal. Her warmth is fading, but that makes her blood no less desirable in Roseline's current state.

She wishes for the candlelight to snuff out so she won't have to look at the body anymore, but even without sight, she will be unable to forget every minute detail of the dead girl. She has been the biggest temptation Lucien has thrown at Roseline so far.

The first three cups of blood left at her cell door are now splashed across the far wall. Thick trails of crimson creep down the stone toward the packed dirt floor. Next came a sheep, its throat slit so deeply its head dangles by a single tendon. Its rotting corpse remains untouched near the cell entrance, but the girl…she is new.

One taste, just one, would ease Roseline's suffering, but it would also spark her transformation. Lucien won't allow Roseline's rebellion to linger much longer. Starvation is not an option.

Roseline rolls onto her side, facing the wall. Her revulsion at what she is becoming wars against her need. The thirst multiplies with each passing moment, and her thoughts have begun to fragment. Voices call to her from the shadows of her mind.

She digs her long nails into her palms, hissing as blood pools around the wounds. She licks her hands, closing her eyes to the metallic taste that barely quenches her need. Her blood will not heal her nor will it keep her thirst at bay for long, but it soothes her parched throat.

A sound shatters the stillness and sends Roseline cowering against the wall. She tucks her knees into her chest and raises a frail arm to cover her eyes as a swaying lantern approaches. She tries to peer around the glow but can't see who or what walks just beyond.

"Hello?" Her voice croaks, so she attempts again. "Who is there?"

She can hear footsteps now. Each step is smooth, as if gliding over the stone rather than actually stepping. When she can't detect any hissing or the foul stench of death on the air, she breathes a sigh of relief. Whoever this is, it's not one of Lucien's snake-like Eltat that attacked her in the Hell Fire Club caverns or the beast that shredded her intestines. She places her hand over her stomach, feeling the sticky blood that still seeps from her wounds.

"Roseline?"

She lowers her hand, nostrils flaring as a new scent invades her senses. It is bold, laced with danger and something more.

"Stay back," she growls, clawing at the wall. Her nails dig deep into the stone as the lock on the cell door rattles. She doesn't need to see past the light to know who is coming. It's *him.*

"What have they done to you?" The masculine cry of outrage is quickly followed by a loud clink as the lock falls to the ground.

Roseline covers her ears and begins to rock as the door screeches open. The sound stabs at her mind, making her long for the return of endless silence. "Don't come any closer, Malachi."

Her warning is multi-layered as the shadow moves through the open doorway. Anger boils in her belly, but even that is not enough to dismiss the delicious aroma of his blood as he draws near.

Shiny black boots stop less than three feet away. When the lantern swings closer, she squints as her eyes struggle to adjust to the light; she has been kept in the dark for too long.

"I came as soon as I could," he says, lowering the lantern.

Clutching her arms tightly around her knees, Roseline glares up through a curtain of matted hair. Her lips curl with contempt. "Why are you here?"

"I had to see that you were safe." He stretches out his hand to touch the top of her head. She gnashes her teeth at him and he yanks back out of reach. "I never dreamed he would treat you like this. Not you."

Roseline barks out a laugh, which quickly turns into a coughing fit. She beats on her chest weakly. When she is able to speak again, her voice is strained with effort. "You didn't think he'd roll out the red carpet for me, did you? Surely you aren't that naïve."

Malachi slowly crouches down to her level. "I tried to stop this, to escape before he came for you, but you were so..." he trails off, shaking his head. "Why didn't you just come with me?"

"You killed my friend," she spits back. Her stomach clinches as she imagines wrapping her fingers around his neck and squeezing the life from him. But would that be enough to kill him? Roseline isn't so sure any more.

"She was in my way." He grimaces, turning his gaze away. "I regret that, but I had no other choice."

"She was a human!" Roseline lunges forward, slashing at Malachi's face with her nails. They tear through his flesh, leaving deep gashes. He cries out and lurches back, cradling his cheek. His eyes grow wide with shock.

Blood oozes through his fingers as he rises. His face disappears into shadow, but not before she sees his expression drain of emotion. "It was her life or yours. I chose you."

Roseline presses back into the wall. Her gaze falls beyond him, landing on the partially open door. She knows Malachi is no fool. He would never leave her a way to escape if he thought her capable of doing so. Obviously, he suspected her frailty before he even stepped foot in this place.

"A lot of good that did."

Malachi's voice sounds distant as he shifts to lean back against the wall. "I didn't know this would happen. I knew he wanted you for something, but I never dreamed it would be for *this.*"

"Yeah, well, now you know." Roseline crosses her arms over her chest. She tries not to think of how thin her arms have become, as if her body is absorbing itself just to survive.

She can feel her strength receding, her mind weakening, the worst possible fate for a warrior. Lucien knows this, planned for it. How much longer can she hold out before madness drives her to feed?

"Why are you here?" She asks again wearily, leaning her head back against the wall. It takes too much effort to keep it held aloft. "Come to torture me yourself?"

"Never!" He crouches at her feet. She pulls her toes back under the protective cover of her dress. She doesn't want any part of him to touch her ever again.

Malachi sinks down onto the ground, pressing his fists against his eyes. "This is my fault. I should have never let you leave England. I should have kept you from fighting Vladimir. Made you go with me. If I had known…"

Roseline peers at him. The sorrow in his voice confuses her. She has always been good at sniffing out a lie, but Malachi has proven himself to be a master of deception. "You really didn't know, did you?"

"No." His head droops so low his chin presses against his pristine white dress shirt. The golden buttons on his cuffs look abnormally shiny in this dingy dungeon. When he glances up, Roseline can see the change: the subtle narrowing of his pupils and the slight tick of his right eyelid. "I can help you."

Roseline tenses. Her gaze flits over his shoulder to the empty hallway beyond. Maybe she could make it. One short sprint would get her down the hall and around the corner, but what lies beyond? She was unconscious when they brought her here. "How?"

Malachi unbuttons his sleeve and rolls it up past his elbow. His skin appears ghostly pale in the dim candlelight that flickers in the passage behind him. Staring Roseline in the eye, Malachi sinks his teeth into his wrist, piercing the artery. Blood flows over his teeth, glossing his lips.

Her hiss echoes against the cave walls. Spasms erupt through her stomach as her eyes roll back. Her breathing quickens, and her pulse thumps wildly in her ears. "Don't," she grunts, shoving his arm away.

"It's ok," Malachi soothes as he stills her feeble protests. "Angel blood will slow the transformation. I won't let you become a monster like Lucien."

Roseline's eyes water as she fights against the heady scent. Delirium steals away the remaining shreds of logic as she dives for his arm. She hesitates only a moment, pausing to look up into his blackened eyes.

"Trust me," he whispers as she sinks her teeth deep into his flesh.

Five

It feels wrong to be in Roseline's room, lying atop her bed when she isn't here. Sadie will never forget the man who took her friend.

He was the one who left Sadie for dead.

His blade sliced through her belly like a knife through butter. Smooth. Quick. Effortless. Although the physical pain is gone, the memory of it lingers.

Closing her eyes, Sadie curls onto her side, wrapping her arms around a pillow and hugging it close. She was too weak to save Roseline before but no longer.

Sadie can feel a new strength now, as if granite has been poured into the marrow of her bones. She can hear the slightest sounds, from the fluttering of Nicolae's heartbeat down in the great room to the frustrated pacing of Fane in his room on the opposite side of the castle.

She is strong, yes, but she is untrained.

Releasing a heavy sigh, she slowly rises to sit on the edge of Roseline's bed. Someone cleaned the floor of her blood, and the bedding has been changed since she awoke from her transformation. Evidence of her near death has been bleached from this room, but it is still there in the tiniest scent of blood that stubbornly clings to the stone floor.

Nicolae probably didn't want her reminded of her ordeal.

A tiny smile tugs at the corners of her lips as she thinks of how attentive he has been since she woke up. Her smile wanes almost immediately at the ever present reminder from Fane that, at any moment, she might develop the desire to rip out Nicolae's throat.

Her nose scrunches with disgust. The delicious scent of his blood is no stronger than his ever-increasing grip on her heart. No, she could never hurt him, nor could she harm William. Not that Fane believes her.

He continues to pace, now just outside her room, waiting for her to prove him right. His watchful eye is beyond annoying. Why can't he see that she isn't a danger to them?

Even as this thought tumbles through her mind, another seeks to replace it, one that is darker and far more terrifying. *What will happen when they leave the castle? When she is surrounded by people she doesn't care about?*

Sadie curls her knees into her chest and perches on the edge of the bed, unsure if she can trust herself. Perhaps it is good that Fane delays leaving. Is he giving her time to adjust or time for Nicolae to come to his senses about her?

Nicolae doesn't know that she has heard his heated arguments with Fane in the stairwell that leads to back courtyard. To say that Nicolae's hunters aren't happy with his decision to save her life would be a grave understatement. It hurts to know that her life has driven a wedge between him and his men, but she likes to think he knew the consequences of his decision when he made it.

Or maybe he wasn't thinking at all, her inner doubts whisper to her. *Maybe he regrets losing Sorin and his hunters, the only family he has ever known.*

Clutching her knees tightly to her chest, tears begin to seep from her eyes. Guilt tugs at her from all directions.

Fane is angry with her. William is terrified but putting on a brave face. Nicolae is far too careless around her. The hunters are mobilizing, planning an attack on the castle. They are coming for her.

Roseline is still missing. Who knows what terrible things might be happening to her at this very moment?

Sadie hangs her head in shame. "This is all my fault," she whispers to the empty room.

"No! Out of the question." Fane bellows as he rounds on Nicolae. His voice echoes loudly through the empty great room of Bran Castle. "I've already told you, there is no way I am letting you two train together."

Nicolae's fists clench at his side. This isn't the first time they have had this argument over the past couple of days and he fears that it won't be the last. "Let us?"

"You know what I mean." The skin around Fane's eyes wrinkles as he glances through the top of the great window toward the castle turret. Nicolae can see a light still on in Sadie's room. He is not sure if Fane actually heard her sneaking down the stairs or if he is trying to pause for effect. "I know you think you can handle her, but she is dangerous. What if she did attack you? Could you really kill her if your life was on the line?"

Nicolae hesitates, sucking in a steadying breath before answering. "She won't hurt me. I know her."

Crossing the room, Fane sinks onto a leather couch. He turns his face toward the blazing fire, as if he could find the answers he seeks in its flickering depths. "I am happy that her transition took, but we don't have time to stop and train her right now. Roseline needs us. We can't just forget that she is gone."

His posture slumps as he stares deep into the flames dancing in the tall hearth. "I don't even know where to begin looking for her."

"I think I may know." Nicolae perches on the arm of a couch opposite Fane. "I spoke with Sadie at length about her ordeal. I thought it might help her to process it all. She told me what we feared, that Malachi was the one who attacked her, but also that he wasn't alone that night. Someone else was on the balcony."

Fane leans forward, resting his elbows on his knees. A fervent intensity gleams in his eyes. "Who?"

Nicolae purses his lips as his doubts flood back in. Of course he believed Sadie was telling the truth, but that doesn't mean it really happened. "She was probably delusional from blood loss..." he hedges.

"Tell me."

Nicolae's finger flinches against the cool leather of the couch. He doesn't want to say, to get Fane riled up, but what if there is even a grain of truth to Sadie's story? Can he really live with himself if he doesn't tell Fane?

"She saw Lucien."

Fane hisses, leaping high into the rafters. Nicolae can hear him running along the aged beams, clinging to the shadows. He peers up into the darkened recesses of the room but fails to catch a glimpse of the enraged immortal. In all the time he has known Fane, this is the first time he has reacted so strongly. A resurrected Lucien is obviously far more serious than he had first thought.

"Do you believe her?" Fane's voice sounds hollow and distant as it drifts down from above.

Nicolae finally spots him near the shattered remains of the great window. The bottom has been boarded up to seal out the strong winter winds that whip through the castle grounds. Another snow storm has unleashed its wrath, slickening the window panes with glistening ice.

"We saw him die," Nicolae says. "It shouldn't be possible, but..."

As he trails off, Nicolae begins to realize that Fane shares his doubts. What if an immortal could come back from the dead? Weren't they technically dead already, at least compared to human standards? In all of his years of training, he never once heard Sorin speak of such a feat, but Nicolae knows not everything is as is seems.

Fane remains in the rafters for several minutes, silent and contemplating. Finally, he drops from above, his brown cloak rippling around him as he lands silently on the floor. His skin is absent of color, his eyes haunted and bright with fear.

"If Lucien is alive, dark magic must have been used to revive him." Fane turns to face the fire, his arms crossed tightly across his chest. "There's no telling what terrible things he could be capable of now."

A ripple of apprehension curls in Nicolae's belly as he stares at the rigid posture of his friend. His expression is tight, and his chest lies still. He doesn't move for several minutes, which scares Nicolae far more than he would like to admit.

Fane has always been a fierce warrior, someone Nicolae begrudgingly admired for his bravery, even in the face of terrible odds. It deeply unsettles Nicolae to see Fane so disturbed by the thought of Lucien's return.

"What do you think he wants Roseline for?"

Fane turns slowly to face him, his eyes glossed over, unseeing. "She killed his brother. Lucien never forgives and he never ever forgets. If he truly has her, I can only imagine what she is being forced to endure."

Nicolae's stomach clenches at the thought of anything happening to her. The childhood hatred he once had for Roseline faded during their time spent together in London. He grew to not only respect her as a warrior but to consider her a friend. The thought of anyone harming her makes his skin tingle with anger. "We have to find her."

"Exactly," Fane nods, breaking out of his comatose pose. "And that is why I can't let Sadie become a liability."

Nicolae stiffens. "What's that supposed to mean?"

Fane takes a step toward him, his expression grave but determined. "I saved Sadie's life because you asked me to, but make no mistake, Roseline is and will always be my first priority. I won't let anything get in my way. Not even Sadie."

His threat falls heavily over the room. A myriad of emotions hits Nicolae at once. Anger. Betrayal. Doubt. Fear. But even as the feelings wash over him, understanding follows quickly behind. He remembers the agony of holding Sadie's hand in his own, unable to do anything to save her. He had grasped onto the only hope available to him, desperate to see her survive. Isn't that exactly what Fane is doing?

Nicolae straightens his shoulders and rises to his feet. "I will take full responsibility for her."

Fane laughs. "And what about your hunters? Do you think they are so willing to forgive their leader's decision to create another immortal? Their enemy? They are planning to attack us, Nicolae. That doesn't sound too forgiving to me."

Nicolae opens his mouth to speak, but no words escape. He knew the consequences of his decision to save Sadie's life when he made it, but at the time it didn't matter. Now, it seems like he will have to fight to protect her again, but this time it will be his family, his brothers-in-arms that he must defeat.

"I thought not." Fane rises and begins to pace before the fire. His shadow lengthens against the wooden floor as he passes. "There may be another option."

His musings capture Nicolae's attention. "Tell me."

Fane swiftly moves to Nicolae's side. "You forced a truce with Roseline when you came looking for me. I know that wasn't easy for you, but somehow you convinced your men to fight alongside her to overthrow Vladimir. Do you think they would be willing to accept a new truce? One between you and me?"

Nicolae nods but with hesitation. "Perhaps, but why?"

"I can take Sadie with me, train her when I have time, but only return when I am sure that she is safe. If we can prove that she is not a threat, your hunters might be willing to spare her life."

Nicolae thinks it over, absently rubbing his jaw. "Yes, it might work, but on one condition."

"And that is?" Fane arches an eyebrow.

"I'm coming with you."

His friend hesitates, clearly none too pleased with this additional requirement. Although he and Fane have created a bond over the past couple weeks, their relationship is still new. There is hardly any chance that Fane would be willing to freely allow Nicolae access to intimate knowledge of the immortal world.

"I have your word that you will not interfere with Sadie's training? We do it my way or not at all once Roseline is safe?"

Nicolae nods. "You do."

"Even if that means turning your back on your brothers? Knowing they will hunt you to get to her?"

He swallows roughly but nods again. "Sadie is my family now."

Reaching into the folds of his cloak, Fane withdraws a serrated blade. Nicolae tenses but does not move away as Fane closes the gap between them. Fane grips the handle in his right hand, never breaking eye contact with Nicolae as he tilts the blade and slices through his left palm. Blood splatters against the stone floor as Fane holds out the knife.

Curling his fingers around the handle, Nicolae presses the blade to his own flesh. "Not too deep," Fane warns.

Nicolae nods and slides the blade across his palm, slicing through several layers of skin. A hiss passes his lips as he holds out his hand. Fane grasps it in his and their blood mingles, sealing the pact.

Lightheadedness overcomes Nicolae as he is released from Fane's grip. The blade clatters to the floor as he sways, unsteady on his feet. "I told you not to cut too deep," Fane scolds as he lowers Nicolae onto the couch.

Warmth trails down his arm as Fane holds Nicolae's hand aloft. It soaks through Fane's white shirt, staining his flesh. Nicolae winces as Fane presses down near the wound. "Ow."

"Sorry about this," he mutters as he draws Nicolae's hand close. "There's no other way."

"What did you say?" Nicolae asks. His vision blurs and he closes his eyes as the room begins to spin.

"Just hold still."

Nicolae cries out as Fane's teeth pierce his flesh, just to the side of his wound. The immortal retracts his teeth and buries them back in again, slowly working his way around the deep gash.

Each time Fane's teeth sink into his palm, Nicolae's fingers jerk in reflex. "I'm not a midnight snack."

"I'm almost done. Stop being a baby." He bites one final time and then rises up, wiping a smear of blood from his mouth with his sleeve. "Next time heed my warning."

Nicolae holds his hand aloft, amazed to watch as his flesh begins to knit itself back together. The pain recedes and the blood flow stops completely. New, pale flesh seals completely over the wound in a matter of minutes. A four-inch scar is the only reminder of his blunder with the knife. He grins up at Fane. "Wicked."

<u>Six</u>

The sound of blood dripping down to the floor is music
to Lucien's ear. He taps his foot to the beat, humming as he
works. His knife is sharp, easily peeling back layers of human
flesh. His stomach growls with need but he reins himself in.
Now is not the time to feed.

The screams of the two priests died off less than an hour
ago. He misses them, the way they carried up to the great
heights of the cathedral, echoing through the vast hall. He had
very much enjoyed their pleas for mercy, offering him anything
in the church's possession to spare their lives.

That made it all the more fun when he started carving.

After the BBC fell silent about the four working girls
slain in the red light district of Amsterdam, Lucien knew he
needed to up the ante. Perhaps the crowds weren't large enough
nor the location popular enough.

He needs to remedy both of those.

Investigators are no closer to finding a lead to tie the two
murders together, nor have they released any details about the
bites. Although the police may have trouble sleeping at night,
the rest of the world is still in the dark.

After tonight, that will not be the case.

He reaches for a cloth to wipe the blood from his hands
and steps back to admire his work. Three crosses have been
nailed to the wall. The two priests hang from the outer crosses,
their hands and feet nailed to the wood. Their clothes have been
removed, save for their shorts, and their chests laid bare, flayed
alive with a knife.

But his eyes are not drawn to them, for they are merely
for effect. The real jewel hangs in the middle.

The girl's head is tied to the side, covering a single bite
mark over her artery, in traditional vampire fashion. Her long

blonde hair brushes against the floor from her upside down crucifix.

Her arms stretch out on either side of her, large galvanized nails piercing her wrists. Her feet have been placed one on top of the other, a nail driven through the tops of them. Blood seeps from the wounds, trailing toward the floor.

She is exquisite even in death.

Lucien kneels, brushing her cheek with a gentle caress. "Whatever are they going to make of you, my dear? Will they be smart enough to realize you are more than human? That your heart recycled the blood of a four-hundred-year old girl?" Surely, her burnt orange eyes should make her supernatural nature obvious to even the most daft of investigators. "It is such a pity to lose such great beauty, but sacrifices must be made."

He presses his lips against her forehead, closing his eyes to the memories of countless rendezvous they shared over the years. If Lucien had been capable of love, Victoria might have managed to capture his heart.

She was ruthless, merciless, stunning…all the things he would have looked for in a mate. But she has served her purpose now. "It has been fun," he whispers.

He rises and lets his hand drift away from her face. No heartfelt goodbye. No final glance. That is not his style.

His long cloak billows about him as he turns and descends from the altar, practically skipping past the church pews. He has left the murder weapon, the mallet and box of nails in the open, laid out neatly in a puddle of holy water. He grins, giddy with the irony of it all.

Lamplight filters in through the stained glass windows of Notre Dame Cathedral, casting an eerie glow on his victims. For a moment, he is tempted to turn back for one final glimpse, but he resists. Let the churchgoers who arrive for Mass tomorrow enjoy the first glimpse of his work.

His laughter echoes through the great church halls as he shoves through the double doors and out into the night.

A *Breaking News Report* symbol scrolls along the bottom of the screen, detailing the gruesome details of yet another killing spree, this time in the heart of Paris.

Nicolae frowns at the tension in his friend's shoulders as Fane paces back and forth, watching the muted screen. William and Sadie are curled up next to each other on the couch, William's drool dripping dangerously close to Sadie's arm. If she were awake, he'd have a black eye by now.

Tiptoeing past the sleeping siblings, Nicolae joins Fane. The flickering light of the TV is the only light in the room. "There's been another attack," Fane says, his voice barely above a whisper.

Nicolae's jaw sets firmly as he nods. Together, they have been watching the news in snippets, trying to keep Sadie and William from hearing the reports. "What do we do about it?"

"I honestly don't know. We don't even know who is initiating these attacks or where they will strike next." He turns to stare at Nicolae's profile. "Have you heard anything from your end?"

Nicolae's stomach clenches at the thought of his estranged brothers. "We aren't exactly on speaking terms at the moment."

"I thought not," Fane says, sinking down onto a chair behind him. He perches on the edge, too anxious to sit back. "We can't let this continue. Whoever is behind this targeted Victoria. She was no fool, Nicolae. It would take a skilled hunter to track her down."

"I don't think it was one of us," Nicolae says, staring at the blurred out images taken from the crime scene. Although the outline of the bodies can be seen, the more gruesome details of the priest's death have been left to front page coverage of newspapers around the world.

"Nor do I and that's what worries me." Fane's fingers dig into the leather arms of the chair. "Someone is trying to expose us. But who? Vladimir is gone. It doesn't make any sense."

"What about someone under his command? Lavinia?"

Fane snorts. "That woman couldn't pull anything like this off. She may be demented, but she's far from methodical. No, whoever is planning these murders is patient, disciplined. I fear this is only the beginning."

Nicolae blows out a deep breath. "What about Roseline? Do you think Sadie could be right? That Lucien really is alive? This sounds like his MO."

Fane dips his head in consideration. He slowly nods, his expression darkening. "It could be. Or maybe Malachi is on a rampage. Who knows? But we can't let it continue. This latest attack is getting major attention. People are starting to get scared. Whispers of fanged monsters in the dark have already begun to surface. A few more of these and there will be people with shotguns and pitchforks breaking down our door."

The thought chills Nicolae. It will be nearly impossible to keep Sadie from being killed by his own hunters, let alone protect her against an entire town or country. Romania is deeply veined with tales of vampires, so if word gets out that the myths could be true, people will flock to Bran Castle to hunt them down.

"We have to leave," Nicolae says, staring blankly at the muted news report.

"I agree. The sooner the better." He looks back over his shoulder at Sadie and William. "We will let them sleep tonight, but tomorrow we head for Canada."

"Canada?"

Fane nods. "You will all be safe there."

"You?" Nicolae's brow furrows. "You aren't planning on sticking around?"

"No," Fane shakes his head. "I have to go after Roseline."

"But that's suicide," Nicolae protests. "If Lucien really is the one behind these attacks, that means he is alive and deadly as ever. What do you think he will do to you when you show up on his front doorstep looking for Roseline?"

Fane rises from the seat, a sad smile spread along his lips. "It doesn't really matter, does it? I have to find her and I know you understand that."

He pauses to place his hand on Nicolae's shoulder before he leaves, closing the door behind him. Nicolae hangs his head, weary of fighting, and death. Will it ever end?

When he looks up, he finds Sadie staring at him in the dark. "How much did you hear?"

"All of it."

Nicolae smirks. "I should have known you were faking it."

She nods, biting her lip. "We can't let him go on his own. He won't survive."

"I know." He sighs and sinks back into a chair, covering his face with his hands. "But what else can we do? I won't risk your safety for his."

"As touching as that is, he is your friend now, Nicolae. Your family. Maybe not by blood, but that doesn't matter. He would risk his life for you."

"So what are you suggesting?"

Sadie slowly unwinds herself from William. He snorts, twisting to his side to clutch a pillow before settling back into a deep sleep. "We need help and I know just where to get it."

Roseline clutches her stomach as her thirst begins to build once more. It comes faster now, more potent with each feeding. Although her wounds start the healing process with each time Malachi shares his blood, as soon as he leaves they begin to fester, pus-filled scabs that leave her weak and debilitated.

She has learned to tell time by her thirst. Malachi comes three times a day— giving blood each morning and night. His visits in the afternoon appear to be for nothing more than to offer her company.

Despite his blood sacrifice, she can't bring herself to trust him. He has been too vague about the length of time she has been here which worries her far more than she lets on. Although he seems sincere in his concern for her, doubt continues to eat away at her.

Why does he want to help her? Surely coming to her aid places his life in danger. Or does it? Is it naïve to believe that this selfless streak runs deeper than even he knows?

It is hard to concentrate now. The voices in her mind continue to grow stronger even as her energy wanes. She grows strong and alert after each dose of angel blood, but its effects quickly fade.

It is only a matter of time before Lucien realizes what is happening. Someone will smell Malachi on her and when that happens, her only lifeline to the outside world will be removed.

She leans her head back against the wall. Her gaze roams the ceiling, searching for an escape route. The ceiling is domed high overhead, much too high to leap through, even if she had her former strength.

The walls are rough but slicked with a layer of grime. It might be possible to climb the wall, but once she reaches the center of the room, her escape will be thwarted by an angel hair wrapped metal grate.

Each time she closes her eyes she becomes acutely aware of the shift within her body, the poison slowly eating away at her soul. She can feel her thoughts being tainted by Lucien's blood traipsing through her arteries, altering her essence.

It sickens her to think of any part of him inside of her. She shudders, loathing herself for growing anxious for Malachi's next visit. She finds herself beginning to rely on him, something she would rather die than admit.

Her thoughts turn to Gabriel and the last time she saw him. He looked different, beautiful, despite the blood that clung to his clothes from the battle. How did he find her? Why didn't he come for her?

The dark plays tricks on her mind, making her doubt the love she felt when he called for her. He could have saved her and Sadie, but he didn't even try.

A single tear slips from her eyes. She brushes it away, angry with her weakness.

Gabriel must have had a reason. It's the only explanation. He will come for her. She knows it.

Seven

Nearly five days pass with no sign of Elias. Seneh remains annoyingly silent, refusing to say anything more about Gabriel's tasks or how they affect Roseline. Elias had told him there would be three in total. He has already passed one. Two more remain.

Katia has taken up the hobby of watching him, studying him at night when the only light in the cabin is from the roaring fire. She remains oddly aloof, always looking to Seneh before speaking directly to Gabriel. He's not sure if that is because of her broken English or if she worries she might say something wrong.

Her relationship with Seneh is an interesting one. In the evening, once the chores are done and the dishes put away, Seneh and Katia settle in for a game of chess. Gabriel has enjoyed seeing a softer side to his guardian. Never before has he seen a more fierce looking man, and yet when he is with Katia, his tough facade seems to melt away.

Even though Gabriel has adapted to this new lifestyle, he yearns for freedom. To race through the mountains and stretch his legs or just to be alone for a while.

He spends his days on the ridge where Katia first discovered him, perched atop a rock or fallen log with his sketch book in hand. Some days he focuses on the minute details of the forest life around him or the endless sea of clouds that span the valley below, but normally his thoughts linger on *her.*

Roseline is ever in his thoughts, taunting him, accusing him. He can't shake the feeling that she needs him. He knows she is hurting, he can sense it. The knowledge that he is helpless to change her fate is maddening. So he draws, digging into the pages with such ferocity that the charcoal snaps in his fingers.

Now all he has left are small crumbs of coal. His fingers cramp as he attempts to squeeze one last picture into Enael's book. There is little room left to draw, save for the borders of the creased pages.

Gabriel groans, chucking the last crumble of coal into the forest. He plunges his hands into his hair, gripping his head as he bends at the waist. He closes his eyes, fighting against the urge to lash out and destroy something.

What am I doing here? This thought has nearly driven him mad over the past few days. *I should be out there, searching for Roseline. She needs me.*

"I thought I might find you out here."

The voice drifts down from above, deep and lilting with laughter. Gabriel stiffens, then his handsome features shift into a deep scowl. "So now you return."

He closes his book and carefully tucks it into his shirt. He despises the scratchy texture of the woolen shirt Katia loaned him. It clings to him, making him feel as if he's suffocating. He never dreamed that he would miss the robes Sias gave him back at the monastery, but somewhere along the way he grew fond of them.

"Where have you been?" Gabriel asks, refusing to look up at his mentor. He knows, judging by the direction of Elias' voice, that the angel is perched in the treetops of the pine a few feet ahead.

"I had a task to attend to. I apologize for the delay." With a great rush of wind, Elias leaps from the tree and lands lightly in the snow. Gabriel glances up, ready to unleash his anger, but he stops short, his mouth dropping open.

Elias' chest bears fresh burns, gaping wounds from shoulder to waist. The flesh around the burns is charred, shriveled and dying. His pants are singed and torn, as if by an animal's claws.

"What happened to you?" Gabriel breathes, surging to his feet.

His mentor motions for him to sit. Gabriel throws his leg over a fallen log and perches with his hands pressed against the bark. Elias winces as he sinks heavily onto the ground. Once his back is against the tree, he scoops great handfuls of snow onto his chest. His teeth clinch in pain, but the grimace slowly fades as the ice begins to melt, trickling down his bare skin.

"I made a mistake," Elias replies. His lips press tightly together as he shifts, digging out a fallen branch from beneath him. He chucks it into the forest before meeting Gabriel's concerned gaze. "I appreciate your obvious concern, but I will be fine. Seneh has mended me from wounds far more serious than these."

Gabriel watches in silence as Elias leans his head back and closes his eyes, exhaling. "You seem on edge, young one."

"I need answers, Elias. I think I deserve them."

"Indeed." Elias nods.

"And nothing cryptic this time," Gabriel rushes to add.

The angel's chuckle is low and rumbling. "I believe it is time for you to learn the nature of your second task."

"But what about Rose—"

Elias holds up his hand, silencing Gabriel's question. "You will have your time to speak. For now, just listen please."

Gabriel reluctantly falls silent, deciding it is far better to get some information than none. Elias begins again. "Your first task forced you to sacrifice something dear to you. You did this by choosing to continue with your mission instead of going to Roseline. I know this doesn't make sense, but it was the right decision. You should know that you are capable of self-sacrifice. The second task is much like it and yet infinitely more difficult."

"How so?"

Elias opens his eyes to look at him. "The first task dealt with your heart. The second will deal with your flesh."

Gabriel shifts against the log, not the least bit comfortable with how that sounds. "And the third?"

"Should you succeed with your second task, the third will focus on your soul."

"Oh," Gabriel says, trying for an indifferent shrug. "Is that all?"

Elias' gaze hardens. "Neither of these tasks will be easy, nor should they be taken lightly. Both will be very dangerous and death is always a possibility."

Gabriel's jaw tightens. He presses his fingers into his thighs until the ache helps to drown out the fear Elias has elicited. "Do I even have a chance of completing these trials?"

"That depends entirely on you."

Gabriel surges to his feet, desperate to move. His hands shake at his sides, riddled with nervous tension. Unnerved, he turns and slams his fist into a pine tree beside him. Splinters tear through his flesh as he withdraws his hand, staring at the hole he punched straight through the trunk.

"Feel better?" Elias asks.

"A bit."

The angel chuckles, shaking his head. "Still ruled by your human emotions I see."

"I am human."

"No." Elias pushes up to his feet. "You *were* human. Now you are an immortal, the *Arotas.* You need to start thinking like one."

"And how do I do that?" He rubs his hand down his arm to remove the splinters from his skin.

Elias steps forward, placing his hand on Gabriel's shoulder. "By remembering that today is fleeting, merely a blink of an eye compared to what lies ahead of you."

"And Roseline?"

A slow smile spreads along the angel's face. "She will be waiting for you at the end."

The sound of blood dripping against the dirt floor ignites Roseline's carnal thirst. She clings to Malachi's arm, unwilling to let go, even when he shoves at her head.

"Roseline, stop. You don't want to overdo it."

She snarls as she retracts her teeth from his flesh. Malachi gingerly withdraws his arm, cupping it with his hand.

The wound is larger than normal, his flesh torn as she fought to gulp down a few extra ounces before he pulled away.

"Sorry," she mutters, swiping the back of her hand across her lips.

Malachi no longer comes dressed like a gentleman. His attire is plain, with jeans, loafers and a t-shirt, a far more suitable fit for this squalor.

"It's getting worse, isn't it?" He asks, cradling his arm against his chest. Blood soaks through the cloth he binds tightly around the wound. It won't take long for the skin to repair itself, but the scent of fresh blood makes it hard for Roseline to concentrate.

"I can handle it." She swipes her arm along her lips, staring at the crimson smear against her pale forearm. The urge to lick at it captures her thoughts for several moments.

Malachi sighs and lowers his mended arm onto his lap. He crosses his legs and leans backward, propped up against the wall. "We've increased your feeding time and it's still not working. The poison is spreading too quickly and my blood can only slow the process, not stop it."

A shiver runs down her spine as she presses back against the cold stone. The chill never seems to leave her now.

It was the first sign that she was changing, shifting. She should be thriving off of this damp cold, but instead she is always shivering. "How long does Lucien plan to keep me here? Surely he has figured out by now that I'm not transforming."

Malachi shifts, turning his face away to hide in the shadows. Her eyes narrow as she detects the increase in his pulse. "What aren't you telling me?"

"Nothing."

She snatches his arm and digs her nails into his flesh. "Tell me."

At first, she thinks he will remain silent, but finally he concedes. He looks at her with concern in his eyes. "Lucien has been…preoccupied."

"With?"

He swallows and pulls her nails free of his arm. "There has been a rash of killings over the past few days. Signs left for humans to discover."

"About us?"

He nods. "It's bad. I can feel a shift in the air. The streets are deserted at night and most of London's nightlife has come to a grinding halt. People are terrified of going anywhere, unsure of where the next attack may occur. A curfew has been put into effect until a suspect is placed in custody."

"But they will never find Lucien!"

"I know," he says, closing his eyes. "There is more. I think he's going after Gabriel as well. Lucien has immortals all over the world hunting for him."

"But why? He has me."

Her panic begins to muddy her thoughts. Wasn't this the whole point of biting her? To claim her for himself? Lucien has already won so what could he possibly want with Gabriel?

"Is it the prophecy?"

Malachi shrugs. "Perhaps. Lucien believes that Gabriel is the only one who can save you, and he refuses to let that happen."

She falls silent, thinking over his words. Can it really be that simple? Kill Gabriel to get to her? No. There must be more to it. She isn't important. There must be something more going on than she knows, and she'd bet her life that Malachi does.

"You're lying."

His jaw clenches and his eyes flash in warning. She has seen this look before but never with him. "I am not."

"Fine, then you're still treating me like a child that has to be protected."

He snorts, rubbing the bandage along his arm. "Aren't you?"

"No!" She shoves him back and leaps on top of him. Her knee buries into his neck, pressing against his vocal chords. She could easily do it, just end his life with one twist of her leg.

She stares down into the fathomless depths of his eyes and sees no fear. On the contrary, she sees pleading. "You want me to do it, don't you?"

Although he struggles to move, she can easily tell he is nodding. She releases pressure and shifts back into a crouch. "Why?"

"I have my reasons." He growls, rubbing the back of his neck. He refuses to look at her.

"There is no honor in willful death."

He shrugs, rising from the ground. "The end result is the same. That's all I care about."

Her eyes narrow as he yanks the bandage off his arm and tosses it aside. She will have to hide that later, probably with the other rags that are stuffed inside the rotting sheep across the room. Roseline thought about moving the girl over there as well but couldn't bring herself to touch her, for fear of losing what little control she still possesses.

"Then why not do something honorable?" she challenges him.

"What could I possibly do now to redeem myself?"

She leans forward, capturing him with her fierce gaze. "Get me out of here. I can stop Lucien. You know I can. I just have to get to Gabriel."

His nose scrunches with disgust. "You think it's that easy to get out of here? This place is swarming with immortals that want your head for Vladimir's death, not to mention more Eltat than I care to count."

He releases a small shudder and Roseline can't help but agree. The red-eyed monsters, with their curled claws and green scaled skin are a hideous sight and lethal. She doesn't fancy meeting any of those down here.

"But this is your home. You know all of its secrets. You could do it," she presses.

He casts a guarded glance in her direction before moving to the cell door. He steps through and the lock clanks back into place. He pauses, staring intently at her. She can see his indecision and smell his fear. "Perhaps."

Nicolae storms after Fane, chasing him past the empty well and charred rubble that used to belong to Bran Castle's front gate. A layer of ice covers the ground, glistening in the early morning light. Small, rough pebbles litter the courtyard, crunching underfoot. "You know I'm right about this. We don't have a choice."

Fane turns so abruptly Nicolae slams into his chest. Nicolae winces at the stab of pain in his sternum, rubbing it gingerly as he steps back. "What'd you do that for?"

"There is always a choice." The immortal's face is rigid as stone. "And do not make the mistake of thinking me a fool, Nicolae. I know Sadie put you up to this."

"So what if she did? She's got a point." Nicolae says, leaning back against the crumbled remains of a wall. A thick layer of damp stone dust clings to his pants and the soles of his shoes. "You fought alongside me only a couple days ago and now I'm suddenly the enemy again? What about our pact?"

Fane releases a long and controlled breath. "You, I like."

Nicolae stiffens. "The hunters are still my family. They will listen to me."

"You care for them," Fane says. "That makes you foolish. You aren't thinking clearly. A truce of that magnitude between our kinds is not possible."

He can't help but notice that Fane actually sounds a bit sad when he says this. Perhaps Roseline wasn't alone in wishing things could be different. She and Fane have been fighting this war a lot longer than he has. If anyone would like to find peace, it must be them.

"Roseline believed it was possible," Nicolae says, watching his friend's reaction. Fane keeps his face emotionless, but Nicolae can sense the turmoil brewing just beyond his eyes.

Nicolae takes a step forward, cautious but unwilling to give up the chance to convert Fane. "Give me a chance to reason with them. They fought alongside you to take Vladimir down and you know they will want a chance at Lucien. This is as much their fight as it is yours."

"But we don't know that he is behind all the murders." Fane grinds his teeth, revealing how unsettled the news reports have made him. "What if all of this is a trick to throw us off Roseline's trail? Or worse, to start a war between immortals and the hunters while he continues to sweep panic across Europe? We can't risk it."

"And what about the new murders? Immortals are jumping on Lucien's bandwagon. People are being murdered in broad daylight. Your world has been thrust before human eyes, and there is nothing you can do to make them unsee the horrors all around them."

"I know." Fane's head hangs low.

Nicolae steps forward, touched by the burden Fane so obviously bears. "You need my men, Fane. Too many immortals have sided against you. Even if you could scrounge together a handful, you would still be sorely outmatched. Without our help, you can't hope to win."

· Fane's jaw tightens as he turns, allowing Nicolae only a profile view as his gaze roams the ruins of his once magnificent home. "There are many who would help me."

"But are they enough? War is coming. It is inevitable now." Nicolae insists, stepping forward.

"Can you risk losing this battle? Can Roseline?"

"Of course not," Fane growls, rounding on Nicolae. His nostrils flare as he bears down. "Do you think me cold-hearted? That I would forget the one person most dear to me just because of all this turmoil?"

Nicolae raises his hands, gently pushing back against Fane's chest. "You know that's not what I meant. I'm simply stating a fact. You can't be in two places at once. Someone must deal with this outbreak of attacks, but we can't just leave Roseline in Malachi's hands. You can't do this alone, Fane."

Fane's shoulders droop as he closes his eyes. Nicolae knows the pull of duty all too well, but he also understands the overwhelming need to save a loved one, no matter the cost. He knows Fane can't argue with his logic.

"There will be a meeting in a few days," Fane begins hesitantly, pausing to open his eyes and stare hard at Nicolae. "My brethren are gathering in the North to create a battle plan. I am supposed to attend, but I cannot leave Sadie alone, so I am forced to take her and William with me."

"And what about me?"

Fane's gaze hardens as a mixture of emotions play across his face. Slowly, his expression loosens. "I trust that you will never do anything to put Sadie's life in danger. As such, I will allow you to join us, but only you."

Nicolae begins to protest, but Fane shakes his head. "You can't control your men, not in a place like this."

"I can try,"

"And if you fail?" Fane presses, stepping closer. "Are you sure enough to risk Sadie's life, as well as that of William and myself?"

"I won't fail." Nicolae swallows roughly, thinking over the consequences if he should fail. Sadie is the enemy now. William would be a causality of war, and Fane...he wouldn't go down without a fight. Nicolae straightens his shoulders, determined to prove Fane wrong.

The ice cracks around Fane's boots as he shifts uneasily. His arms cross tightly over his chest, his posture rigid. "You realize what it is you ask? If your men join our fight, the truce would be tremulous at best, our quarters tight and with a fully stocked armory between us. The chances of there being a massacre among our ranks before we even reach the battlefield are very high."

Nicolae nods solemnly. He knows the risks. He also knows that everyone he loves might die, but can he really back out now, when he has so much personally invested in this? Sadie has become his brothers' enemy. He can't allow them to treat her as such. And the murders...how long will it be before the humans start to fight back, hunting down Fane's kind out of fear?

The world is quickly tumbling into chaos and he is going right along with it, one way or another. "You have my word."

Fane stares hard at him before nodding. "Let's hope that is enough."

Eight

Gabriel can't help but feel odd as he stands in the fierce embrace of a girl he only met a few days ago, realizing that she has become an important figure in his life. Katia's fierce hug surprises him as he pulls back. "It was nice to meet you. Once I am able, I'd like to come back and visit you again."

"You welcome, brother." She wipes away the tears from her wind chapped cheeks.

Gabriel looks back over his shoulder to find Seneh and Elias grinning. "You told her?"

Seneh shrugs. "Who is she going to tell?"

He turns to smile at Katia. "I won't forget you."

"Or bear stew."

Gabriel laughs, knowing how true that was. He would rather eat grain from the hen house floor for the rest of his life rather than swallow down her cooking. "Take care of yourself. I'll make sure to send Seneh back when I'm done with him."

Her smile seems tinged with sorrow as he walks away. An odd sense of homesickness lingers over Gabriel as he wraps his arm around Elias' neck and they rise into the air. "Will I see her again?"

"Someday perhaps."

"And you're sure she's safe here?" He can't help but shake the fear that has gripped him since the first moment he found out they were related. If someone were to discover their secret, she could be used against him. She is his family now, and he will do whatever it takes to protect her.

Gabriel secures his hold around Elias's neck before waving one final time to Katia. As the roof of her cabin blends in with the rest of the forest, he turns to see where they are going.

"Now can you tell me where we are going?" he asks, speaking directly into Elias' ear.

"It is an ancient place, one no man knows still exists. People have sought it out for centuries, but they have been looking in the wrong places."

He pauses as he dips his wings and changes direction, soaring on the mighty gusts of the frozen land. Seneh rides just off Elias' right wing, ever the watchful eye.

"Many years ago, a great flood came over the earth. Water fell from the sky, filling all of the land until only the sea remained. Mountains sank into the depths, and the land shifted and reformed. Nothing was as it was before."

"You're talking about Noah, right?"

"Indeed." Elias nods. Gabriel retightens his grip as they keep to the clouds to remain unseen. The fine mist tickles his face as Elias pumps his wings powerfully and they shoot forward at a greater speed.

"I thought that was just a fairy tale to tell children."

A deep rumbling laugh rises in Elias' chest. "You are riding on the back of an angel right now. At what point will you begin to believe in the impossible?"

"Fair enough." Gabriel releases a frustrated sigh. "Go on."

"This great flood did more than wipe out an entire people. It also hid one of the most precious places in all the land. A place forbidden for man to re-enter."

Gabriel frowns, sifting through childhood memories for a story that might fit. His mind trails back to a tale of a sneaky serpent, one that could speak and tempt. "Whoa, hang on a second. You're not talking about Eden, are you? The garden Adam and Eve were cast out of?"

Elias turns his head to cast a grin back over his shoulder. "See, you know more of your history than you thought."

"That's not history, that's…"

"A fairy tale?" Elias laughs. "Hardly, although is a tale of sorts. Eden is our destination. We should be there by nightfall."

Elias pumps his wings, soaring to greater heights. Gabriel's head breaks through the clouds, and he is blinded by the brilliant sun. He cries out and presses his face into the downy softness of Elias' wings, sure that somehow the angel is pulling his leg. To think that such a place could still exist is crazy. Aren't millions of dollars spent each year by people trying to disprove the Bible? If it were true, wouldn't someone have found evidence of this garden at some point? There's no way such a place could still exist and humans not know about it.

And yet…they don't know he exists either.

Pain ricochets up Roseline's spine as she slams against the ground. She grunts, reaching under herself to clutch her bruised ribs. Rough, scaly hands curl around her arms as they pull her aloft. Fingers twine through her hair and yank her head back, forcing her to stare into the beady eyes of the green monster. The Eltat's stench is overwhelming and foul, forcing her to hold her breath as she comes face to face with it.

Her right eye is swollen shut, and her lower lip is split and seeping blood. Her legs buckle under, no longer able to hold her weight.

She squints, struggling to adjust to the bright light shining down on her. The room is vast and unnaturally lit by fluorescent lights that dangle on chains from the towering ceiling above. The walls are made from stone, smooth as granite. Four doors line each of the walls, leading further into the maze of this underground labyrinth.

Roseline blinks, suddenly realizing she has been brought to the room where she was first reintroduced to Lucien. How vastly different it looks in the light.

Her head begins to throb as the Eltat's grip tightens, pulling strands from her scalp. She would love nothing more than to rip his heart from his chest with her bare hands, but her strength has waned again. Malachi hasn't been back to see her since her plea for help. Has she offended him? Has he changed his mind about saving her from this horrible transformation?

Screams echo from somewhere beyond this room, screeching and high-pitched. Roseline tries to turn toward the sound but surrenders to the pain from her hair ripping from her scalp in large chunks. The Eltat releases a pig-like grunt that she can only assume to be laughter. She vows that he will be the first to die if she has a chance to fight back.

The scream grows louder over the next minute and Roseline braces. She has a bad feeling about what is about to come through the door.

She isn't exactly sure of what she expected to appear, but a teenage boy dressed in a filthy umber robe was not it. His head is shaved clean, but his chin sports clumps of poorly grown beard.

His cheeks sag, evidence of rapid weight loss. His robe piles around him on the floor as he crawls toward the room. Roseline watches as a shiny black boot appears in the doorway and kicks the boy in the backside, sending him sprawling face first into the room.

Anger simmers in Roseline's belly as Malachi comes into view. His face is hard as stone, his features etched with disgust. He raises his boot again to kick the boy. "Stop it," she screams, lunging against the Eltat's grasp.

She can feel trickles of blood trailing down her temple and onto her cheek. Although Malachi's demeanor doesn't shift, his eyes soften just enough for her to know he is pained by the sight of her discomfort. He nods curtly and lets the boy rise shakily to his hands and knees.

As the boy raises his head to look up at Roseline, she notices two things— recognition and determination.

"Don't look at her," Malachi grunts, kicking out one of the boy's hands. He slams back to the ground and grunts in pain.

"Why am I here?" She tries to put as much strength into her demand as she can muster, but the waver in her voice betrays her. If not for the Eltat's claws digging into her arm, she probably wouldn't be upright.

Malachi looks away. "He wants you to see something."

She snorts and sways back into the Eltat. The scaled beast releases a grunt of disgust and shoves her away. In her mind, she knows she's about to fall, but her body refuses to help. She stumbles, knees buckling just before she tumbles to the ground.

The sound of her nose shattering sounds unusually loud in her ears. Thick blood drains down her throat, gagging her. Roseline swallows, grimacing at the feel of sharp bone fragments lodging in her throat.

"I said she was to remain unharmed," a voice calls from her left. A frantic mewing sound rises behind her. She closes her eyes at the spray of blood that splashes against her face. The Eltat falls to the ground beside her, a gaping hole remaining when its throat used to be.

Hands wrap around her arms, lifting her to her feet. She blinks away the blood from her vision to glare at Lucien. Malachi closes the gap between them, allowing her to lean back against the length of his body so that she doesn't fall again.

"I have a gift for you," Lucien says. His breath hisses through the narrow slits of his nose. His breath stinks of rotting flesh and blood, making her stomach roil violently as she presses back into Malachi's chest.

"You killed that thing. That's good enough for me," she spits back.

"Ah, yes. I never liked that one anyways. He had shifty eyes and he always smelled like garlic for some reason." Lucien shrugs and turns his attention onto the boy.

Lucien's long black cloak flares about him as he drops to a crouch and lifts the boy high into air by his throat. Lucien laughs as the boy claws at his hand, his eyes bulging at the pressure on his windpipe.

"Pathetic, isn't he?" Lucien turns him to the left and back to the right, examining him as if he were a meal. Which, Roseline knows he most likely will be. "So frail. So breakable."

"Did you bring me here to lecture me on the inevitability of his death? Because honestly, I'd rather go back to my pit and stare at the wall for the rest of the day." Roseline's words end in a racking cough that doubles her over. Malachi's grip tightens to support her.

Lucien tsks, tossing the boy aside. "You disappointment me, Roseline. I would have thought you would like this boy."

"And why is that?"

He glides close to her, his eyes searching her face. "Because he reeks of Gabriel."

She tries not to show her surprise, but it is impossible. Her breath hitches as she looks past Lucien toward the boy. She has a very vague, blurred memory of seeing him before.

Sorin's dungeon!

Roseline remembers now. He was with the group of monks that took Gabriel away from her. That poisoned her so she couldn't fight back. She stares at the boy as he lies with his cheek pressed to the ground, blood seeping from his hairline. His eyes flutter open to look back at her.

How could she not smell Gabriel on him? Have her senses dulled that much?

"So that's why he's here? To torment me?" Her voice cracks. Her hands begin to tremble at her sides at the thought.

"Oh, no. You misunderstand," Lucien coos, running his finger along the length of her cheek. "He is here to help us find Gabriel. You want to see him again, don't you?"

She wavers on her feet, dizzy. The room spins about her, faster and faster as her eyes sink back into her head and she falls limp in Malachi's arms. As he lowers her to the floor, the boy's screaming begins.

Nine

The tension in the vast great room of Bran Castle is palpable as Nicolae enters through the towering doors with Sadie close at his side. Their footsteps echo around them. He squeezes her hand, reassuring her. "It will be ok."

"Tell that to them," she mutters, glaring at each hostile hunter's face in turn.

Nicolae knew this meeting wouldn't go over well. The hatred for immortals is deeply ingrained in his brothers, but he hopes after today they might be able to bridge a gap.

"Grigori." Nicolae nods as he takes a chair across from the tall man. Grigori's nose sits slightly crooked, a reminder of a time before the truce was begrudgingly forged with Roseline. Nicolae can't help but wonder if he will be able to extend the same truce to Sadie.

"Nicolae," Grigori grunts, never letting his gaze fall away from the spunky girl at his leader's side. Grigori is a fierce warrior, unwavering. Nicolae tightens his grip on Sadie's hand as her muscles lock down, her lips peeling back from her teeth.

"Easy," Nicolae whispers, tugging her toward two empty sets at the end of a long, rectangular table. He holds the chair for her as she sits and then remains behind her seat, his hands gripping the high wooden back.

"I called this meeting tonight to speak of peace—" Nicolae begins, but is instantly cut off by loud protests.

Fists pound against the glossed surface of the cherry wood table. It stretches the length of the room, large enough to seat twenty people easily. Hand carved chairs tip over backward, clattering to the floor, as his brother's lurch to their feet in protest. He closes his eyes, fighting for a calm he doesn't feel. "Peace, brothers. This is the time to speak, not act. I only ask that you listen."

"Those are fine words for someone who brought a traitor into our midst," a man with a strong, square jaw and wild mane of ginger hair growls from the corner of the room. Nicolae squints but struggles to put a name with the man's face.

"I am your leader by birthright." Nicolae pauses to look at each man in turn. "You know that Sorin raised me to one day take his place. I didn't ask for it to be so soon, but I assure you that I am more than capable of filling his shoes."

A laugh rises from a man at the far end of the table. Even though concealed in shadow, Nicolae knows him to be Bodgan Ardelean, his uncle's swordsmith. The barrel-chested man who sits stroking his favorite battle ax is not one that Nicolae would usually like to take on, but this is not a normal situation.

"You aren't fit to lead us. Sorin knew you were weak, and now you're always spouting off about making peace with that filth. Your uncle would turn over in his grave if he saw you today."

Nicolae grits his teeth as he releases his hold on Sadie's seatback and steps into the space before his own chair, taking up his rightful place at the head of the table. "I am well aware of what you all think of me. I know you feel betrayed, and I don't blame you for that. For generations, we have been taught to hunt and kill immortals, but we can't live in an archaic society forever. Roseline and Fane have proven that not all immortals are bad. They helped you take down Vladimir Enescue and this is the thanks they get?"

"They are different." Grigori holds up his hand to silence the protests. "They have proven themselves to be honorable. Your girl hasn't."

Nicolae's grip tightens on the edge of the wooden table. His knuckles pop as he tries to withhold his anger. He should have known Sadie would be the first topic on the agenda.

"She is under Fane's protection and has no desire to harm any of you."

"Are we supposed to just take your word for that?" Nicolae turns to look over his shoulder at Costel Petran, a well-respected leader among the European hunters guild. He is short

and rotund, but Nicolae knows him to be deceptively strong.
Although he has only seen the man from a distance, he knows
his uncle thought very highly of the man, and that worries
Nicolae. This man must despise immortals just as much, if not
more, than Sorin did.

Costel's dark brown eyes look nearly black in the dim
light of the dining room of Bran Castle. Nicolae would feel
much better if they could light a fire, to add more light to the
dreary room, but he knows the heat disturbs Sadie so he resists.

"She is none of your concern."

"I beg to differ." A man with raised red scars lining his
arms stands up to join the argument, easily the tallest of the
hunters in the room. Danut Lupei became a hero after the fall of
the Berlin Wall. He led a small group of hunters over the ruins
of the wall and rooted out an entire coven residing in the
Kremlin. His brutality is nearly as legendary as Vladimir's, so
Nicolae has always been glad to have him fighting on his side.

Nicolae turns to face the man. "Is that a challenge,
Danut?"

The heavily muscled man grins, appearing excited at the
prospect of a fight, but Grigori holds up his hand. "Enough.
This is getting us nowhere. Nicolae called us here for a reason,
so let's hear him out before there is bloodshed."

Never before has Nicolae been so grateful for his
second-in-command. He has never particularly liked Grigori,
but Nicolae could almost kiss him right now. Clearing his
throat, Nicolae stares each of the men down until they slowly
sink back into their seats.

He glances at Sadie, who perches on the edge of her
seat. "It's ok."

She nods stiffly and relaxes back but looks far from
comfortable, despite the fact that Fane paces in the hall beyond.
He was less than happy when Nicolae asked him to remain
outside. Although Fane's presence may have been accepted by
several of the hunters, Nicolae vowed to do this on his own, to
lead his men without any outside help.

"You have all seen the news reports," he begins, pausing
for effect. The shift in the room is instantaneous as each man

nods. "Someone has taken up Vladimir's quest and they must be stopped. The killings have been spreading through Europe and are now popping up all around the world. We must stop this before it gets out of hand, but we can't do it on our own."

Nicolae hesitates and braces for the anticipated uproar but is shocked to find that none of the men speak. He raises an eyebrow in surprise but Grigori nods at him to continue. "Someone is trying to send a message, and I don't think it's just for the humans. We are being called out."

"By whom?" Costel leans forward.

"We have reason to believe Lucien Enescue is behind all of this."

The room explodes around Nicolae. He waits several minutes before speaking. The angry whispers cease as he continues. "I have already sent a team to each of the crime scenes to see what details they can uncover, but it doesn't look good. Initial reports show teeth marks and the victims drained of blood. I think Lucien wants the humans to know about immortals."

"But that's insane!" Danut pounds his fist against the table top. It shudders, the wood groaning in protest. "Those beasts have spent thousands of years hiding their existence. Why would they come into the light now?"

"Because they want to shift the food chain," Sadie whispers.

All eyes swivel to land on her. She blinks, startled to find herself in the spotlight. "What did you say?" Nicolae whispers.

She stares back at him, unsure if she should speak or not. He smiles, encouraging her. Slipping to the edge of her chair, she clears her throat and addresses the group.

"You may not like me, and to be honest, you're not so likable yourselves right now, but I know both sides of this story." She pauses to lock eyes with each man sitting around the table. "I can smell your fear even though you try desperately to hide it. I can hear every quiver of your heart as you think about the global battle you have on your hands, and you are right to fear. Lucien knows what he is doing. He wants the entire world to fear him, to know that immortals are the top of the food chain now."

A heavy silence fills the room as her words trail off, and she leans back in her chair. Nicolae can't help but smile at the effect she has had on his men.

"Can he really do this? Flip the food chain on its end?" Grigori mutters, clenching his hands into fists.

"They can and they are. Already humans are terrified to leave their homes at night. People are afraid to travel or to even say hi to their next door neighbors. Mass panic is beginning to spread around the world. Lucien's murders are becoming more brazen, more gruesome. These attacks are increasing by the day."

"But there has to be more than one person doing this," Bodgan says, running his thumb along the edge of his battle ax. A small sliver of blood appears and Sadie stiffens beside Nicolae. Every hunter fixes her in their gaze as she releases her breath and turns her attention away. "No man can move from country to country so quickly."

"He doesn't need to," Nicolae muses, leaning forward and resting his palms against the table. "We know from Sorin's reports that Vladimir had pockets of immortals already stationed around the world. China. Russia. Australia. The United States. Spain. Africa. South America. Who knows how many thousands of them there are? I'm still waiting for the Intel, but I'd bet my life that these pockets have been mobilized. It's only a matter of time until this spreads into a worldwide epidemic and we won't be able to stop these murders. This panic will only grow unless we can end this now."

A stout hunter, with marbled hair and a weathered face leans forward into the light. Nicolae eyes the older man, dredging up his name from memory: Andrei Ungur. "So you want to join up with Fane and go out in a blaze of glory, is that it?"

Nicolae smiles. He slips out from behind his chair and slowly makes his way around the room, placing his hand on each man's shoulder in turn. "I'm giving you the chance to avenge your loved ones. Never before has there been a battle such as this. Your names will be infamous. You will bring honor to your families."

A low rumble begins in the back of the room, and Nicolae decides to take that as affirmation that he's on the right track. He steps behind Grigori's chair. "All I ask is for a temporary truce. Long enough to track down these fiends and put an end to them. Isn't this what we were created for? What you have spent your entire lives training for?"

Another rumble of assent is followed by a few random head bobs. Nicolae begins to speak but is shocked into silence as Sadie rises and stares down at his men. "I may be new to your part of the world, to immortality, but I tremble standing before you, not because of your weapons in hand or the gleam in your eye, but because of the pride I see in this room. You are fierce hunters, and you have earned your name among your kind and mine. I would be honored to fight alongside you, to shed blood and rend limbs to bring order back to our world. Will you fight with me? Will you fight for Nicolae?"

Nicolae's mouth gapes open at the obnoxious pounding of fists against the table as his men rise and cheer. He turns to stare at Sadie, dazzled not by her eccentric beauty but by the leader she is becoming.

He rounds the end of the table and pulls her hand into his, leaning close to whisper into her ear. "You are so hot right now."

She laughs and pulls back, her cheeks flushed with excitement. "I bet you say that to all the girls."

Malachi has heard his fair share of screams over the years, but none have compared to this. After half a day of torture, the old man still won't break, but the sound of his agony rises with each hour that passes.

Malachi places his saw on the wooden table beside him. Fresh blood speckles against the floor. He moves his feet back to avoid being stained. "I can end this, you know. No more pain. No more screaming. It can all just go away."

The man's head hangs low, revealing a growing bald spot at the top of his head. His whiskers are long, unkempt, and soiled. His eyes are bloodshot, and his mouth hangs open as he sucks in great gulps of air.

Malachi can't help but admire the man's courage, no matter how foolish it might be. He has tortured many men and brought them to their knees, begging for death, but this man hasn't said a single word. Malachi ripped out his fingernails with pliers and shoved a branding iron against his stomach, but the man remained mute.

He screamed. Oh yes, he did plenty of that, but he never spoke a word.

Lifting his head, the man stares defiantly back at Malachi from his one remaining good eye. His left eye rolled off the table and into the corner about an hour ago after being extracted from its socket.

"You have maintained your honor, old man. Let me give you a swift death to end your suffering." He can feel himself almost pleading with the man, not for the sake of gaining the information he seeks, but so that he can show mercy

The man spits at his tormenter. A mixture of shattered teeth and blood smack against Malachi's cheek. He sighs and shakes his head as he grabs a scalpel. "So be it."

Gabriel's knees have gone into complete lockdown by the time they finally arrive at the edge of an unusual body of water. The shallow, briny lake is rimmed with white sand and encircled by dark forests of eucalyptus trees. The ocean is not far away; a narrow strip of white dunes separate the lake from the frothing waves that crash against the shoreline. The water is clear near the coast, beautiful turquoise spilling into the vast spread of deep blue sea.

But the water that laps against Gabriel's feet is nothing like that of the ocean or any other body of water he has ever seen. Even in the fading twilight, he can see the pink hue that permeates the water.

"How is this possible?" he asks, turning to speak to Elias. Gabriel's mentor huddles not far away, deep in whispered discussion with Seneh.

They both look up, cast their gaze beyond him and seem completely unphased by the amazing sight. "Some scientists claim it is caused by the algae living within the lake, while others have ruled out that theory. Humans have only to look to the beginning to see what has caused this amazing marvel."

Gabriel stares past Elias to Seneh. "Are you going to put that into English for me or do I have to waste my time guessing?"

Seneh laughs. He stretches out his broadsword, carefully rubbing a warm stone along its edge. "He speaks of the rains that fell from the sky, creating the flood. Some versions speak of the water rising from the depths of the earth. Others say that it fell in the form of rain. Both are true.

I don't get it," Gabriel steps out of the water. Sand clings to his damp feet as he sinks down onto a log beside the two angels. "How does that make this water pink?"

"Some say that the sunlight coming through the flood rains made it look pink." Seneh shrugs. "I don't really know. We were busy on the front lines."

Gabriel's eyebrow rises. "That happened a long time ago, right?" Elias dips his head in approval. "So then that would mean you guys are really old. Like ancient, even."

"Age, growth, the passage of time…all of these are human terms, created to help you understand your place in the cycle of life. As you can now see, when eternity expands out before you, time no longer matters." Elias says, stretching out his wings, like a cat after a long nap in a warm window.

Gabriel turns to look out over the lake. Its surface is eerily calm considering the winds that have begun to whip around them. "It feels weird here."

Elias nods. "Humans can sense there is something peculiar about this place. Some would say magical even, but none can truly figure out the secrets of Hiller Lake."

"So, what now?" Gabriel rises and approaches the tall grasses that grow at the edge of the beach, sinking to his knees. The heat of the day has begun to flee and a chill hangs on the early evening air, refreshing and eerie at the same time.

Australia looks nothing like he imagined. It is too beautiful, too rugged. He can appreciate the primitive nature of the land and if it weren't for the heat, he could see himself making a home near the ocean.

"Now," Elias pauses, stretching out his legs as he sinks down onto the edge of the sand, "you swim."

"Whoa, hang on a second," Gabriel says, marching back toward him. Seneh's lips curl into a smirk as he silently sharpens his blade. "You can't be serious. That lake is probably full of hungry monsters."

"Oh, to be sure." Elias grins, crossing his arms over his bare chest. His eyes glint with humor. "Don't tell me you're afraid of a little crocodile."

Gabriel straightens his shoulders, annoyed with his mentor's taunting. "Laugh all you want, but I'm not going in there alone."

"Of course not." Seneh rises to his feet. "I'm going with you."

He should have known his guardian would follow him to the ends of the earth. "Fine," Gabriel kicks at a sand dune, not the least bit excited about this. "But if I get eaten, this is all on you, Elias."

His mentor leans forward, all traces of humor gone from his face. "What lives in the lake is not what you should be worried about, Gabriel. Fear what you will find in its depths."

Ten

Fane paces the length of the hall just outside the great room of Bran Castle. He is deeply unsettled by the presence of so many hunters in his home. It doesn't feel right. Despite his reluctant agreement to host the hunters here, he is definitely having second thoughts.

He spins around when the doors to the great room open inward. Nicolae pokes his head out and waves him over. "It's a go."

"Are you sure?"

When Nicolae grins, his youthful appearance does little to instill confidence in Fane's heart. "I told you to trust me."

"We haven't made it to Canada yet," he mutters as he follows Nicolae into the room.

Dozens of beady eyes rise to meet Fane's as he approaches the foot of the table. The air feels thick and oppressive as he tries to take a breath. *This is a mistake. I should never have allowed this.*

A tall man stands and a hush falls over the room. Fane eyes his large frame, noting the scars along his face and the slight twist to his nose. "Grigori," he nods in acknowledgement.

They have tussled several times over the past few years. He knows the man's strengths as well as his weaknesses. Unfortunately for Fane, the man possesses very few.

"Are we correct in assuming this was not your plan?" Grigori asks.

If he was human, Fane is sure he would be sweating profusely by now. Instead, he remains cool and aloof. "You are correct."

"And yet you agreed?"

Fane clears his throat and casts a tight glance at Nicolae. The boy stands straight and proud at Fane's side. Perhaps

Nicolae really could pull off being a leader. "Reluctantly, but Nicolae can be rather…persuasive."

Grigori cracks a hint of a smile. "Gets that from his uncle."

At the mention of Sorin Funar, Fane struggles to conceal the growl rising in his throat. No matter what friendship he might have formed with Sorin's nephew, he has no intention of ever forgiving the deceased man for luring Roseline to his dungeon.

Nicolae steps forward to intercede, but Fane places a hand on his arm. "No, it's fine. I'm sure he taught you to be a good leader."

Murmurs rise around the table, but Fane ignores each of them. "I realize the need for your help in this matter, but I must impress upon you the danger that you will be facing. I cannot guarantee your safety."

"Nor should you try," a man with a bushy red beard man calls out from the far end of the table, his eyes flashing with barely concealed anger. Fane nods in agreement, thankful that they at least understand each other.

This truce will be fragile at best. Neither side wants it, but both know they need it.

"The trip to Canada will not be an easy one. The journey will be long and taxing on you. The summers are cold and the winters fierce. You will need to pack warm clothes."

"We are mountain men, immortal," a man beside Grigori protests. "We know how to handle the cold."

Fane leans forward, his knuckles popping as he applies weight on them. "I assure you, you have never felt winds like this before."

Sadie shifts uneasily in her chair as the men around her puff up with indignation. Nicolae covers his face with his hands, shaking his head. Fane understands his frustration all too well, but he wonders if the boy truly comprehends what he is about to face.

"This compound is deep within the northern territory of Canada. It is called the Senthe base, run by a group of highly skilled immortals. Some of you may recognize them from previous skirmishes. This remote location offers frozen wastelands and death to any who dare to enter. Most of your men will not survive the cold, let alone the battle. The ones that do may wish they hadn't."

"That sounded pretty intense," William says, plopping down onto a couch in Bran Castle's library, soup bowl in hand. Walls of books tower to the high ceilings above. A fire crackles in the hearth, spilling warmth into the room. William tugs a blanket into his lap. "Everything ok?"

"It went as expected," Nicolas nods, lifting his head from the map he has spread on the table before him. Try as he might to find any sign of the Senthe base Fane mentioned on the map, he finds only barren, raw wilderness. Of course, he should have figured that. No immortal would create a hideout where hunters could easily penetrate.

"I heard we are leaving." William tips his bowl just enough for Nicolae to see three enormous scoops of ice cream.

Nicolae shakes his head, laughing. "Only you would eat ice cream when it's the dead of winter."

"I've got a blanket and a cozy fire. I'm good." William shrugs. "So what's the deal with this base then? Sounds kinda weird."

Nicolae leans back in his chair, pinching the bridge of his nose. His eyes are tired from reading under candlelight, and the muscles in his neck and back are stiff from sitting far too long. "I don't really know much about it, for obvious reasons. Fane says it will be the safest place for you and Sadie."

"And you agreed to this?" William lifts the bowl to lick off a drip of chocolate.

"I did." Nicolae begrudgingly nods. Even though he likes to think he can trust Fane, agreeing to place himself in a small building with other immortals isn't exactly on his top ten list of things he wants to do before he dies. "There is a war coming and this will be the safest place for you."

He pauses and looks to where Sadie is curled up in an armchair in the far corner of the room, as far from the fire as she can get while still remaining in the room. "Fane has agreed to let me train with Sadie, but only when he is present. I guess that's something."

Sadie's expression turns sour. "He still thinks I'm going to bite you, doesn't he?"

Nicolae closes the map before him and pushes up from his chair, moving to sit beside her in the oversized chair. It's a tight fit but he doesn't mind it one bit. "It's not you that he's worried about. It's me. He's worried that if you attack me, I'll have to stake you in the heart."

"Alright, Buffy," Sadie chuckles, smacking him on the arm hard enough to leave a bruise. "Easy on the staking bit, will ya?"

"Did someone say Buffy?" William asks, his head craning back to look at them. "That girl is one hot chick."

Sadie rolls her eyes and snatches a pillow to throw at him. William cries out as his bowl tumbles to the ground, his spoon splattering melted ice cream everywhere as it bounces off the hard wood. "Oh! Not cool, Sadie. Not cool."

He dips low to retrieve his bowl, groaning loudly at the puddle of goo underfoot. Nicolae smirks, leaning back to rest his head atop Sadie's. This feels almost normal. Almost.

"So what about these Senthe? Are they a different type of immortal or something?" Sadie asks, watching as William leaves the room to grab a cloth.

"I've never actually heard of them before, which is odd since Sorin had spies everywhere." He glances over at the map and frowns. "Apparently the immortals were still a step ahead of us."

"Don't feel so bad." She places a hand on his chest as she snuggles close. "We are *way* cooler than you."

He barks out a laugh as he encloses her in his arms. "That is debatable."

The door to the library opens and William steps in. When he looks to where they sit, his nose scrunches up and he makes a show of covering his eyes. "Ah, come on guys. There is way too much PDA going on in this room."

Sadie laughs and leaps up from the chair, tiptoeing lightly across the back of the couch before doing a front flip to land silently before her brother. When he opens his eyes to see her standing an inch from his nose, his shriek of terror is priceless.

Nicolae howls with laughter, clutching his stomach as William flails back, bouncing hard off the door before sliding to the floor. His face goes from white to red in a matter of seconds as he comes up, spluttering.

"What are you doing? Trying to give me a heart attack?"

"Nah. I think she was looking for a snack," Nicolae calls, grinning mischievously.

William's face drains of color once more as he darts a nervous glance at his sister. "He's just joking, right?"

"Oh, come on, Will. You know I'd never bite you."

"Why not?" He asks defensively.

"Well, you kinda stink."

Nicolae erupts with laughter as William's mouth gapes open. "I…I do not stink!"

Leaning forward, Nicolae makes a show of sniffing the air. He scrunches up his nose. "You do kinda stink."

William scowls and crosses his arms over his chest. "The soap here is weird. It's not spring fresh the way I like it."

"You're such an idiot," Sadie snickers. "I'm not talking about your soap preferences. I'm talking about your blood."

The laughter in the room instantly cuts off. William and Nicolae exchange a worried glance. Sadie's smile fades. "What? I'm not allowed to admit that I notice stuff like that?"

"No, of course you can. It's just…"Nicolae trails off, unsure of how to explain without hurting her feelings.

"It's creepy," William finished for him.

"Wow, way to earn subtlety points," Nicolae growls.

"Be that as it may," Sadie says, interrupting the tension in the room, "it's still the truth. And you, dear brother, reek."

Nicolae shifts his gaze toward Sadie, confused. "I thought blood would smell good to you."

"It does. Like yours, it's really nice." She grins, punching him on the arm. "But William's has this…sour scent to it."

"Hmm." He purses his lips. "I wonder why."

"Because they are related." Fane winces as he steps into the room, blasted by the heat billowing out from the fire. Nicolae rushes forward and tosses a bucket of dirt onto it, dousing the flames.

Fane smiles his thanks as he moves to the bookshelves and traces his finger along the leather bound bindings. He plucks random books from the wall, looks at them and then replaces each as he continues his search. "Immortals never look upon their own flesh and blood as food. That would be…disgusting."

"Oh," William gulps loudly, rubbing at his neck. "Good to know."

Sadie sticks out her tongue at him. "See. Told you."

Fane clears his throat. No one realized he had shifted to join their group. Nicolae frowns, reminded of how eerily quiet immortals can be when it serves their purpose. "William may be safe, but Nicolae is not. Sadie's control over her thirst is impressive, but it is not infallible. One of these days she will fail, and when she does, I pray that she does not regret it."

His words hang heavily over the silent room. The only sounds are the howling of the wind beyond the castle walls and the sputtering of the dying fire.

"What are in those books?" Nicolae asks, trying to break the somber mood in the room. He can tell Sadie is caught between fuming and fear that Fane might be right.

Fane turns and hands a book to Nicolae. Its cover is made of supple black leather, obviously much newer than the other books housed in this great library. "This book will tell you everything there is to know about the Senthe base. They are no different than Sadie or me. The Senthe is an organization, a secret society among my world, if you will."

"Oh, great," William groans, sinking back to lean against the wall. "Because history has shown us that secret societies only exist for the good of the people."

Fane's lip curls with humor. "This one actually does. We were created by a noble founder. I believe even you, William, can find no fault in Roseline."

"Hang on a second," Nicolae says, gripping tightly to the book. "You're saying Roseline helped form this group?"

"No." Fane turns to look at him. "I'm saying it was her idea to create it in the first place."

The sound of dripping has returned. Roseline groans, rolling to her side. The dirt floor is cold beneath her and the light dismal. She is back in her pit.

"Roseline," a voice nearby rasps.

She bolts upright, instantly wishing she hadn't. Her head spins as pain lashes out with a vengeance against her mind. She clamps her eyes shut, praying for the torment to end.

"I knew it was you."

Barely opening one eye, she searches for the voice. It comes from a person hanging from the far wall, nearly fifteen feet overhead. Thick, rusted chains hold the boy aloft. Blood clings to much of his bare skin, evidence of the earlier torture she passed out before.

His face is a mess of gashes and his right eye is swollen completely shut. Numerous knife wounds slit across the flesh of his throat and arms. Crimson droplets trail slowly but steadily down his leg, pattering onto the floor.

She groans and buries her head in her hands. She can't handle this. Not this.

"Are you ok?" He calls down to her.

"No," she croaks, releasing her head to clutch her arms about her curled knees as she begins to rock. It has been too long since she last had a bloodletting with Malachi. She can feel the poison beginning to take control. "You shouldn't be here. This is bad. Very bad."

"Tell me about it. I had reservations for dinner tonight."

Her mouth gapes open as she lifts her head to stare at the boy. "Are you...did you just make a joke?

"Yeah, it's just this thing I do right before I pee myself." He tries to look down to see if that has already happened, but his chains keep him from seeing. He goes limp, giving up. "My uncle always said I'd make a terrible prisoner. Guess he was right."

Roseline opens and closes her mouth, unsure of what to say, or even if she should believe he is here. "Are you real?"

"Afraid so. Can't you smell me?" When she swallows roughly, he winces. "Sorry. Poor choice of words."

"I agree." She releases her hold on her knees and presses her palms back against the wall, inching her way to her feet. She can feel the weakness in her legs but refuses to acknowledge it.

"I've seen you before." She leans back to rest against the wall. Just the effort it takes to stand is exhausting, but she needs to see his face.

The boy nods. His chains shift, casting him just far enough into the light to confirm it for her. "I remember... I nearly snapped your arm in half when you tried to touch Gabriel." An irrational rage begins to simmer in her stomach, intense and highly explosive.

"My name is Enael."

She is only vaguely aware that he spoke as she closes her eyes and sways, remembering the dart that burrowed into her chest, leaving her paralyzed and helpless to save Gabriel. Her lip curls into a snarl. "You took him from me."

Roseline stumbles forward, her arm outstretched to try to grasp his foot. He cries out as her nails graze his big toe. He thrashes about as her face contorts with anger. "You took him from me!"

Her cry echoes through the room as she swipes wildly at him. He bucks his legs to remain out of reach. She growls, pacing beneath him like a wild animal, desperately trying to figure out how to sink her claws into him.

Even as she moves beside the wall, beating her hands in frustration, she knows she is overreacting. The lucid side of her brain tells her that she needs to stop, screaming that this boy could help her find Gabriel, but she can't seem to break free from her rage.

"We never hurt Gabriel. We helped him," Enael shouts, tears streaming down his gaunt cheeks. Roseline pauses to stare up at him. "He was my friend."

Her hands slide off the wall. "What do you mean?"

"Gabriel has a destiny. One that he couldn't fulfill if he remained with you, so my uncle Sias and his men brought him back to our monastery. Sias taught him how to fight and how to understand the changes he was going through while he waited."

Roseline pulls back the matted hair covering her face to see him clearly. "Waited for what?"

"The angels."

The quivering begins in her feet, slowly working its way up her ankles and calves. By the time it ripples up to her head, she knows she's about to lose control again. She tries to slow her breathing and to regain some sense of calm, but her own body is fighting against her.

"His destiny was with me," she growls. Her head lolls to the side as the whispers come, crawling from the shadows to torment her. Their guttural growls and hisses consume her mind.

"Go away," she moans, clutching her head in her hands as she doubles over.

"Of course his destiny is with you, but not in the way you think."

Her moaning cuts off. She uncurls her fingers from around her head as she slowly rises to look up at him. "What do you mean?"

"The prophecy is very specific about the fact that you are as much a part of Gabriel's success as he is yours. He can't win without you. You and he are meant to—" His eyes bulge as the manacles around his arms begin to shift, the chains clanging as they are retracted into the wall. They pull from opposite directions like an old fashioned rack.

"No!" Roseline screams, clawing at the wall. Enael's cries shift into desperate wails as the chains pull taut. As his joints begin to crack, Roseline searches for the winch that controls the chains. Her gaze runs along the metal links until they disappear into the wall. There is no way for her to shut down the machine.

"Help me!" Enael screams. His face contorts with pain as his muscles and tissues begin to tear. It's only a matter of seconds before his shoulders dislocate and a few more before his flesh begins to split.

Sudden clarity returns as she contemplates leaping and grasping onto his feet to yank him down, but that would shatter everything below his waist. Her only chance is to climb to the chains and pray that they aren't wrapped in angel hair.

Enael's screams rise to sickening levels as his right shoulder pops out of socket. "Roseline!"

"I'm coming," she growls.

Digging her fingers deep into the stone, she refuses to acknowledge the pain of dislocating her own fingers as she frantically tries to climb. She slams her toes repeatedly into the wall, trying to carve out footholds. She howls in frustration as her bones shatter and her footing gives way, leaving her dangling from the wall. There is nothing she can do to reach him.

She plummets to the floor as Enael's shriek cuts off. Her head whips up to see his left shoulder popped out of place. Enael's head bounces against his chest as he finally passes out. Urine trails down his leg, pattering into the floor below.

Roseline crouches to the side and pushes off the floor, her crooked fingers stretching to reach his feet, but he is too far out of reach now. She collapses to the ground, tears of defeat swimming in her eyes. She has never felt so helpless.

She closes her eyes as Enael's flesh begins to tear, knowing that it will all be over soon. She covers her ears and buries her face in her knees, unable to watch. The last of the candle flickers out, leaving her in complete darkness.

Eleven

A cluster of Eltat scatter as Malachi shoves his way through the crowded hallway. "Get out of here," he growls, kicking at a scrawny creature beside him as his boot connects solidly with its spine, sending it sprawling to the floor.

It turns and hisses up at him. Its forked tongue is black and swollen, flitting out of its lipless mouth. He ignores the idle threat as he turns his back on the little monster. It won't touch him. None of them can. Not until Lucien gives them the order and, for now, that hasn't happened.

As he reaches the base of a wide double door, he shoos away a small olive-skinned creature, a midget among his kind. It stands only three feet tall. Its scales are bleached much lighter than the others. Its tufts of hair are brown instead of black. Malachi can't help but wonder if he was the bastard of the bunch.

"Off with you, Phio. You know he doesn't like it when you snoop."

Its beady red eyes narrow as a low growl rises from its throat. It doesn't speak. Ever. It hasn't since the first day it arrived at Malachi's home and that is just fine by him. He never has liked the grating tone of their voices. The Eltat language is nothing more than disjointed hissing and clicking of tongues. He finds it to be rather annoying.

He waits for the sound of Phio's clacking claws to fade away before slipping through the doors. They open silently on well-oiled hinges. A human wouldn't even hear his entry, but he knows Lucien has already sensed his presence.

The entry to Lucien's chambers is narrow and the ceiling low. Although Malachi doesn't have to duck, there is little space between the top of his head and the stone above. His footsteps are silent as he moves steadily along the passage. He peers through the dark, noting the disturbing lack of light.

His unease grows more intense as he senses an odd rise in temperature. The air in the room feels close and humid against his skin. Lucien's chambers are normally kept cool.

"Master?" He calls, stepping from the hall and descending three steps to the main floor of Lucien's chambers.

The room opens up into a nearly perfect circle once out of the hall. The walls, from waist height upward, are adorned with bookshelves, each one heaving under the weight of an enormous collection of ancient books. Malachi has never been allowed to touch a single one although he would dearly love to. His own collection is far inferior.

"I am here," a raspy voice drifts from above

Malachi cranes his head back to peer into the great heights of the room. Much work went into creating this space to widen the caverns to give Lucien a mansion like room. Stone arches have been carved from the bedrock, providing an excellent vantage point for anyone capable of reaching such heights.

If it were not for his ability to see in darkness, Malachi would have struggled to pinpoint Lucien's location. Finally, he spies him in the far corner, his large shadow hunched and turned away from him. "You sent for me."

"Indeed." The shadow moves, one second there, the next slithering along the ceiling and toward the bookcase.

A single lamp rests in the center of the room. Its mellow light offers a warm golden glow on a small circle of chairs, each set low to play mental games with anyone who enters. Lucien has always enjoyed games and loves making his victims feel less than they really are, not that he ever needed chairs to accomplish this feat.

When Lucien reaches the far wall, he turns and begins to climb down the ladder-like bookshelves, head first. Malachi frowns, disturbed by Lucien's new trick. "Are you well?"

"Never better," his master hisses, leaping backward from the wall and landing on all fours before Malachi. His grin widens, revealing multiple rows of teeth, as he raises up.

Up close, it is impossible not to notice the changes in Lucien. His arms and legs are nearly double their original size.

His scale-like skin is transforming into something reptilian, almost like living body armor. Each scale glows an iridescent red, even in the dark, as if a fire burns deep within. His eyes are a deep scarlet, vacant of eyelashes.

His lips have receded to the point of being nearly non-existent. His ears are shrunken at the sides of his head and his hair has begun to fallout in great clumps.

"It just that you seem a bit…different," Malachi hedges. He forces his muscles to relax, even though every fiber of his being says to flee. He scolds himself for not noticing these changes sooner, but he has been consumed with his work. It took much longer to kill the old monk than he would have liked.

"Humans believe in evolution, and although I find their theories to be highly flawed, I do think they are intriguing." He lifts his arm and turns it this way and that, grinning at the way the light glints off his scales. "Perhaps they are not entirely wrong after all."

Goosebumps rise along Malachi's neck. Whatever is happening to Lucien is not good. "How did this happen?"

Red eyes shift to stare at him. Malachi refuses to show the fear growing in his chest, threatening to suffocate him. "Roseline did this to me. It is a gift. Soon I will be able to share the joy of this transformation with her."

"She'll be like you?"

Lucien's gaze narrows at the obvious tremor in Malachi's voice. "You say that like it's a bad thing."

"Not at all. Just…clarifying." Malachi's brow grows damp. He clears his throat and tries to focus on why he is here. "The monk didn't give up any information on the boy's whereabouts."

Lucien nods, slowly turning his back on Malachi. He weaves back and forth, more snakelike than human. "That is because he did not know."

Malachi blinks. "You knew this?"

"Of course," Lucien laughs, deep and throaty. "The man was a fool. Nothing more."

"I skinned him alive," Malachi whispers, haunted by the memory.

"Yes," his master hisses with delight. "Pity I couldn't be there to watch his final moments. I'm sure they were…excruciating."

He has never seen a human withstand such pain before. It was a relief to finally shove the knife into the old monk's heart to ease his suffering. "I disposed of the body as you asked. The old man should be found in the Thames within the day."

Lucien's chuckle sounds wet as he turns around to face Malachi. "That will keep the local police busy while we move to a more…suitable location."

"You have yet to tell me where that will be, Master." Malachi bows low, aware of Lucien's critical gaze. A tiny bead of sweat escapes his brow, betraying him.

"You need not know all of the details for now." He waves off Malachi's questioning glance. "You have another job to perform before we begin to pack."

Malachi rises slowly, tilting his head just enough to make the sweat drip into his eyebrow instead of running freely down to his cheek. "Another job?"

"Why yes," Lucien says, sounding surprised as he turns back. "Have you forgotten that we have another monk staying with us? Surely he knows of Gabriel's whereabouts."

"And if he doesn't?"

A jagged, toothy smile spreads across Lucien's face as he gazes down at a quilt of leathery flesh that adorns his floor. The large patches have been sewn together, each one varying in pigment. The newest addition is still moist to the touch. "Then I will have another skin for my collection."

Nicolae grips his armrests tightly. The foam padding escaping from his bucket seat tumbles about the floor as the plane lurches in the air.

"We're gonna die. We're gonna die." William chants with his head buried in his hands.

"I promise I won't let that happen." Fane clasps him on his arm. "I'd never hear the end of it from your sister."

Sadie sticks out her tongue at him before dipping her head to look out of the window again. Nicolae relaxes a fraction as the small by plane rights itself and they begin to slow.

He hadn't really stopped to think about their final destination. The Northwestern Territory of Canada had sounded bad enough, but when you add in the bit about being above the arctic circle Nicolae knows he greatly underestimated his ability to adapt to his surroundings.

Nicolae notices that Fane failed to mention anything about the perpetual twilight that covers the land. "What time is it?" He asks.

"Who cares?" William groans, clutching his stomach. His skin has taken on a sickly green hue. "I just want to be on the ground again!"

Nicolae shoves a small metal bucket toward William. The pilot handed one to each of them when they boarded this internal flight only a short time ago. William has already filled two and is working on his third.

"It's a little after noon," the pilot calls over his shoulder as the plane shudders and turns for its final approach to the small airport terminal. It is tiny, far smaller than any Nicolae has ever seen. In the blustery winds, it looks descrtcd.

The plane jolts suddenly as it is caught in an updraft, causing William to shriek and Nicolae to dig his fingers into the seat yet again. He can hardly feel the shudder of the wheels as they lower into place. His eyes focus only on the wheel as the pilot calls for his final permission to land and lines up with the runway.

The landing itself goes much smoother than he could have anticipated, but the icy slide afterward leaves his stomach back on the runway. Finally, the tiny plane slides to a halt less than a hundred yards from the terminal.

"And thank you for flying Air Canada." Their pilot chuckles to himself as he begins powering down the engines.

William clutches his bucket, glaring up at Fane as the immortal pries it out of his hands. Sadie grunts as she works to unbuckle the belt from around William's rotund belly. "I think you're taking this a bit to the extreme."

An airport worker bangs his fist against the outer hull just before the seal around the door breaks. Fane leans out and helps to lower the foldable stairs to the ground.

"You've got to be kidding me," William swears and burrows deep into his coat as the first blast of icy winds swirls about the cabin.

Nicolae wraps his arms about himself, following Fane's lead from the small aircraft. Cruel winds toss Nicolae's hair about his face, hindering his vision, not that he cares to keep his eyes open for long. The dismal temperatures of the Arctic Circle are not to be underestimated.

"Welcome to Inuvik, Canada," Fane calls. Nicolae can hardly hear him.

"What's with the sky?" William shouts.

"Don't you know anything? It's dark here in the winter," Sadie says, closing her eyes as she lifts her face to the wind.

"Dark? As in the sun never rises or sets? Oh man," William groans, sinking further into the layers of his coat. "I saw that movie, *30 Days of Night*. Those vampires tore up that town!"

He casts a contempt-filled glare at Sadie and Fane. "You two sure now how to show a guy a great time."

"And you look like a fool," Sadie chides, poking William in the area his stomach should be under all of his layers.

A muffled curse emerges from the general direction of William's head. "Why do you people always hide in the freakin' snow?"

Sadie laughs, tossing out her hands as she twirls in the rising winds. She is dressed in only a light sweater and jeans. If she'd had her choice she probably would have stripped down to her underclothes just to feel the snow against her bare skin. Her hair whips about her forehead as she laughs. "It feels amazing. I wish you could experience this, Will."

"I'd give my left arm for a hot water bottle down my pants right about now," he grumbles back. His head disappears into the folds of cloth, reminding Nicolae of a very grumpy turtle.

Nicolae's cheeks burn and his nose has become a leaky faucet. His eyes water when he cracks them and he fears they will ice closed. "William does have a point. It's freezing out here. How long until our next flight?"

Fane pulls the sleeve of his black woolen coat up enough to look at his watch. At least he has the decency to pretend to be affected by the weather. "That was it. A car will be along within the hour to pick us up."

William groans and begins to waddle back toward the terminal, muttering something about dismal weather and terrible airport food. Nicolae quickly hurries behind him, desperate to regain feeling in his extremities.

The rush of warm air that hits him when the airport doors open sends a shiver through him. He shoves past William into the warmth and lifts his face to the blower overhead. He is only just starting to come out of his ice coma when Sadie sneaks up behind him and slides her hands under his shirt.

"Sadie!"

She giggles and retracts her frozen fingers. "Oops. Sorry."

"Can you at least pretend to be human?" Fane growls as he shoves past her. He makes a show of brushing snow off his coat before adding a shiver for good measure.

Sadie pouts. "Are you always this grouchy when you fly?"

"I am when I'm forced to babysit a toddler."

His sharp retort makes her nostrils flare with anger. Nicolae watches as she grits her teeth. "I am not a—"

Stomping on her foot, Nicolae wraps his arm around her shoulder and steers her away. "People are watching," he hisses in her ear.

He marches straight toward a door on the opposite side of the arrival lounge, which is really nothing more than a few benches and a questionable looking burger stand. He shoves open the door and pushes Sadie through it. "I think you need to cool off."

"I can do that outside, not in a smelly bathroom."

He glares at her until she turns and slams the door in his face. Suppressing an irritated sigh, he turns and heads back over toward Fane.

"Thanks for backing me up."

"I didn't do it for you," Nicolae mutters, sinking into a seat beside William. It's a tight squeeze with all of William's extra layers. "You act like she should know how to be a perfect immortal, but it's only been a couple of days. Cut her some slack."

Fane leans over to speak into his ear. "The Senthe won't be as kind as I am. She is a liability they will not stand for. She has to learn now."

"Then stop egging her on," William says as his head pokes out of his oversized coat. His hair is shaggy, tangled and matted with newly melted snow. "Sadie has always loved to make waves. She's like a bull. The more you ride her, the harder she is going to buck you."

"So what do you suggest I do?" Fane places his weight on one side, jutting out his hip. Nicolae can tell that he's struggling to keep his cool around the humans. Even he has to admit that Sadie has been working overtime on Fane's nerves since they left Romania.

"Just ignore her." William turns away to examine the reddened tips of his fingers. "That's what I do."

Fane glances at Nicolae, who only offers a shrug in response. "It might work. Or you could just let me work with her."

"Not going to happen. Not yet at least."

"Why not?"

Fane leans in close. "Because you're a hunter. I'm going to have a hard enough time keeping the Senthe from killing you at first sight!"

It is eerily disconcerting for Gabriel to realize that he doesn't actually need to breathe as he swims deeper into the lake. The water is much warmer than he would have liked. It is almost like dipping into a sauna instead of a cool pool. The salt water stings his eyes, making it hard to see through the murky water.

So far, nothing has crossed his path, but he is on alert for a lake monster. Seneh swims beside him, his great sword locked tightly in his teeth. Although separated by nearly ten feet, Gabriel is comforted by his guardian's presence.

Water plugs his ears, making it impossible to detect any sounds. Night has fallen above so he can barely see his hand in front of his face now.

A tap on his shoulder startles him. He flails, trying to escape but fingers grasp tightly around his arm. Seneh waves his other hand in front of Gabriel's face, trying to gain his attention.

Gabriel releases the hold on his lungs and water floods in. He chokes on the brackish taste. Seneh's grasp on Gabriel's arm tightens as he pushes with his powerful legs, propelling them closer to the bottom.

Within minutes of letting Seneh take over, Gabriel begins to sense a difference in the water. The temperature has risen and a faint light glows from below.

Gabriel grunts, tapping Seneh's hand excitedly but the angel is already nodding. That is their destination. Excited at the prospect of being free of the water, Gabriel surges forward.

He points his toes and pumps his legs, ignoring the screaming muscles in his calves and arms. The multi-colored light grows brighter as he draws near. It almost looks like it's pulsating or alive.

Doubts begin to filter through his mind as he maneuvers toward the opening. What is on the other side? Will he be the first person to step foot in the Garden of Eden since Eve's time?

Seneh's hands clasp his feet, propelling him through the narrow tunnel. It tapers sharply, making Gabriel wince as his back scrapes against the top of the narrow passage. He wiggles and worms his way forward, his finger clawing deep into the sediment to pull himself through.

Just as Gabriel begins to fear he will never be free, the shaft takes a sharp turn upward and he emerges into a pool of clear, ruby red water. He splashes to the surface, gulping in great breathes as he claws his way up onto the sandy shore.

The sand is pristine white and warm to the touch, as if it has been under the sun all day. The walls of the cave are made of glistening rock and the ceiling twinkles like the night sky, appearing to be in constant motion.

Seneh rises up from the depths behind him, his long braid plastered to his chest as he thrashes about. Gabriel laughs and holds out his hand, helping the large angel ashore. "You could have warned me it was so narrow."

The towering black angel grunts, ruffling his feathers to release water from them. Gabriel notices that many of the feathers have been yanked free or bent. Blood dots his back. "I guess you didn't know, huh?"

Seneh shakes his head. "This is my first time here, young one."

Gabriel rises and brushes the damp sand from his clothes. It clings to his skin, chafing in places he'd rather not think of. "Do you know which way to go?"

Each way he looks, a long dark tunnel stretches out before them. Both are equal in size and apparent distance, with no light at the end of either of the passageways.

"Elias said to follow you."

"Oh brother," Gabriel mutters as he pauses to peer into the right tunnel. Cold air escapes from within, scattering goosebumps along his arms. He steps toward the left and feels a shift. It is subtle, but infinitely more appealing.

"I think we should go this way."

"You are sure?" Seneh asks. He clutches a bunch of broken feathers and yanks them free. He winces in pain as he lets the handful float away. Gabriel notices there is a slight current in the water, leading away from them toward the back of the cavern.

"No, but it's a fifty-fifty guess, right?"

Seneh shrugs but instantly clutches his shoulder. "Lead on."

Gabriel turns and walks into the pitch black with his hands stretched out before him. The air is slightly warmer here, a perfect temperature to dry his skin and clothes but not too warm to feel smothering. His steps are slow and hesitant at first, but the tunnel continues on for what feels like miles.

"Maybe we took the wrong path," he suggests, starting to doubt his instincts.

"No," Seneh whispers just over his shoulder. "Look ahead."

Gabriel squints into the darkness, staring so hard he makes himself see a pinprick of light. No, not just one pinprick but hundreds. "What is that?"

Seneh doesn't respond verbally, but the pressure on Gabriel's shoulder increases as his guardian urges him forward. Gabriel's wet shoes slap loudly against the floor, picking up speed as he breaks into a jog.

The light grows brighter and more defined as they draw near. He soon realizes that it isn't a hundred single lights but the flickering of millions. A swarm of creatures hang before them like a curtain of lightning bugs but entirely different at the same time.

Their wings are florescent, glowing in brilliant blues, oranges, purples and yellows. They have two arms and legs, a broad torso and tiny neck. Their heads seem oddly large for the size of their bodies. Their eyes are wide and colorless.

Gabriel spins beneath the blanket of light, in awe of this strange beauty. "What are they?"

"They are Faer. I believe humans would call them faeries." Gabriel lifts his hand to touch one, but Seneh pulls him back, shaking his head. "It is not wise to touch anything here."

"Why?"

"Because we are walking on sacred ground."

He steps past Gabriel, taking the lead as they move beyond the hanging cloud of Faer. Gabriel wishes he could

linger and study these unusual creatures, but he doesn't want to
risk being separated from Seneh.

"How many other mythical creatures are real?"

"What is mythical to you now was once fact to many
people. Just because certain creatures have not been seen in the
present day does not mean they do not still exist."

"Sort of like the creatures of the deep? Those giant
squids you see on the Discovery Channel?"

Seneh turns to look at Gabriel, his brow deeply
furrowed. "I am not sure of what you speak."

Gabriel laughs, shaking his head. "Sorry. I forget that
you don't watch TV."

He follows Seneh further into the dark, leaving the cloud
of light behind. After several minutes he begins to hear a
strange sound. "Is that…wings?"

Seneh nods, his grip on his sword tightening. "Stay
behind me."

Apprehension seizes Gabriel as he shifts to walk in the
footsteps of his guardian. What could possibly be making that
sound? Another creature lost to history books?

The sound of rushing wind is countered by the plodding
of heavy feet. Gabriel tries to peer around Seneh, but the angel
blocks his attempts. "What you are about to approach has not
been seen by a human in thousands of years."

"But I'm not human."

Seneh glances back over his shoulder. "That is merely a
technicality."

When he steps aside, Gabriel's mouth drops open. He's
not sure if it is awe or terror that glues his tongue to the roof of
his mouth, but he would guess it's a bit of both.

There, standing on either side of a gleaming archway,
are two of the most unique creatures he has ever seen. Their
heads and facial features appear to be human, but that is where
the resemblance ends. They possess the fierce, powerful body
of a lion with two wings on either side.

They stand nearly taller than Seneh, double the height of
Gabriel. He gapes up at the beasts, his eyes shifting from their
imposing figures to the sword that turns between them, blocking

the path beyond. The blade is tall, silver and straight. Blue and orange flames lick across the surface, weaving an intricate pattern across the blade.

Just beyond, Gabriel spies an endless forest, rich with wildlife and vegetation. Sunlight appears to filter down through the leaves, casting a warm glow on the woodland. A calm falls over Gabriel as he stares at the garden. It feels so tranquil and perfect.

"Be mindful, young one," Seneh warns as he lowers his sword before him. "The Cherubim will not give up their sword easily."

"Seriously? You want me to take that sword from them?" He can't even fathom how he could survive such a confrontation.

"No." Seneh shakes his head. "You will have to prove your worth. Then, perhaps if we are lucky, they will give it to you."

"And if not?" Gabriel questions, peering uncertainly up at the creatures.

Seneh's eyes darken as he raises his sword. "I would rather not find out."

Twelve

The whisper of silk and the rapid clack of heels from down the hall alerts Malachi to Ainsley's presence. He glances at the clock, surprised by her early return. He assumed she would be gone the entire day, happily spending his money shopping on Oxford Street.

He takes a deep breath and pushes aside the book he's been pretending to read for the last hour. Although it has always been a favorite, it has not been able to capture his attention today. Not after meeting with Lucien and seeing the changes he's undergone.

His stomach knots painfully at the thought of Roseline becoming a thing. He can't let it happen, that much is clear, but sneaking her out of here, especially in her current state, will be nearly impossible. Malachi is no coward, but going against Lucien Enescue is sure suicide.

Taking a long sip from his chilled cup, he contemplates several options. The cool blood slides down his throat, easing the nagging discomfort he has felt since exiting Lucien's room. Normally blood is not an attraction for him, but today he is making an exception. As the sedative slowly takes effect, he exhales and waits for the door to open.

The staccato of heels pauses just outside his study door. The doorknob turns and the door sweeps silently inward.

"Well, isn't this cozy." The sultry tone of Ainsley's voice used to send shivers of desires racing down his spine. He once would have done anything for that woman, but no longer. Now she puts him on edge, always wary.

They used to be quite the pair back in the day: bloodlettings at Stonehenge, parties at the Hell Fire club, dancing around the fires and plagues that tore through London. Those were good times.

But those times are long gone. Malachi isn't the same guy any more.

"Back so soon? Did you max out my credit limit already?"

Her lower lip puckers into a pout as she closes the door behind her. "Don't be like that. You know you like treating me to little gifts."

She slinks around the edge of his desk. Her skintight black dress rides high on her thigh as she uses the heel of her knee-high leather boot to push his chair back from the desk. She sinks down onto his lap, tugging at the collar of his shirt. "I'm surprised you even noticed I was gone. You've been so busy the past few weeks and I've been lonely."

Her pout used to make his toes curls, but now he stares back dispassionately. "You know I've been working."

"Working?" she snorts, batting eyelashes that shimmer with silver. Her lavender eyes open wide, defined by dark eyeliner and smoky eye shadow. "With musty old books? Don't tell me you've forgotten how to have fun?"

"Fun," he mutters, pushing her back as she slowly begins unbuttoning his shirt. "I'm not in the mood for *fun*."

He lifts her easily from his lap and places her on his desk. He averts his eyes as she slides down onto the glossed wood while trying to entangle him with her legs. Skirting past her, he takes great care in replacing his book to its rightful place on the shelf.

"You care more about those books than you do me."

His shoulders rise and fall with a deep sigh. "I don't have time for this, Ainsley."

He moves to walk around her, but her leg flashes out, blocking his path. She rises up onto her elbows, staring him down. Her smile is gone and her gaze is sharp as a razor. "You always were a terrible liar."

His expression darkens. "What's that supposed to mean?"

She pushes off his desk, placing herself in his path. "I know where you've been going. What you've been doing. The walls have ears, Malachi, and they like to sing."

He keeps his face void of emotion as he leans forward. "I have nothing to hide."

With a hard shove, he removes her from his path and walks by. She stumbles two steps, her hip connecting painfully with the edge of his desk before righting herself. As he stretches out his hand to open the door, a heel slams into the back of his head with enough force to crack a human skull.

Malachi bounces off the door and turns slowly, his nostrils flaring in anger. Ainsley defiantly stares him down. "What do you think Lucien will say when he finds out that *you* are the reason the girl hasn't changed? How many hours of torture do you think you will have to endure while he peels your skin off, like you did to that old monk?"

His fingers press into the flesh of her throat before she even has a chance to blink. "You will say nothing, is that understood? If I so much as suspect that you've tried to snitch, I swear I will tie you to a mooring ball and toss you in the ocean, where you can spend eternity praying for death."

Her eyes flash with anger. "You wouldn't dare."

"Wouldn't I?" He slams her back into his bookshelf, smashing through the wood and cracking the stone beyond. His precious books tumble to the floor, but he doesn't stoop to reclaim them. Instead, he turns on his heel and slams the door shut behind him.

Roseline holds her ear, praying that the crying will stop. The wailing started up not long after the candle burned out. It must be the voices taunting her again.

"Please, just stop," she moans, rocking. Her tailbone is bruised and bleeding, but she can't seem to stop. She fears if she does, the voices will catch up to her.

"Shut up. Shut up. Shut up!" She doesn't know how much more she can take.

The pain in her fingers and toes pulsates, reminding her of her pitiful attempt to rescue Enael. She slams her forehead against the stone, trying to erase the memories. "I am nothing. I am nothing. I am nothing," she chants.

"That's not true," a raspy whisper comes from the dark.

"Shut up!" She screams, slamming her head against the wall again, so hard her forehead splits open and blood trickles down her nose. "It's talking to me again. It won't leave me alone. It just calls and calls and calls."

"I'm not a voice. I'm Enael, remember?"

"No. Mustn't speak to it. It's bad. Bad voice," she croons, plunging her hands into her hair. "Enael is dead. Gone. In pieces."

"I know where he's gone," the voice whispers again.

"He?" Roseline pauses. "He who? I'm not a he."

"Gabriel. I know where he's going."

She blinks, brushing back the nest of sweaty hair from about her face. "Gabriel? You know him? I miss him."

"I know you do. If you can get me down, I can tell you where to find him."

Her rocking resumes. "Can't. Not allowed to jump. Toes don't like it."

"Please," Enael calls from above. "They're going to kill me!"

"Not dead. Can't die. Just a voice in the dark."

"Do I smell dead to you?"

She cocks her head to the side and takes a deep breath. Her pupils dilate as she cranes her head back. "You smell good."

"That's it," he calls down. "See. I am real."

Rising slowly, Roseline begins to sway back and forth. Her tongue flicks rapidly out between her lips, tasting the air. "I smell blood. Smells yummy."

"Uh…" She can hear his chains shifting above as she circles below him, like a vulture stalking its prey. "Roseline? You do know that I'm not for eating, right?"

"Eat?" Her stomach growls on command. The bones in her fingers crack as she curls them into her fists. She steps beneath a slow drip of blood that falls from above. Droplets splatter against her cheek and she smears it toward her lips, inhaling the scent. "Hungry."

"Help!" The chains clatter overhead. "Someone help me!"

She giggles, moving toward the wall. "No help. Nobody cares."

Propelled by the basic need for food, she clings to the wall and slowly begins to climb. Her toes are useless as she digs her nails deep into the stone and pulls herself upward. Enael thrashes above her. She cackles, inching higher. "Die. Die. Die."

The clattering of chains seems to be all around her now, above and below, echoing through her mind. She pauses, pressing against the wall as she prepares to spring backward.

Enael shrieks. A hand clasps around Roseline's foot as she leaps and she plunges to the ground. She hits hard, her cheekbone shattering on impact.

"Roseline!" Strong hands yank her upright, holding her face. "Oh god. It's already begun."

"She just tried to eat me!" Enael screams.

"Shut up," Malachi yells, yanking up his sleeve. Her head lolls against his lap, her vision hindered by the light of his lantern. She rolls to the side as the room begins to spin, sure that she is about to vomit all over his pretty shoes. "Hold on, Roseline. Just hold on."

The warmth of his flesh startles her. The scent of his blood is too sweet to resist. She instantly buries her teeth into his flesh, relishing the hiss that passes his lips. She drinks deep, her eyes rolling back into her head as she gives way to need.

The cold splash of water does wonders to cool Sadie off. She cups her hands under the bathroom faucet and douses herself repeatedly. Water drips from the end of her nose and off her long eyelashes, splattering against the rusted sink drain.

"That's a good way to get hypothermia," an elderly woman says as she opens a stall door behind Sadie. The sound of the flushing toilet follows her out.

She steps up to the sink beside Sadie, staring at her wrinkled reflection in the mirror as she turns on the hot water tap. "Not dressed properly either," she tsks.

The woman's wrinkled face is about the only thing that can be seen. Despite the heat pumping adequately from the vents overhead, she is bundled from head to toe in warm animal skins. She looks like she belongs on the back of a dog sled instead of waiting around in an airport.

Sadie laughs, dabbing the excess water from her face with a paper towel. "I like the cold. It's invigorating."

The woman's eyebrow rises. "Cold? Honey, you ain't felt cold until you step out those front doors and into the heart of the arctic. You'll learn. They always do."

Arthritic fingers tear off a paper towel. The woman wipes her hands for nearly an entire minute before turning and tossing the used towel into the trashcan. She hobbles toward the door, her shoes shuffling along the polished floors. Sadie stands and watches the woman.

"Are you from here?" she calls out.

"Born and raised," the woman croaks. "Lost my first toe when I was nine. Lost two more before I hit puberty." She turns back, casting a hard look at Sadie. "You youngsters think you know it all. One of these days you will be old, wise and toeless like me."

With a cackle that sounds disgustingly chunky, the woman opens the door and disappears. Sadie continues to look at the space where the woman stood, unnerved by her words.

The old crone was right. She should be huddled in ten layers of clothes like William or pacing anxiously like Nicolae, but instead she feels nothing.

Turning to look at herself in the mirror, Sadie stares hard at her image. Her cheeks show no signs of windburn. Her lips aren't cracked or bleeding. There isn't even the slightest hint of redness on the tip of her nose or a single goosebump to be found on her skin.

She is completely immune to the cold. Worse…she thrives off of it.

Sadie grips the edge of the sink as a heaviness lodges in her stomach. The girl staring back at her shows no signs of the human she used to be. Her eyes are the same, albeit brighter and more defined by the longer lashes. Her cheeks have been enhanced and the slight kink in her nose has been smoothed out.

Her forehead is higher than before and her hair has taken on a glossy sheen, several inches longer than before. Her skin is ivory, flawless in its creaminess. The slight pudginess of her stomach has been refined into toned abs.

The tiny scar on her chin, from when she and William were wrestling in grade school and hit the edge of the coffee table, has vanished. All of her imperfections are gone.

Sadie is gone.

Clenching her fingers against the basin, Sadie tightens her grip until the pipes begin to groan and the tile around the sink forms a spider web of cracks. She wrenches her hands back, horrified at her strength.

"It will get better," a voice says from behind her.

She spins to find Fane looming in the doorway. The door slowly swings shut behind him, sealing them in. "Get out. You're not allowed in here."

He moves forward, his steps purposeful but non-threatening. "I have been waiting for this moment."

"To stalk me in a freakin' ladies room? You're sick!"

Fane ignores her jab as he steps closer. His stride shortens as he draws close to her. "There comes a time in every immortal's life when the thrill of speed and beauty fades and the truth replaces it."

She crosses her arms over her chest, fighting for an air of indifference but she knows he hears the waver in her voice. "And what truth is that?"

The hard planes of his face soften and his stance relaxes ever so slightly. "That you are no longer human."

Her breath catches and her lips part to shout back, to refute his incredible claim, but she knows he is right. Of course, he is right. She has known this for over a week now, but why has it only now sunk in?

Her gaze sinks to the floor as she leans back against the cold porcelain sink. "How do you do it? Accept it?"

"You don't."

She looks up, startled. She had expected him to have some great words of advice to help her, but she was wrong. "You don't?"

"No." He purses his lips, appearing to be unsure of how to proceed. She waits impatiently, held back only by the growing fear that constricts in her chest.

"I helped Roseline adjust to immortality," he whispers. Fane refuses to look at her. His gaze is riveted on the dingy off-white grout in the tile floor. "I swore she would be the last."

"Then why are you here?"

When Fane looks up, it is as if a hollow man stares at her. "Because she loves you and so I must as well."

Numbness falls over her like a blanket as she looks at the broken man before her. Not as her mentor. Not even as her friend. He is the reject, the lover cast aside. No matter how Roseline may have tried to ease his pain, it is still haunting him. "You really do love her, don't you?"

His nod is jerky and his skin is paler than normal.

"I'm sorry," she whispers, unsure of what to say. She never has been very good with making people feel better. Humor and snarky jokes are her strong point.

Fane clears his throat and straightens his shoulders. The hollowness in his eyes expands to encompass his facial features. "I realize that I haven't been the best mentor to you. Part of that I blame on myself, but you must take a portion of the blame as well. There is much that you must learn, Sadie, but if you continue to fight me, I will not waste my time on you. Do you understand?"

She does. Painfully so. This is her one shot to get help. If something happens to Roseline and Fane refuses to help her, she will have no one to aid her in adjusting to this new life. Even though Nicolae would try, he will never truly understand how she feels.

"I can't promise I won't complain," she hedges.

The ghost of a smile crosses his face but vanishes as quickly as it appeared. "I would think less of you if you didn't."

Sadie laughs. "I'm not very good with taking directions either."

He nods, shoving his hands into his pockets. "And I'm not very good at not being obeyed."

"Well that's obvious." She rolls her eyes but catches herself. "Sorry. Force of habit."

Fane lips curl into a smile, not forced but not entirely welcoming either. "I must ask one other thing."

He pauses, waiting for her to consent. Her hesitation doesn't go unnoticed but her eventual compliance seems to satisfy him. "I need you to stay away from Nicolae."

"No way!" She pushes off the sink, coming to a halt mere inches from his broad chest. "You can't keep us apart."

Fane holds up his hand and she falls silent. "It is not for his safety that I ask this but yours."

Her face crumples with confusion. "I don't get it."

"You will once we arrive at base camp. Once the hunter's arrive, you will finally understand just how dangerous all of this truly is." He pauses, turning to look at the door. "I just hope we all survive the next few days."

Thirteen

Roseline blinks sometime later, disoriented as she sits up. Her head is pounding and the pain is splitting straight down the middle of her skull. "Where am I?"

"Home sweet home," Malachi grins, helping her back against the wall.

"I feel terrible." She clutches her stomach as cramps roll through her intestines. She feels sated for now, but there is something wrong. She's not healing.

"The poison is spreading. It's my fault. I tried to get back sooner but Lucien had me…occupied."

A disgusted snort comes from across the room. "Occupied? You skinned my friend alive."

Roseline jerks her head around. The movement causes her far less dizziness than it did before. She squints up at Enael, shocked to find the boy alive. "You died and you…" she turns to stare at Malachi. "Did you really skin his friend?"

He winces, nodding. "It was my job. I did it. End of story."

"End of story?" Enael struggles to rise from the ground. He has been freed from the manacles. The sleeves of his robe have been torn away and used as a sling for his right arm. His left hangs at an odd angle but appears to be at least partially of use. "How can you speak so callously about Ordin's death? It was the epitome of cruelty."

"No," Malachi glares at Enael. "I let him die. That was mercy."

Enael sinks back against the wall as tears fill his eyes. Roseline watches him, touched by his remorse. "I'm sorry for your loss."

He stares at her warily. "Do you still want to eat me?"

She laughs. "No."

"Oh." He inhales deeply. "Well…then good. I accept your sympathy."

"Who is this guy?" Malachi whispers into her ear.

"Someone who knows where to find Gabriel."

Malachi stiffens and stares once more at Enael. His gaze narrows as he looks up at the chains. "So that's why Lucien wanted you dead. You really do know how to find the kid, don't you?"

Malachi shakes his head. "I should have known the instant I found him here with you."

Roseline turns to look at him, wary of his tone. "What do you mean?"

"Lucien is no fool. He placed that boy here for two reasons. The first to speed up your transition, which is pretty obvious by the state I found you, but also for information. He knew the boy would tell you where to find Gabriel. He used you."

"But why?" Roseline stares at the chains overhead. They dangle lifelessly, only ten feet below the grate overhead. Anyone could have been standing there listening to them. What a fool she had been. "Someone tried to stop Enael from talking earlier."

Malachi leans forward. "Lucien knows there is more going on with this prophecy than he knows. I'd guess that he is desperate to stop Gabriel from doing whatever it is that he's doing. If that means killing everyone here, including you Roseline, I think he would do it."

Roseline turns to fix her gaze on Enael. He stiffens, obviously not too thrilled about being the object of her intense scrutiny again. "You never told me where Gabriel was going."

"No. I didn't exactly get the chance, did I?" He casts an evil glare up at the chains, rubbing his wrists.

"No," she shakes her head, "you didn't. Why not?"

Malachi turns to look at her. "What are you getting at?"

"Lucien set us up, right? So why wait until the exact moment of the big reveal to silence Enael? It doesn't make sense."

"Unless…" the boy starts but falls silent.

"Unless what?" Malachi asks.

The boy glances between both immortals, obviously weighing his words. "Someone didn't want me to tell."

Roseline watches him closely, noting every facial tick and flicker of his eyes. She instantly notices a pattern. Apparently, Malachi does as well.

"You think *I* did it?" Malachi asks incredulously.

"It makes sense," Enael says.

"Why would I do that? I work for Lucien."

Enael laughs and rests his head back against the wall. "And yet you are here, helping us. I wonder why that could be."

Malachi shifts beside Roseline. "That's none of your concern, boy."

"No," she agrees, turning a cold glare on Malachi. "But it is mine."

He opens his mouth to protest but he falls silent. His jaw clenches as he glares at the boy across from him. "Fine. I stopped you. I couldn't risk someone overhearing what you had to say."

"Why?" Roseline gasps, horrified at the things Malachi is willing to do.

"Because then you would be expendable," he spits out. His features pinch with anger as he looks away. "I couldn't let that happen, ok?"

"So you thought it better to rip my arms off?" Enael shouts, his cheeks reddening with anger. He tries to lift his left arm on his own but it's no use. The flesh is badly torn and the tendons in his arm are beyond repair.

Malachi waves him off. "You're in one piece, aren't you? Just be thankful she couldn't reach you."

"She wouldn't have had to if you weren't tearing me to pieces!"

"How do you think this ends for you, boy? Do you think someone will come for you? Rescue you from this pit?" Malachi's face is thunderous as he leans forward. "You have information that Lucien wants. He didn't get it from your friend, no matter what I did to him and trust me, I have never failed to extract information before. That old man is a hundred times braver than you are. What do you honestly think your death will be like?"

Enael clams up. Tears slips from the corners of his eyes, but this time he doesn't even try to hide them. Roseline places a hand on Malachi's arm. "Go easy on him. He's young."

"He's a dead man walking, that's what he is. He needs to learn that real quick." Malachi pulls out of her grasp and crosses his arms, fuming.

A heavy silence falls over the room, each person weighing out their lot in life. Enael is as good as dead and they all know it. Malachi is too if Lucien discovers he's the reason Roseline has held on for so long. And what about her? Once the transformation is complete, will she even care about Gabriel anymore?

"We have to escape," she says to no one in particular. "All of us. Today."

Malachi snorts, shaking his head. "That's impossible. The boy's too weak to move and you are hardly better. Even if I could get you out of this pit, there are Eltat swarming the grounds. We'd never make it."

"So we should just sit here and wait to die?"

He winces at her biting words. "No. I'm not saying that. I just don't think now is the right time."

"When then? How long have I been here, Malachi? How long until Lucien forces human blood on me? You know we don't have a choice."

He exhales loudly, closing his eyes as he leans back against the wall. "This is a really bad idea."

"Best one I've heard all day." Enael's quip fades to the background as they begin plotting their escape.

Nicolae eyes Fane and Sadie with suspicion when they exit the women's restroom together. It doesn't set well with him that Fane went in after her, not because it's somehow morally wrong, but because it should have been him by her side.

"You ok?" He whispers as she plops down beside him. It's obvious that Sadie has been crying. He can see the puffiness around her eyes.

She offers him a small smile and nods. His suspicion grows as she falls silent instead of badgering William or loudly complaining about their wait time. Something is different.

"What happened in there?" He asks, leaning toward her.

Fane glances in their direction but says nothing as he marches away toward the double doors of the small airport. Nicolae hopes he is going to find a taxi to take them the rest of the way. Something safe would be nice, with all four wheels on the ground.

"It's nothing," she responds vaguely.

Nicolae frowns. "You're evading me."

"Not really." She smiles. "Just nothing really to talk about. Fane says I need time to adjust is all."

"And he understands what you're going through better than I do," Nicolae finishes for her, exhaling loudly.

Sadie laughs, sounding almost like her old self. "Is that jealously I detect?"

"Maybe." He slumps low in the chair, regretting having asked in the first place.

She tugs on his arm until he allows her to take it into her lap. She strokes the back of his hand. Although he feels embarrassed by her style of affection, there is no way he's about to pull back. It feels wonderful to have her touching him, even with William sending annoyed glances their way.

"You know Fane is a pain in my backside." She soothes. "He could never replace you."

"Course not," William says, rising in his seat. "No one can be a bigger jerk than Nicolae."

"Ha-ha," Nicolae scowls, kicking William just below the knee with the toe of his boot.

"That hurt!" William howls and grabs at his kneecap, swearing under his breath.

"Are you children done yet?" All three look up to see Fane standing before them, a scornful glare in his eye. "Yes? Good. Our ride is early."

"Thank God. I'm dying for a hot shower and a big juicy hamburger," William groans as he bends to stretch out the kinks.

"You will find neither of those where we are going," Fane replies. He reaches down for their bags, easily lifting all of them in one hand. Nicolae frowns in disapproval at the obvious lack of human qualities, but upon further examination, he realizes the airport is almost empty. Their flight must have been one of the last for the day.

"Tell me you at least have a heater," William pleads, tugging his backpack over his shoulder. It is loaded down with snacks and magazines, the essentials he no doubt feels he needs to survive this trip.

Fane tosses a look back over his shoulder that gets William moving toward the door. Nicolae places his hand on the base of Sadie's back as he leads her toward the exit.

He expected the blast of cold air to take his breath away, and it certainly would have if it hadn't been for the three imposing figures standing just beyond the double doors, obviously waiting for them.

The first is a pixyish girl with flaming red hair chopped short enough to leave her ears exposed to the brutal winds. Each lobe is lined with ten small silver rings. Another glitters just below the hem of her halter top, at the base of her exposed belly button. Her green eyes shine like a cat in the night.

"Whoa." William's mouth gapes open. The girl winks at him and blood rushes to fill his cheeks.

Fane steps forward. "No flirting with the human, Daelyn."

Her pout draws a muffled moan from William. Daelyn shoots him a conspiratorial smile before she turns and prances toward a large SUV.

"Don't even think about it," Fane says, pulling William back. "She's nearly two hundred years older than you."

"You're determined to ruin all of my fun on this trip, aren't you?" William grumbles, crossing his arms over his chest. Even Nicolae can't help but laugh at him, with his arms nearly three times their normal size in his overstuffed parka.

Fane doesn't seem to see any humor in the situation. "We are not here to sightsee. Either you obey my rules or I send you home. Got it?"

When Fane turns his back to speak to the two remaining immortals, William sticks out his tongue at him. William leans in close to Sadie. "If I wanted you to break his fingers while sparring…"

Sadie grins. "Consider it done."

Nicolae shakes his head, laughing as the two siblings move toward the car, plotting Fane's demise. He steps up to the small group and braces for what he expects to be a less than warm welcome.

The two remaining immortals are as different as night and day. The one beside Fane is short and lean, with hair as dark as coal. Dimples appear on his cheeks when he smiles. His white eyes and tiny pupils are startling in their brilliance, reminding Nicolae of a huskie he once owned.

The other immortal is much taller. His poise and perfectly manicured goatee give him an air of dignity. His shiny black hair is long, brushing the tops of his shoulders. His eyes are green and deeply set in his porcelain-like face.

Neither one seems happy about Nicolae's presence, but they don't appear hostile either. Fane steps back to allow him to join the group. "I'd like to introduce you to Theus Luthor and Julian Le Roi. Both are friends from long before you were born."

When Julian dips his head, his goatee brushes against his pristine, white button-down shirt. Somehow, despite the blizzard brewing up around them, his clothes remain perfectly pressed and muck free.

"Nice to meet you." Nicolae dips his head in greeting toward Theus, noting that the immortal is only an inch taller than him. "Thank you for allowing us to come here."

"There will be more of you, yes?" Theus queries, his words clipped with a strong southern accent.

"Yes." Nicolae shifts his weight, suddenly uncomfortable with the idea of having his men in close quarters with these immortals. Maybe Fane was right to protest after all. "They are anxious to fight alongside you."

"I'm sure they are," Julian says with an air of mockery.

Fane places a hand on his friend's arm. "Peace, Julian. Nicolae will keep his men in line."

Julian looks down his long nose at Nicolae, sniffing indifferently. "We shall see."

With that he turns and marches toward the blacked out SUV. Nicolae blows out a breath he hadn't realized he was holding. Theus smiles at him. "Don't worry about, J. He's always got his panties in a twist."

Fane laughs, clapping the immortal on the shoulder. "As do you, my friend. Still trying to forget your age, I see."

Theus smirks and motions for them to follow him to the vehicle. Nicolae slips into the back seat, grateful to discover that Julian has chosen to ride up front. Fane shoves William out of the way as the immortal tries to fold his large frame into the third row.

The ride through town is uneventful. A couple stop lights later they are already leaving it behind. Nicolae twists in his seat, staring longingly at civilization.

"Going to miss the humans?" Sadie grins conspiratorially.

"If I say yes, will you hit me?"

She shrugs and then, with lightning fast reflexes, slams her fist into his bicep. He yelps and grasps his arm. "I didn't say anything."

"You were thinking it," she laughs as she rides down her seat to rest her head on his shoulder.

Nicolae sinks back into the supple leather seat, enjoying the feel of Sadie against him as the SUV barrels toward the barren wasteland stretching out before them.

Fourteen

Great black eyes stare down at Gabriel, sizing him up. He tries not to let his nervousness show, but it's nearly impossible in the face of such a terrifying beast. Seneh motions for him to step forward but holds out his hand to stop Gabriel when he comes level with Seneh.

"What do I say?" Gabriel whispers.

"Greetings." The cherubim's tones are deep, speaking in perfect unity. Their rolling voices vibrate through Gabriel's chest. "You have traveled far to find us."

"Yes," Gabriel moves forward half a step, leery of leaving Seneh's side. Somehow the cherubim even manage to make the angel's hulking size appear small. "I am in need of your sword."

The creatures turn to stare at each other, unblinking and unmoving for several long minutes. Gabriel shifts, wishing he could turn and run away, but he has come too far. Elias is expecting him to pass this trial. Without completing this task, he may not be able to save Roseline. Failure is not an option.

"We are aware of your mission, young one," the voices say. The two heads swivel back to stare down at him, pinning him in place with their steely gazes. "But are you worthy of such a gift?"

Isn't that what I've been wondering this entire time? He wonders.

The creatures' gazes narrow. "We sense fear in you. Doubt. Anger."

Gabriel risks a glance back at Seneh. He curtly shakes his head, and then looks toward the lion creatures. "I am human."

"Your mother was human. You are something more." Their words echo through the chamber. Beyond them, the leaves of the trees vibrate. "But you rely on your human weakness as an excuse."

"An excuse?"

"Yes." They dip their heads in unison. "You fear failing so you do not try. This is the heart of a coward."

"Now hang on a second—" he begins to protest but Seneh places a warning hand on his arm.

He glances down and notices the claws of the cherubim curling around the ledge on which they perch, their nails digging into the stone. "Be careful," Seneh hisses as he release his tight grip. "Do not disrespect them."

Gabriel has never seen Seneh so on edge. He nods and exhales slowly, fighting to let his anger subside. The creatures watch him take three calming breaths.

"The enemy that you face is stronger than you. Are you aware of the risks?" they ask.

"Yes." Gabriel nods solemnly. He has spent every night dreaming of his own death mingled with those of Roseline and his friends. Elias keeps reminding him that he is the key, but what if he isn't enough to save them?

"And what of the girl?"

Gabriel stiffens at the mention of Roseline. "What about her?"

"We sense love in your heart, but is it pure?"

"It is," he responds with certainty.

The creatures' wings shift, expanding out to their sides until they touch wingtip to wingtip. "We know your heart, young one, and we know your thoughts. What you say is what you believe, but only time will tell."

Gabriel grits his teeth in frustration. Why do these creatures speak in riddles? Why not just come right out and ask him for what they seek?

"How can I prove my worth?"

The cherubim dip their heads, closing their eyes. He waits with growing impatience as the sound of their heavy breathing surrounds him. Seneh rises up onto his toes, coiled and ready for battle, which makes Gabriel extremely nervous.

He stares up at the sword, unsure of how he will grasp the fiery handle even if he is allowed to get that far.

The room begins to brighten, the brilliance appearing to emanate from within the creatures. Gabriel retreats, unsure of what is happening. Raising his hand to shield his eyes, he realizes there is a growing heat along his forearms. His *Arotas* cross tattoos have flamed to life, pulsating wildly as the two creatures' wings begin to beat rapidly.

Seneh shoves Gabriel, barking at him to stay back. The angel's face is deathly grim as he stares at Gabriel. "Get the sword and return to Elias. This is your mission."

"I don't understand," Gabriel shouts. The creatures' voices rise in unison, chanting in a language he can't understand. "What is happening?"

"You have been found unworthy," Seneh shouts as he leaps forward, his sword poised to strike.

Roseline holds out her hand, examining it in the flickering candlelight. There is a definite green tint to her skin now. Although she can't quite make out the individual scales yet, she can feel them developing. She scratches at her arms, loathing how dry and flaky she has become.

"That's probably why they hide out here," Enael says, watching her.

She lets her hand fall away. "What are you talking about?"

"The moisture. Above ground their skin would dry out faster. Here it's damp and cool. They can survive."

"Not to mention the fact that they are really ugly and people might take notice," she barks out a bitter laugh, trying desperately not to wonder if she will someday be confined to the dark like them.

"Can you see me?"

Enael lifts his head, pausing from tracing patterns in the dirt floor. "You're not a ghost."

"I mean the real me."

Leaning his head back against the wall, he searches her face closely. "I see your fear. I see small things, like how you hold your head or how you sometimes stick out your tongue, as if to taste the air, but you look the same."

"So I don't look green to you?" She holds out her arms for him to examine.

"No, but I know you are."

She sighs and presses back into the wall, her fingers splayed against her crossed knees. The pain in her fingers and toes has vanished, thanks to her healing with Malachi, but the transformation is progressing. He can't stop it forever and she's not sure how much longer she can hold on.

"You said you were friends with Gabriel..."

He nods, wiping his dirty finger against his filthy robe. "I've spent most of my life studying the words of the prophecy. My uncle Sias devoted his entire life to doing the same. Our brotherhood has been searching through the ages for the *Arotas*, so you can imagine how excited I was when we finally tracked him down."

"To Sorin's dungeon?" she mutters.

He nods. "What my uncle told you was true. We meant Gabriel no harm. Although Sias never said so, I think it really bothered him that you care for Gabriel. It isn't natural."

Roseline laughs bitterly. "Tell me about it."

Enael shifts forward, tucking his legs under him as he sinks back on his heels. "Do you know why?"

"No." She shakes her head, hearing the same question that has plagued her from the first moment she met Gabriel Marston. *Why?*

"You're a part of this too. You always have been."

Lifting her head, she stares hard at the boy. "Explain."

He winces. "I'm not really sure that I can. I never was too good at reading the old languages. I just know that the *Arotas* was meant to be balanced by another person, a yin to his yang if you will. If one falls, the other does as well. He can only succeed in his quest if you live."

"And if I become this...thing?" she motions to herself.

Enael shrugs. "I don't know, but I'd guess if Lucien wants to turn you, he has a really good reason for doing it."

The words weigh heavily on Roseline. Her resolve to escape this pit increases a hundred fold as she stares at the cell door. How long has Malachi been gone? An hour? Four? An entire day?

Already she can feel the effect of his blood waning, but she can no longer tell time by that. The poison is rampaging through her at a much faster pace.

"Do you think he will come back?"

She refocuses on Enael. His cheeks look horribly sallow when he turns to the side to stare at the cage door. She can't help but wonder when he last ate. "He promised he would."

"And you trust him?"

Roseline remains silent for a moment. "I don't have a choice."

Fifteen

Sadie clings to Nicolae's hand for support. Neither of them is sure how this first meeting will go. The running bet within the base is that today's arrival of hunters will end in at least one severed limb and human blood staining the snow. Sadie refused to place a bet, but if she had, she would have sided with the immortals.

"Are you sure about this?" She asks, turning her face from the blustery winds.

"No, but it's too late to back out now." Nicolae huddles down into the upturned collar of his coat. His hair flaps in the wind, lashing against his face, and his lips are chapped. Sadie feels bad that she's thriving off the cold weather while Nicolae suffers in silence.

The metal door to the Senthe base opens behind them and Fane exits with two immortals at his side. Sadie smiles at Claudia. Although the woman is nearly one hundred years old, she and Sadie formed an instant bond.

Claudia's thick German accent and wicked sense of humor endeared Sadie to her the moment they first stepped foot onto the base. She didn't even mind it when Claudia showed signs of interest in William, not that he could scrape his eyes off Daelyn's backside long enough to notice. At least Claudia's quick wit helps to make up for the sparse and uncomfortable surroundings of their new home.

The compound is literally in the middle of nowhere. Sadie doubts that even a satellite could find them way out here.

The main building was built into the ground, its walls made of thick steel and its roof is a natural layer of solid ice. William's teeth haven't stopped chattering since he arrived, although he man's up pretty quickly when Daelyn walks into the room.

It took Sadie a couple days to learn the layout of the base. Several tunnels wind off into the dark, burrowing deep into the underground cavern system. Fane has warned them not to go wandering. Even though the immortals have been surprisingly gracious hosts, he doesn't want to press their luck.

The other immortal, a pretentious woman named Ambrose Creighton stands a hairs-breadth from Fane's left shoulder. Sadie disliked her from the moment they first met. With her nose always curled into the air and her ample chest bulging out of her low cut top, Sadie easily pegged her for the harlot of the group.

Ambrose's laugh is borderline obnoxious and her teeth perfectly straight, bleached as white as the snow all around. Her smile never reaches her eyes, even when she's pawing at Fane's arm. Sadie can't help but love the fact that Fane barely tolerates her presence.

Thank goodness William is too smitten with Daelyn to pant after Ambrose.

Fane stands rigidly beside Nicolae. Sadie narrows her gaze, peering across the vast plain of white for any sign of their approach.

"Can you see anything?" Nicolae asks.

"No." She starts to shake her head but stops when she spies a small black speck bouncing over the top of the crest. "There!"

Nicolae grips her hand tightly. He turns toward Fane, a smirk tugging at the corners of his lips. "Did you have to let Enoch drive?"

"No, but I thought it might be fun." A ghost of a smile crosses Fane's lips before he settles back into a grim expression.

This initial meeting is crucial. If even one of Nicolae's hunters steps out of line, there will be blood on his hands. "They know their place," Nicolae mutters with little conviction to himself.

Fane glances over at him. "Let's hope so."

Sadie squirms beside Nicolae, trying to get his attention. She rises up on her toes to plant a kiss on his cheek. "It's going to be fine. You worry too much."

"They want your head too, remember?" Fane says. Her smile fades slightly.

"They'll have to go through me to get it," Nicolae growls.

Pride and love swell in her chest at the proclamation, but is it quickly tainted by the fact that she knows such a thing would destroy him. She knows he would never let anyone lay a finger on her, and yet these men are his family. To ask such a thing of him would be unthinkable.

As she turns her gaze on the two immortals beside her, she realizes that her allegiance has shifted as well. She isn't human any longer. Her place is at Fane's side as his student, and yet her heart yearns to be by Nicolae's side as well.

If only it were possible for the truce to last beyond this turmoil. She has heard Nicolae speak of it several times in private with Fane. His conviction is so great that she can almost believe it's possible. Almost.

The sound of ice crunching beneath rubber tires makes her refocus. She can hear swearing mingled with shouting from within the vehicle when it draws near. Although the windows are blacked out, she can see the hunters within being tossed about as Enoch twists the wheel this way and that, sliding dangerously on the ice.

Nicolae grits his teeth. "He's just begging for a fight."

Sadie tightens her grip on his hand. "At least they will be in no shape to draw a weapon when they arrive."

He turns to stare down at her, his brow raised in surprise. "Are you laughing?"

"Of course." She grins. "Aren't you?"

She can tell he struggles to keep a straight face as he shakes his head. Any other time he would be laughing right alongside her, but today he is a leader and must act like one or risk his men losing faith in him.

He steps forward as the SUV slides to a halt less than ten feet ahead. His boots punch through a newly fallen layer of ice. The blizzard broke earlier this morning, leaving clear blue skies overhead. It is beautiful here, remote, but absolutely beautiful.

The doors open and hunters spill out onto the ground. A couple of them clutch their stomachs as they double over onto their knees. Others grip the car doors with pale fingers as they will their legs not to give out on them.

A broad shouldered black man slips out from behind the steering wheel, his grin wide and genuine. "Made it in record time," he boasts.

Fane steps forward, his lips drawn into a line of displeasure. "You could have gone a bit easier on our...guests"

Enoch waves off Fane's poorly veiled reprimand. "They had fun. Just look at them. Like kiddies on a merry-go-round."

Sadie smothers her grin as Enoch claps Nicolae on the back and trudges past. He tosses a wink at Sadie before disappearing into the compound.

"I trust your flight went well," Nicolae says, stepping forward to grasp Grigori's hand.

His scars stretch tight as he scowls. "Much better than the drive here. Three hours with that maniac. Who's idea was that?"

"Mine." Fane steps forward. "Although I warned him of the danger of provoking you and your men."

Grigori's chest puffs up slightly. Sadie smirks behind her hand, impressed with how well Fane is able to stroke Grigori's ego when necessary. "Well, I'm sure it was just a bit of harmless fun, wasn't it, Bogdan?"

The man swears loudly as he pushes up to his feet from the snow. His skin is pale and almost sickly in appearance. His hands shake slightly as he clutches his stomach. "If you think I'm going to let that beast treat me like that, you've got another thing coming!"

Claudia and Ambrose hiss behind Sadie. Although she can't see them, she knows they have dropped back into a fighting stance. "We are not beasts," Ambrose snarls.

Bogdan's laughter rumbles deep in his chest as he flexes his hands, as if itching to reach for his sword. Costel Petran places a warning hand on his companion's arm. "He was merely having fun."

Sadie watches as he squeezes Bogdan's arm tightly. The swordsmith relents, but not without a withering glare in Ambrose's direction. Claudia sheathes her blade. Sadie turns, surprised that she never even heard Claudia remove it. Claudia winks at her but quickly returns her attention to the hunters.

Sadie has often wondered what sort of fighter her new friend is. Claudia walks with the stealth and quiet of a lioness on the hunt. She always keeps her waist length blonde hair wrapped into an intricate braid at the back of her head. Sadie watches as Claudia places her hand on her hilt, realizing that she is seeing the deadliest of hunters: One that is always prepared for battle.

"Your rooms have been assigned. They aren't much, but they should suit your needs." Grigori dips his head in acknowledgement at Nicolae and then motions for his men to follow. There are eight of them. Sadie only recognizes a couple of them from the truce meeting in Romania a couple days before.

"Is this it?"

"No." Nicolae shakes his head. "This is just the first group."

The clanging of metal startles Roseline from a dream. For the briefest of moments, a smile graces her lips, but reality comes crashing back in as she spies the beady eyes of an Eltat through the bars.

"Dinner time," it rasps. Its teeth are long and pointed, spilling out over its lower lip. This one has a blue tint to its scales, but its eyes are still as red as freshly spilled blood.

She turns, raising her nose to the air as she catches a faint scent of something.

Enael is on his feet, racing forward before the food even hits the floor. He clutches the moldy bread, shoving it into his mouth before Roseline can stop him. He moans, sinking back against the wall as he struggles to chew.

"You're not very bright," she mutters, wrapping her arms about herself.

Enael glares at her, obviously offended. "I am so."

"Oh really?" She sits forward, wincing at the tenderness of her tailbone. "How long has it been since you last ate?"

His neck muscles cord as he works to swallow the thick lump of bread that's stuck at the back of his throat. He winces as it slowly descends. "First time since I got here."

She nods. "And why do you think that would change now?"

His brow furrows as he thinks. Slowly, realization hits him. He rolls to the side and shoves his finger down his throat. Roseline closes her eyes to his gagging. "Lucien put you here for a reason, make no mistake of that. Whatever that was that he placed in your food would probably have killed you within seconds."

Enael retches one last time then rises, wiping his mouth with the back of his sleeve. "Thanks for that."

Roseline shrugs. She has her own problems to deal with, and she doesn't need the boy causing her any more. Obviously, Lucien wants the boy dead. No doubt, he felt that she would be more willing to drink from him if he were dead. The trouble is…he is probably right.

"Just do me a favor and stay alive."

He snorts, tucking his robe tightly around him. "That is the plan."

"How long was I asleep?"

"Hard to say," he says, pulling his legs into his chest. "A couple hours. Maybe more."

"Malachi has not returned?"

Enael shakes his head. His patchy beard is more pronounced than it was when he first arrived. A light stubble of growth clings to his chin. She grinds her teeth, infuriated over the impossibility of judging the passage of time. "He should have been back by now."

"Yep. Told you he wouldn't help us. I know his type. They save their own skin, no matter the cost."

Roseline clenches her fists, hoping that Enael isn't right. For once, she thinks he probably is. "We're going to have to do this on our own."

"How?" He stares at the metal grate overhead. "You're not strong enough to reach that and there's no way I can."

Slowly rising to her feet, Roseline takes a close look at the grate. Eight bars run in a crisscross pattern across the opening. They are made of steel, by the looks of it, easy enough to break for an immortal.

She narrows her gaze, searching for any sign of angel hair wound around the bars. It is nearly impossible to see in this light but from what she can tell, the bars are not protected, unlike the reinforced cage door.

"He wants me to escape," she whispers.

"That's insane."

She looks down, startled to find Enael beside her. Her gaze flits over the dried blood caked on his skin. The scent of his open wounds makes her stomach turn over as Lucien's plan begins to unfold before her.

"It makes sense." She steps back from him, exhaling before she draws in a breath of musty air. "With your blood I will ignite the final stages of the transformation. I would be strong."

Looking at the grate overhead, she knows she is right. "That's our way out."

"We've been over this. You aren't..." he turns and stares at her, shaking his head as he backs away. "No. No way! Don't you come near me!"

"Calm down, Enael. I won't take much. Just enough to get us out of here."

"Are you insane? I'm not going to just let you bite me. Don't you remember what you became earlier? That thing?"

Roseline winces but nods. "Yes, but you're not going to let that happen to me."

"I'm not?" he asks, surprised.

"No. I get us out of here and you help me find Malachi. He can counteract the blood and remove it before it does too much damage."

Enael pauses, looking longingly at his source of freedom. "You really think it will work?"

"It has to…for Gabriel."

With a curt nod of approval, he steps up to Roseline and rolls his neck to the side. "Get it over with."

Her forehead crinkles with disgust. "This would be a lot easier if you weren't so disgusting. No offense, but you smell like you been sleeping in a garbage dump."

"Look who's talking."

"Fair enough," she laughs. "Now hold still. This will only hurt for a second."

"And then you'll stop, right?"

Without pausing to respond, she wraps her fingers around his neck and pierces his flesh. The delicious metallic taste that flows over her lips mingles with the scent of unwashed skin, turning her stomach.

She tugs at the vein, clutching him tightly to her chest as heat races through her body. The fires burn hotter than ever before, almost to the point of unbearable pain. She groans, fighting to remain latched to his neck.

Enael beats at her arm, screaming at her to let him go, but she doesn't. Not yet. She needs just a bit more.

Seneh's cry of pain shakes Gabriel from his paralysis as the angel falls to his knees, a wide gash opened in his side. "Seneh!"

"No," the angel holds out his hand to stop Gabriel from rushing to his aid. His palm glistens with fresh blood, his voice strained with pain. "Get the sword. It is your only hope."

"I won't leave you," he protests, taking a step toward Seneh, but he stops at the glint of determination is his guardian's eyes.

"Get the sword."

Gabriel turns and sprints forward, diving just beneath the wide sweep of a cherubim's claw. As he passes under, he notices blood dripping from its sharp nails…Seneh's blood.

Gabriel feels the whoosh of air as the paw passes back over him again. He leaps to his feet, sprinting toward its tail, but the second creature is waiting, wings beating the air into an almighty gale. Gabriel leans into the wind, fighting to remain upright.

Forced to his knees, he lowers his head and waits, praying that his senses are not dulled by the beating of wings. The pressure on him shifts just before the mighty claws swing down at him. He manages to roll out of the way at the last second, but not before the razor sharp nails tears through his shirt.

Gabriel can see the sword blazing high overhead but realizes that it is still too far out of reach. He frantically searches for a way to climb high enough to leap for it, but the walls are smooth as glass, offering him no help. He spins and grunts as a tail smacks into his stomach like a whip, knocking the breath from his lungs.

He goes down hard, cracking his knees against the stone. Pain lingers in his chest as he grasps at the tail, holding on as it rises high into the air. It flails about, trying to shake him loose, but he clings to it with all his might.

Refusing to let go, he digs his fingers into the creature's fur, searching for flesh. The cherubim's muscles are strong and broad, even in its tail. Gabriel holds on, praying to inflict enough pain to buy him some time.

A growl echoes through the room as Gabriel claws at its flesh. With an almighty whip of the tail, Gabriel is thrown off, slamming hard against the wall. He slides down to the floor, shaken by the brunt force.

Seneh limps several feet away, his sword barely held aloft and his spare hand trembles as it covers his wound. Gabriel calls out to him, but Seneh doesn't appear to hear him over the thrashing of the cherubim.

Gabriel's gaze trails up the curve of the beasts' back, and a crazy idea forms in his mind. He looks to the sword and then back to the writhing creature.

I'm really going to regret this, he thinks as he rises unsteadily to his feet. He crouches low before leaping onto the Cherubim's hairy back.

The monster whips around, trying to throw him off, but Gabriel is prepared this time. His fingers anchor into its flesh, pulling him along. It bucks wildly, like a horse trying to unseat its rider. "Seneh! I could use some help over here!"

The angel nods, grimacing as he staggers on his feet. His chest heaves as he takes a deep breath and, with a mighty bellow, launches his sword deep into the meaty flesh of the cherubim's chest.

It roars in pain, rearing high into the air. Gabriel clings to its furry mane as it whirls around to face Seneh. Just before it lunges, Gabriel leaps from its shoulders and soars through the air, over the second cherubim's raised claws.

Gabriel crows with victory as he plummets to the ground, the fiery sword clenched tightly in his palm. The heat in his forearms instantly cools as the glow of his tattoos fades away. His ankles buckle under him and he goes with it, rolling several times before rising to his feet. "Seneh! I got it."

The cherubim's head whips around, its massive face a mask of rage. Gabriel's smile falters as he looks down at its foot and finds Seneh impaled on its claws.

"No!" He screams, rushing forward.

Blood bubbles up from his guardian's lips as he raises his hand in warning. "Must...get...Elias..."

Seneh's hand falls limp, landing atop the creature's hairy paw. His head lolls to the side, the whites of his eyes showing just before his eyelids fall shut.

Numbness rolls over Gabriel as the creature shakes Seneh off its bloodied claws. The once majestic angel flops against the ground, broken and lifeless. Gabriel's anger floods in as he stares into the remorseless black eyes of the creature.

Gabriel holds the sword aloft, a growl rumbling deep in his chest. He crouches, ready to attack, but the cherubim begin to back away. "Stand and fight me," he shouts.

They bow their heads and step back onto their pedestals, murmuring their chants. The light in the room begins to dim. They sit back, perched once more in their rightful place. They look at Gabriel one final time before raising their gaze to stare into the tunnel beyond him.

Gabriel's grip on the sword tightens. Rage swirls in his mind and heart, begging for him to seek revenge, but as he stares down at the broken body of his friend, he knows it is wrong. Grief weighs heavily upon him as he sinks to his knees, placing a hand atop the scarred chest of his guardian.

His howl shakes the trees in the garden beyond, echoing off the walls. Breathing heavily, he lets his forehead fall onto Seneh's chest, his fingers splayed against Seneh's arms. "I'm so sorry."

Tears stream from his eyes as he sits back. He reaches out and grasps Seneh's sword, placing it over his chest. Then he grabs the warrior's great hands and places them on top.

"You gave your life for me," he whispers, slowly rising to his feet. "I promise I will not let your death be in vain."

Sixteen

A fire begins in Roseline's mind, scorching and all consuming. She retracts her teeth from Enael's artery, letting him drop limply to the ground. His skull connects with the packed dirt with a low thud. His head rolls to the side as his eyes fall closed, sinking into unconsciousness.

Doubling over, she presses her palms to the sides of her head, screaming. The blood fuses with her veins, sealing in the damning poison. Roseline teeters on the edge of euphoria and agony as she sinks to the ground. She doesn't hear her name being called until Malachi is right beside her. Her cry cuts off when he grabs her hands, forcing them to her sides in a vise-like grip. "What have you done?"

"Had to…get away." She falls limp against his side, moaning as heat spirals through her body. She can already feel everything shifting, the lengthening of her muscles and strengthening of her bones. She is changing. "Too late."

"No!" Malachi shouts, holding her with one arm as he bites into his sleeve and tears the fabric free. He presses his arm to her lips but she turns away.

"Full."

"Drink!" He shoves his wrist at her again, but her eyes roll up into the back of her head. Darkness swirls around her, mingled with pain and fire.

"Wake up, Roseline!"

A rough crack to her temple breaks through the haze. She rears up at him with her teeth bared. He grabs the back of her head and impales her teeth onto his wrist.

Cleansing blood gushes down her throat. She sucks greedily as the pain begins to fade. Malachi gasps as she wrenches his arm around, spilling both of them to the floor. Roseline writhes on top of him, straddling his waist as she digs deeper into his flesh, nearly tearing through his arm.

"Roseline, stop! There isn't much time."

A low growl rises from her chest, fire blazing in her eyes. She won't let go. Not now that the pain is receding and Lucien's blood has begun to be caged within her cells, sealing out his damning poison.

Roseline watches as Malachi's expression shifts toward the boy but she doesn't relent. In the span of a heartbeat, Malachi draws a long, silver blade from a sheath at his hip and buries it into Enael's chest. Roseline cries out, releasing her hold on Malachi's arm as she stares at the blood pouring from Enael's chest.

The dagger stands upright, protruding from his chest. The sound of his blood leaking from his heart chills her as she flings herself away from Malachi, clawing at Enael with shaky hands. "What have you done? He was only a boy."

"What I must," Malachi says, wiping the blade on his pants before tucking it away. He rises, ripping at his shredded sleeve and tying it as a tourniquet around his wrist. He uses his teeth to tighten it. "Trust me, this was far faster than what I was sent to do to him."

Roseline lashes out at him with the intent of swiping her nails across his face. Instead, she tumbles to the ground, coughing and wheezing as Malachi props her against the wall. "What is wrong with you? Do you have a death wish or something?"

"Maybe." She grunts, cradling her stomach. It roils with the addition of his blood. "How could you kill him? He was my only hope of finding Gabriel."

She stares at the lifeless boy, shocked that after all he has been through this would be his end. Enael's mouth gapes open and yet somehow manages to look peaceful. She is grateful that he was unconscious when Malachi attacked. At least he didn't feel fear.

Apart from when I attacked him, she thinks. Quickly, she pushes that thought from her mind. She didn't kill him. She rubs her hands against her filthy clothes, trying to clean his blood from her hands.

"We have to go." Malachi grabs her arm to pull her to her feet.

"No!" She yanks out of his grasp. The blood rushing through her veins has made her strong and defiant. "I'm not going anywhere with you. Enael was right. You're the monster. You only do what's best for yourself."

His jaw flinches as he grabs her arm, unwilling to let her go this time. "If you stay, you will be the monster. Is that what you want? To become like Lucien? Trust me when I say, it's not a pretty sight."

"What do you mean?" Her voice wavers far more than she would like.

Malachi looks away. "I think he is evolving into something else, something more. I don't know what happened to him, but I think whatever is in your blood is affecting him."

Roseline stares down at the young monk, wishing that she'd been able to save him, to repay him for the kindness he showed Gabriel.

"What about the other monk? Did he say anything useful?"

"No. He never spoke." Malachi's expression pinches with regret. "If I had thought there was any chance he could help you…"

"Save it. I don't want excuses or false regrets. You did what you did, end of story, now let's get out of here." She slowly rises to her feet. "Do you think we can make it?"

"Doubtful," a voice calls from behind them.

Together, they whirl around to find a red-haired woman slinking in the doorway to the pit. Roseline's brow furrows as she tries to remember where she has seen this girl before.

"Ainsley," Malachi growls, pulling Roseline up beside him. His grip is firm, leaving little doubt to the danger he perceives. "You should have stayed away. You know this won't end well for you."

"No," Ainsley shakes her head. Her hair shifts in waves of fire about her beautiful face. Her cheekbones are high and her eyes wide and expressive, filled with hatred. "You are the one who's going to pay. You betrayed me, Malachi."

"Lover's tiff?" Roseline asks.

Malachi grinds his teeth and nods, not breaking eye contact with Ainsley. "If you walk away now, I will let you live. If not…" he lets his threat trail off.

"You won't hurt me, Malachi. We are bonded." Ainsley steps forward out of the shadows, and Roseline catches the glint of steel as she raises a sword. Its blade is curved and newly sharpened. Ainsley drops low into a crouch. "You belong to me."

Roseline opens her mouth to speak but finds herself flying through the air. The sound of snarling echoes around her as she slams into the wall and crumples to the floor. The impact hurts far more than it should have after a healing.

She rolls to her side, clutching her chest. Her fingers press deep into her side and she gasps. She actually broke a rib from that push. Although she feels strong, evidently she is still fragile.

Rising gingerly to her feet, she watches the death match before her. Malachi moves with smooth, fluid motions while Ainsley is more abrupt.

Lunge. Parry. Repeat.

The clash of steel against rock sends sparks raining onto the floor. Ainsley grunts and slashes at Malachi's stomach. Her arc is good but her footing is off. Malachi spins and shoves her face first into the wall. Roseline smiles at the sound of crunching bone.

Curling his fingers into Ainsley's hair, Malachi yanks her head back. Her shattered nose gushes blood into her open mouth. Her lips curl into a snarl as she spits out several broken teeth.

Malachi snatches the sword from her hand and presses it against her throat. Ainsley laughs. "You don't have it in you."

Roseline pushes off from the wall. "Just get it over with or I will. We don't have time for this."

Ainsley locks her vicious glare on Roseline, spitting droplets of blood in her direction. "This is all your fault. He loved me."

Malachi growls and whips her around. Reaching to the back of his head he yanks out a few strands of hair and lassos them around her neck. Her gargled protests rise as she claws at her throat, clearly terrified.

The angel hair digs deep into Ainsley's flesh. A line of blood seeps from the wound as Malachi grunts, his biceps flexing as he pulls tighter. Roseline can feel her stomach churning, overloaded with far too much blood, but she refuses to turn away when Ainsley's gurgling cries cut off. His hair slices cleanly through her spinal cord and she falls limp in his arms.

Malachi breathes heavily as he shoves the body away and approaches Roseline. Blood stains his hands and clothes. Roseline draws her gaze away from Malachi's fallen lover.

"How do you feel?"

He shrugs, stepping a wide path around her. "I feel nothing. She would have run straight to Lucien if I hadn't taken care of her. It's better this way."

Roseline nods in agreement. "You cared for her?"

Malachi looks up to meet her gaze. "She was a bit of fun. Nothing more."

Although he hides his emotions well, she can tell he's lying. At one time he did care for Ainsley, much like she cared for Fane. She shivers at the thought of ever being put into a position where she must make such a choice.

Roseline walks past the fallen immortal without giving her another glance. Ainsley was a traitor, loyal to a man who has caused only pain and fear in Roseline's life. Good riddance.

"This way." She follows Malachi's lead as they step through the reinforced cage doors. The hallway is empty, as are the three corridors beyond that. The maze of tunnels seems to stretch on endlessly as they weave around corners, ever alert for what might be lurking on the other side.

The fact that they have seen neither immortal guard or Eltat is a concern. Where have they all gone? Has their escape been noticed? Are they are walking into a trap?

Although her sense of direction is greatly hampered underground, Roseline gets the distinct feeling that they are moving away from the main part of the house. "Where are you taking me?"

"Through an old escape route. Lucien thinks he knows all of the tunnels down here, but he's wrong. This one will bring us out on the outskirts of town."

Roseline glances down at the state of her clothes in the flickering candlelight. "I'm pretty sure someone will notice me."

Malachi snorts. "Well, they'll certainly be able to smell you."

Lucien paces in his room, annoyed with Malachi's delay. He sent for him nearly half an hour ago. "What is keeping him?"

The Eltat guarding his door appears to shrink within itself. Small needle-like spines run down its neck and disappear into its shirt. Its skin has a bluish tint and its forked tongue flickers out into the air, no doubt testing to see just how angry Lucien really is.

But Lucien isn't angry. He is enraged. Malachi has never made him wait before because he knows better. When he is summoned, he comes.

"Go find him!"

The Eltat squeals and whirls toward the door, accidentally burying its claws deep into the wood. With a grunt, it yanks back on its arm to free itself and topples backward onto the floor. Lucien closes his eyes, squeezing the bridge of his nose as he sucks in a deep breath.

"I'm waiting."

"Yessss Massssster." It hisses in common tongue, scurries to open the door and then slams it behind him.

Lucien drops heavily onto his couch, tapping his fingers against the supple leather. Something is wrong. He can feel it.

Lurching to his feet, Lucien crosses the length of his room in four long strides and throws open the doors. A small group of Eltat guards are huddled together near the end of the hall. Upon hearing the door open, they immediately part and stand to attention.

"Find Malachi. Bring him to me. Now!"

Seventeen

Fane raps the back of Sadie's legs with a tree branch stripped of leaves and bark. This time is harder than the last. With each mistake, he increases the pressure. Already a large array of welts has risen along her thighs and calves.

"Again."

Sadie's eyes flash with anger as she tosses her sword away and plops down on the ground. "No."

"No?" He steps forward, his fingers tightening around the branch. "You do not have time for childish tantrums, Sadie. War is upon us and I would think that you would like to survive it."

"I'm not going to if you insist on beating me like a dog," she spits back. With the back of her hand, she swipes away the sweat clinging to her brow. The sun beats down on her from overhead, counteracting the blissful Arctic winds.

Fane grits his teeth. "You are the most stubborn—"

"I'd stop right there if you have any hope of her getting up today," William calls through a tiny crack in the compound's front door. "Berating her only ticks her off even more. I should know."

Sadie grins, nodding in wholehearted agreement. Fane releases a heavy sigh. "So what do you suggest?"

William snaps the collar of his coat around his neck and pulls his furry hood over his face before stepping out. He hisses through his teeth as his boots punch through the ice. Hardly any skin has been left bare to the elements and yet he begins swearing almost immediately, as if frostbite has already set in.

Fane crosses his arms over his chest. His short sleeves pull taut over his lean muscles. To say that he is annoyed by William's distaste for cold weather is an understatement. The boy has not stopped moaning about it since he arrived.

"Let her work with Nicolae. You know he's got mad skills," comes William's muffled reply.

"You trust him with your sister's life?"

"Sure. The guy is crazy about her." When he shrugs, his entire parka rises and falls about him. "Besides, you know he'd never let anything happen to her."

"And what about his safety? His life?"

William snorts. "That's his decision to make. Not yours."

Fane looks away. William's words settle uneasily in the pit of his stomach. Hadn't he told himself the same thing about Roseline? Yet, look what has happened to her.

"I'm not sure that's a good idea," he hedges, but the firm set of Sadie's mouth tells him that she's not about to budge. He shakes his head. "Fine. If that's what you want, then fine, but don't think for a second that his hunters will like this any more than I do."

With that, he brushes past William, nearly toppling the boy to the ground. He ignores William's cry of alarm as he pinwheels to stop himself from making an unwanted snow angel. Fane yanks open the front door as Sadie bursts into laughter.

The wind slams the door shut. His boots clomp loudly on the floor. He is angry but unsure if he has a right to be. Is it so wrong for Nicolae and Sadie to be together? Yes, it goes against everything he believes in, but things are changing. Hunters are here among his brethren. Perhaps their relationship is exactly what is needed right now.

He turns the corner and throws out his hands to stop himself from slamming into the broad chest of Nicolae's second-in-command, Grigori. "Sorry," Fane mutters and steps aside for the man to pass.

But he doesn't. Grigori moves to intercept him, waiting for Fane to look up. When Fane does, he's surprised to see something resembling a smile on his face. "Can I help you?"

"That depends," Grigori says as he leans back against the wall. When he crosses his arms over his chest, Fane can easily see each well-defined muscle under his pale skin. Grigori has always been a worthy opponent, so to stand here in a narrow passage with him feels disconcerting.

"On what?"

"On whether or not you know how to keep Nicolae in check. I've tried and failed miserably. I thought perhaps you might have a suggestion."

Fane's eyebrow rises. "What has he done this time?"

"The boy is smitten. I can't get him to focus for longer than ten minutes on anything."

A rueful smile stretches across Fane's face as he nods in agreement. "Sadie is the same way. Her brother seems to think they should train together. I told them it's a bad idea."

Grigori nods, absently rubbing the jagged scar that runs from his temple to his neck. Fane looks away, remembering the night he received that scar. He'd had nothing to do with it personally, but Lucien did. He can only imagine how Grigori longs to repay the favor.

"Will you allow it?" Grigori asks.

Fane blinks, unsure if he heard the man correctly. "You condone this idea? What about your men?"

The tall man grunts and shifts away from the wall, letting his hands fall back to his side. "I will keep my men in check if you keep that girl of yours from sinking her teeth into Nicolae's neck."

"Fair enough." Fane dips his head as Grigori passes. It's a tight fit but they manage to pass without touching each other.

As Fane continues toward his room, he can't help but wonder what horrible thing he did in his past to be landed with the responsibility of babysitting hormonal teenagers.

Gabriel claws his way from the lake exhausted and heavy of heart. The flaming sword extinguishes the instant he releases his grip on it. Too numb to care about how the sword works, he buries his face in his hands and rolls to his back.

Seneh is gone. The reality of this loss is almost more than he can bear.

Strong arms wrap around Gabriel's chest and pull him from the water. Elias hauls him off the beach, moving him toward the fire near a cluster of eucalyptus trees.

"What happened?" Elias asks, propping Gabriel against a log. Elias dips down low to look at Gabriel, waiting for him to respond, but he can't. He doesn't have the heart to speak. Instead, Gabriel rolls onto his side and closes his eyes, silently mourning the loss of his friend long into the night.

When he wakes up the next morning, the sun is beating down on his face. His skin feels dry and scaly with residue of the salt water clinging it. He groans and pushes up from the sand, rubbing his face with his shirt. A heavy dampness clings to the worn material.

Gabriel freezes as memories from the previous night begin to flood back in. His lips pinch together as he fights back tears. He wishes it was all a dream that he could wake from.

Elias shifts, his back to Gabriel as he stares out over the lake. "Seneh never surfaced," he says softly. "I waited all night for him to return."

He pushes to his feet and turns to face Gabriel. His eyes are swollen and his skin is paler than normal. "He isn't coming, is he?"

Gabriel's words catch in his throat, threatening to come out in a low moan instead of something coherent. He shakes his head as tears form in the corners of his eyes. The image of Seneh's shredded body will forever be etched into his memory.

Elias' shoulders sag, his wings drooping so low the bottom feathers blanket the sand. His head hangs with sorrow. "Goodbye, my friend."

Stumbling to his feet, Gabriel rushes to the edge of the ocean grass as the contents of his stomach tumble out. Acid burns his throat while tears sting his eyes.

"It's my fault," he whispers, wiping his mouth with the back of his hand. His shoulders quake as he fights to keep it together.

A strong hand falls atop his shoulder. He looks up into Elias' pained face. "Seneh loved you, Gabriel. He would want you to complete your trials."

Gabriel lurches to his feet, shoving Elias away. "How can you even talk to me about trials right now? Seneh is dead! Don't you get that?"

Elias' jaw clamps down hard. "Death is inevitable. It will come for us all."

"Can you even hear the words coming out of your mouth?" Gabriel rages, plunging his hands into his hair, tugging at the blond strands. "This is insane. Seneh is dead because of my mission. Because of me. I can't carry on like nothing happened."

"No one expects you to, young one."

Gabriel raises a shaky finger at Elias. "Don't ever call me that again. That's what *they* called me."

He spits at the ground, feeling soiled and violated by the words. *Never again,* he silently vows.

Elias holds up his hands in surrender. "Seneh believed in the prophecy and in you. If you end this now, you will dishonor his memory."

Gabriel laughs bitterly, shaking his head as he sways in place, feeling as if he might truly be losing it this time. "Don't use a guilt trip to get what you want out of me, Elias."

"It is not meant to guilt you into anything. It is a fact. The reality of your birth and your destiny has not changed since the time you entered that lake. Your friends and Roseline are still in very real danger. Will you forsake their lives just to wallow in your grief?"

Gabriel sucks in a breath, shocked by the cold reprimand. "How can you feel nothing?"

Dropping his gaze, Elias sinks to the ground. "Do not think that I am not in mourning for my friend. He was the closest thing to a brother to me, but he would not want this."

He raises his head and for the first time, Gabriel notices how Elias' hands quiver against his thighs. "I am asking for you to fulfill your destiny so that more innocent lives may be spared. Evil is coming. It is spreading across your world and only you can stop it with this."

Holding the fire sword aloft, he tilts the blade and offers it to Gabriel. "I never said your trials would be easy. I warned you the opposite. This blade will aid you in overthrowing your enemy, but there is still another trial to come. One that will weaken your soul and test you to the edge of your limits. I need to know if you are prepared to face it."

Gabriel takes a deep breath and slowly blows it out. His mind screams at him to say no, to fight against a destiny he never asked for, but instead he nods.

Elias smiles wanly. "Good. Then we must go."

"Go where?"

"To Canada. Your friends will be waiting for you."

Lucien's cloak billows out around him, brushing against the roughly hewn cavern walls as he rushes toward the pit. The greenish blood of the incompetent Eltat messenger still drips from his fingers. The nameless creature's head will look good mounted on his wall.

Gone. How can they be gone?

A growl builds in his chest as he races around one corner and then the next, burrowing deeper into the earth. The air is cooler here and deliciously moist against his scaled skin. His tongue flickers out between his thin lips, tasting the air for her scent.

She can't be gone. She will ruin everything!

"Out of my way," he grunts as he shoves through a thick group of Eltat. Their hisses and mutterings instantly cut off in his wake. Lucien stops abruptly at the cage door.

He lifts his nose, breathing deep. He can smell blood. Fresh blood.

"Bring me Malachi's body," he snaps, curling his claws into Matis' filthy rag shirt. Lucien doesn't usually keep fallen ones as servants, but this one was a gift to Malachi nearly two thousand years ago. As vile as the beast is, Lucien has always had a bit of a soft spot for it. Matis is smart enough to know where his loyalties truly lie.

"I cannot," Matis squeaks as Lucien's grip tightens.

"What do you mean?" Pressing his face dangerously close to Matis, Lucien watches the boils on its face quiver in fright.

"That is not him."

Lucien jerks upright and releases Matis. The fallen one scrambles backward. The instant he has his feet under him again, he shoves his way through the peering crowd of Eltat. Lucien is only vaguely aware of his departure as he kicks open the gate and steps inside.

A large pool of blood glistens near the center of the room. It trickles slowly along the gentle slope of the ground toward the rusted metal grate. He can hear the random pattering of blood hitting the ground below and grits his teeth.

He doesn't have to look long to realize who the victim is. "Ainsley," he growls, whirling around. His anger burns deep as he reaches for the first Eltat, easily ripping its head from its body. Its spinal cord drips green blood upon his cloak, but Lucien hardly notices as he grabs another and another.

Limbs smack against the wall as the bodies mound up. Blind rage nearly makes him slip as he reaches for the final victim. Its colorless eyes are wide with terror as it's claws rake deep into the flesh of Lucien's arm, but he hardly notices the pain.

"Find him, Phio. Make him pay. Then bring her to me."

With a mighty roar, Lucien launches the creature down the hall. It cries out as its leg shatters. The pitiful mewing sound grates on Lucien's nerves as he storms down the hall. "Never mind. I'll take care of them myself."

His fingers clamp down on the creature's head. With a flick of his wrist, it pops off. Warm blood pours from the severed head and over his hand. Lucien grins and steps over the body as it falls to the ground, his rage sated for the moment.

Eighteen

Nicolae sucks in his breath as Sadie takes a swing at him, the tip of her blade narrowly missing his stomach. "Good. That's good. Attack again. Don't give me a chance to regain my footing."

He leaps as she drops to the ground and swings out her leg, narrowly missing him. The instant his feet are on the ground he slides to the left to parry a blow as she rises. She is light on her feet, much more so than he would have anticipated. "Those self-defense classes must have been amazing," he laughs as he ducks to the side.

The clash of steel rings around them. On and on she attacks, never seeming to slow or tire. The longer they spar, the harder Nicolae has to work just to keep out of reach. She laughs as she advances, hooting with delight as she manages to back him into a corner.

"Give up?" She grins.

"Never!" He lunges. With the tip of his blade he slaps her wrist and unsettles her grip on her sword. Dropping low into a kick, he sweeps her feet out from under her and she topples to the ground, her blade clattering several feet away.

Sadie laughs, covering her face with her hands. "Oh, the horror. A mortal bested me."

Nicolae chuckles as he drops down onto his knees beside her. "I have been doing this a lot longer than you have."

She peeks out from behind her hands, a smirk tugging at her lips. Before he can react, she slams her hand into his arm. As his weight shifts, she rolls on top of him and pins him to the ground, straddling his waist. Her smirk widens with triumph.

"Oh, you're good," he laughs, placing his hands on her thighs.

Despite the thick layer of snow that he's lying in, Nicolae can only feel the warmth of Sadie on top of him. Her smile softens, growing sultrier as she leans down and whispers in his ear. "You let your guard down."

He nods, the back of his head sinking further into the snow. "Only for you."

She tries to laugh off his words, but a flush rises from her neck, staining her cheeks red. Nicolae grins as he grabs her waist and rolls her onto the ground beside him. He doesn't let go of her waist as he stares at her, happy to be in this moment.

For once, Sadie remains quiet. It's completely out of character for her and yet it seems perfect. "Cat got your tongue?" He teases.

He never realized how beautiful her lips are when she smiles. They are lush, full and insanely kissable. He clears his throat, his palms growing clammy as he looks away.

"What?" she asks, her voice hardly above a whisper. Her tone is deeper than usual, taking on a rougher quality.

"It's nothing." He rolls onto his back, choosing to stare up into the overcast sky instead of the depths of her eyes. He can see emotion there he's not sure he's ready to acknowledge. He knows that she likes him, that much is obvious to everyone at the compound. But there is something more between them, something he feels could be far more permanent if he allowed it to be.

"What are you thinking?" She rolls onto her side to stare at his profile. He stares resolutely at the low hanging clouds above, desperate to think about the coming storm instead of the conflicting emotions stirring in his chest.

Tucking his hands behind his head, he ignores the cold soaking through his layers. Leather is a great insulator, but the temperatures are dropping rapidly. They can't stay out much longer, but he hates being confined indoors all the time.

"What am I?"

She blinks, rising up on her elbow to look at him. She rests her cheek in the palm of her hand as she looks down at him. "A hunter."

He nods, glancing at her from the corner of his eye. "And what are you?"

"I'm Sadie."

He sighs, turning to look at her full on. "You know what I mean."

"Of course I do, but I don't see how it matters. I'm still the girl you knew back in Chicago. Nothing has changed."

Nicolae pushes off the ground, drawing his knees inward. He clasps his hands around his calves. "Everything has changed. Sorin is gone and the leadership of the hunters falls to me. There are certain responsibilities and expectations that I have to fulfill now."

Her eyebrows dip into a deep frown. "Is this your way of blowing me off? Because if it is, it's the most pathetic excuse I've ever heard."

She starts to rise, but Nicolae pulls her back. "You know I like you."

"Urgh," she rolls her eyes, wrenching out of his grasp. "Seriously? Do me a favor and save me from the 'friend' speech. I've heard it."

She shoves his hand off and lurches to her feet. The ice cracks around her feet as she stomps over to her sword, her hair whipping wildly in the rising winds. Tears roll down her cheeks as she dips low to retrieve her weapon.

Nicolae is on his feet before he even knows that he's on the move. He grabs her hand, taking on the weight of her weapon. He is insane to do this, to risk giving her the advantage when she is so emotional, but he can't let her leave, not like this.

"It's just not that easy for me, Sadie." His protests sound pathetic even to him. He tightens his grip on her hand and slowly turns her toward him.

"I'm crazy about you," he says, lifting her chin to meet his gaze. Something flashes in her eyes but she quickly squelches it back down. "All I'm asking for is time. Things are volatile right now. We've got more hunters coming in tonight, and I can't risk one of them challenging you because of me."

"You don't think I could take them?" She huffs indignantly.

"You can hold your own, but they aren't me. Please, listen to me. My men are very protective of their way of life. You defy everything they believe in and what I believed in."

"So now I'm an abomination?" Her voice grows shrill as she yanks at his firm grip. He is strong, but she is far stronger. She shoves at his chest, knocking him backward into the snow.

Her cheeks glisten with tear tracks as she sheathes her blade at her waist. "Just stay away from me, Nicolae."

She turns and stomps toward the compound door, slamming it behind her. Nicolae throws himself back into the snow, hating himself for upsetting her.

Why can't she understand? How is he supposed to choose between family and love when the two sides are beginning to dangerously blend together?

Footsteps from the north catch his attention. Nicolae sits up, squinting against the twilight sky.

"You sure handled that well," Fane says, offering Nicolae a hand. Fane's blond hair flaps behind him. His cheeks pale yet void of any signs of chill.

Nicolae grasps Fane's hand and hauls himself upright. "I had no choice."

"Of course you did." Fane releases his grip on Nicolae and steps back. "Do you think my relationship with Roseline was easy? Vladimir would have had my head, and hers as well, if he'd discovered us."

"So then why did you do it? Why take the risk?"

A gentle smile softens the hard planes of Fane's face as he turns toward Nicolae. "Because *she* was worth it."

Malachi emerges from the tunnel before Roseline, poking his head up through a rickety wooden trapdoor that was previously concealed with heavy, damp sod. A light freezing mist hangs in the air as he helps Roseline through the opening.

The moist ground soaks through her ragged clothes as she struggles to crawl out of the tunnel.

When she stands, she squints to see through the dark of night. Low clouds hang over the city beyond. A bed of fog lies over London, creating halos around the lights. A small suburb spreads out below them with empty, winding streets. She doesn't know its name, but judging by the sounds of the approaching train, it must be one of the main line stops.

"It will be dawn soon. We need to move." Roseline says.

Malachi nods in agreement, and then he turns and sweeps her up into his arms. She begins to protest but his grip tightens. "You aren't strong enough or fast enough to get us into London before the sun rises. Like it or not, you need me."

Roseline fumes silently, loathing the fact that he is right. The underground trek has worn through her energy reserves. The poison has begun to burn through again, at a much faster rate than before. She is losing this battle and is terrified that it is only a matter of time before she stops caring.

As Malachi slips through the shadows of the town, the strange voices return. Slowly at first, and then more pronounced, increasing in volume. She swats her hands at them, frowning at their presence. Malachi casts worried glances down at her from time to time, picking up speed the closer they draw to London.

She hardly remembers the final hour of their journey. With the sun cresting over the horizon and cars pouring into the city, Malachi works hard to keep their presence undetected.

"Finally," he grunts as he rounds the corner of a seedy looking street. Roseline blinks to clear her vision, forcing herself to focus.

She blinks again. "You brought me to Torrent? Are you insane?"

"No." He sets her onto her feet and pounds on the door. "Just wait."

Several minutes pass before she hears the sound of someone approaching. She wavers on her feet, leaning heavily against Malachi's side to remain upright. When the door swings open, she is hardly standing at all.

The man stands as broad as a bull, with a silver ring thrust through his nose. He casts a despairing glance at Roseline's bowed form. "Piss off, Malachi. I'm not taking in another one of your junkies."

Malachi bares his teeth and winds his fingers through Roseline's hair, lifting her face. The man's gaze hardens and he stands straighter. "Of course. Bring her in."

He sucks in his paunch as Malachi lifts her into his arms and carries her into the dark. It is blissfully cold inside. Roseline's skin is shiny with sweat. Her head lolls against Malachi's arm as he rushes down the hall, taking the stairs in a single leap. He lands on two feet, as silent as a whisper.

The red door looms ahead. He hardly slows as he kicks through and carries her into the bar. She opens her eyes, staring blurrily at the empty room about her. It feels odd to not have the eardrum shattering music blaring in the background. The cages are empty and vacant of their human fountains.

The bar is clean. Each stool is propped up on the table, waiting for that night's patrons to arrive. The shifting blue light of the bar is off, leaving behind only the thick slab of dark ice.

"Through there," the bouncer grunts, motioning Malachi to a room at the back of the bar.

Malachi turns, carefully lifting her over the bar top to fit through the narrow gap between it and the wall, and hurries beyond the taps and into the dark room beyond.

Roseline can smell the heady scent of human blood more strongly here. The soft chatter of female voices instantly cut off as Malachi pushes through a door. They enter into a room filled with cages, each lined along either side of the wall, like a kennel.

Frail girls cling to the bars, their clothes in no better shape than her own. Their eyes are glossed with fear and their fingers tremble against their cages. Malachi moves past with hardly a glance. Roseline rolls her head back to stare at the girls, suddenly struck with a desire to help free them. She vows that someday she will.

Malachi curls Roseline into his chest to keep her from hitting against the doorframe as he rounds the corner and heads for the staircase at the back. He climbs three flights and pauses to kick through a closed door at the top of the landing.

Roseline flinches away from the sunlight streaming in through small holes of the grimy apartment window. Malachi crosses the room and gently sets her down on a dingy brown couch. It smells of mold and mothballs. She stills her lungs as she pushes up against the fabric to sit. Her gaze rises to glare at the hulking man filling the doorway. Although large enough to scare any human who foolishly attempts to push their way into the club, Roseline knows him to be a pushover.

"What are you looking at, Castor?" she growls.

He stiffens, darting a worried glance at Malachi. "Why is she here? She's supposed to be at your place."

"Plans changed." Malachi shrugs indifferently as he stoops low to ease Roseline's legs onto the couch. She fights the urge to recoil from his touch. "I felt it would be safer to keep her here."

She can tell the man doesn't agree but he lets it slide, obviously deciding Malachi is more in the know. "The loo is in the back but it's shot. Radiator is crap, not that you're gonna care about that. Fridge is shoddy but should have something in it. I think I left some packets of AB in there for a rainy day."

"Thank you." Malachi doesn't turn to usher the man out, but the sharp edge to his voice leaves little doubt that the conversation is over. Castor hesitates one final moment, his gaze flickering over Roseline before disappearing back down the stairs.

She waits until she hears him clomping past the cages before she speaks. "What is this place?"

"It's a safe house. When people get into trouble they come here to hide."

He rises and walks into the kitchenette, dipping low to look into the small fridge. He grunts with disgust when he pulls out a half empty blood packet. "Disgusting."

Roseline's stomach growls loudly and he casts a pointed glance in her direction. She stares back, unashamed. That fact should worry her. She shouldn't be craving blood, especially human blood, but her body speaks for itself.

Malachi's boots shuffle along the hardwood floor. He pauses before the stained sink and tips the blood down the drain. A beetle skitters out of the rusted piping and across the yellowed laminate countertop before disappearing into the coils of the rusted stove.

Roseline closes her eyes and presses her hands against her stomach. Although her thirst may have waned slightly, her need has not. The pain is returning with a vengeance. How long will she be able to withstand it this time?

"I'll have the girls moved further away from your room," Malachi mutters, as if checking off a to-do list. "You should probably get cleaned up. I'll find something decent for you to change into."

The thought of being clean is enough to get her moving. She stumbles away from the couch, refusing Malachi's aid as she reaches out for the wall with shaking hands. Her legs are weak and her head is spinning.

She can feel the delirium returning.

"The shower doesn't work," Malachi calls from behind her.

"Figures," she mutters as she uses the wall to keep her upright.

The floral wallpaper is horrid, peeling off like dead skin on a snake. The sticky texture makes her nauseous but she pushes on, trying not to think of what coats it.

Cracked bits of porcelain slice through the soles of her feet as she nears the bathroom. The once powder blue tile has been mutilated in places, leaving only a fine dust behind. Large shards of glass from the window over the shower litter the floor and tub. She winces as she steps into the confining room, feeling several splinters from the mirror bury deep into her heel.

Blood squashes out from around her wounds as she leans heavily on the sink. The aged grime cracks beneath her grip, pattering in chunks onto the porcelain sink basin. The mirror is mostly gone, cracked and littering the floor, but a few large chunks remain.

She leans forward, staring at herself in the mirror. Her eyes are sunken and her cheeks waxed. Dark circles ring her eyes and her lips are nearly transparent. Her right shoulder sticks out of her threadbare dress, revealing nothing but pale skin stretched taut over bone. The dip in her collarbone is pronounced and her shoulder blades are jutting out of her back.

Roseline closes her eyes, fighting against the tears that threaten to fall. She is literally wasting away. Will there even be anything left for Gabriel to find when he does come for her?

It's a struggle to unstick the faucet because the corrosion is extensive. Gritting her teeth, Roseline yanks against the knob until it releases with a squeal. The piping in the wall shifts and thunks loudly.

She can hear gurgling as the water winds its way toward the third floor. She waits, leaning heavily against the medicine cabinet on the wall for support. Brown bubbles splatter from the faucet first but is eventually followed by a small trickle of dark sludge.

Tears slip from Roseline's eyes as she silently begs for clean water. When the water begins to shift from dark brown to something resembling clear, she cups her hands beneath the tap and brings them to her lips. The metallic taste is horrible but she gulps it down all the same.

Roseline wriggles out of her clothes, gasping as each muscle group threatens to lock down on her. Finally, she drops the cloth to the floor and gingerly steps on it, leaving bloody footprints.

A growl rumbles from her stomach, echoing off the tiled walls in the small space. She lifts her face, observing the hollow of her neck as she wipes a handful of water over her skin. Discolored water drips back into the basin as she washes away weeks of filth.

She takes her time, bathing each part of her body with more care than she has energy to spend. Her entire body trembles as she slowly works her way down her stomach and legs, scraping off the sludge from Lucien's pit. Some of her wounds have scabbed over while others look angry and swollen with infection.

The cold water only eases the burning of her skin temporarily. Her temperature continues to climb and her thoughts become as fractured as the mirror before her.

It's hard to think or focus on anything beyond the feel of the water against her skin. She closes her eyes, savoring the feel of the droplets inching down her waist and onto her hip.

A bold scent hits her. Her eyes pop open as she bares her teeth and spins around to find a gawking Malachi standing in the doorway.

"I uh...I didn't mean to stare."

A growl rolls deep in her chest, rising into her throat as her fingers curl into claws. She doesn't see him. Her other senses are dulled by his scent.

Mouthwatering. Maddening. Irresistible.

Roseline lets out a blood-curdling shriek and launches herself at him.

Fane watches Sadie and Nicolae from a distance. The strain on their relationship hasn't gone unnoticed. William has begun to spend far more time at Sadie's side, trying to cheer her up but each time fails miserably. Nicolae huddles with his men at mealtimes, somber and silent unless spoken to, and even then he only answers in short bursts of emotionless conversation.

Grigori meets Fane's gaze from across the meal hall. Fane mirrors his concern.

Fifteen more immortals arrived today and none of them appear to be very happy with the living arrangements. Although Fane has done his best to keep the two groups separated, space is limited in the compound and a couple of the new arrivals are bunking next door to Enoch and Theus. Already, Fane has had to break up one minor scuffle. They might not be so lucky the next time around.

Grigori jerks his head toward the door. Fane nods and gathers his metal bowl, still nearly full with the soup Claudia prepared for the group. He doesn't have the stomach for food. There is too much on his mind.

Between the ongoing stress at the compound, the rise in global killings and his ever growing fear for Roseline's safety, his patience has grown dangerously thin. One more outburst from the hunter's table and he might be the next one to snap.

"Where are you going?" William asks as Fane rises. He can tell the boy doesn't want to be left alone with his sister. Glancing over at the unshed tears dampening her lower lashes, he doesn't blame him. "I have things to attend to. I will return when I can."

His words are abrupt and straight to the point. As William's face returns to its sullen expression, Fane feels a pinch of regret. It must be hard being the only true human in the room. The hunters don't count. They are lethal, highly trained warriors. William is just a high school runaway whose addiction to TV and girls is sorely lost in the arctic.

Perhaps he should speak with Claudia. She certainly seemed to have a soft spot for the boy. Maybe it wouldn't be a bad idea to have her distract him long enough for them to prepare for battle, hopefully without getting him maimed or killed. She would certainly be a better option for him than Daelyn. Her flirting has crushed more hearts over the years than he cares to count.

Nicolae hardly notices when Grigori stands beside him and exits the room. Fane frowns, annoyed with the boy's lack of action. Nicolae either needs to let Sadie go or yank her into the armory and bar the door for an hour.

Fane slips out of the room, careful to close the door softly behind him. Grigori waits further down the passage, just outside the arch of the flickering hall light. "Something on your mind?"

Grigori nods and motions for Fane to follow him, and they walk in silence. Grigori passes a series of small square rooms with cots lining the walls. This is the hunter's section of the compound. Fane frowns as they move beyond, toward the main meeting room.

Grigori holds the door open for Fane, who passes him and perches on the edge of the long rectangular table. "This seems a bit private."

"I thought you might prefer the seclusion, considering what I have to say." Grigori seals the door behind him and moves around to the other side of the table. He draws back a chair and motions for Fane to sit as well.

Fane's frown deepens as he sinks down onto the hard metal chair. "If this is about Nicolae and Sadie, I want no part of it. I've already given him my advice. If he chooses to take it, so be it."

Grigori waves him off. He leans forward, steepling his fingers before him. "This is about Roseline."

Goosebumps race along Fane's bare arms, chilling him far more than the winds that beat against the compound. "What about her?"

"We found her. I received word just before dinner. I wanted confirmation before I said anything to you."

Fane's hands clench the table's edge. The metal groans in protest as it begins to mold to his fingers. "Where is she?"

"London. Torrent actually."

He blinks, struggling to process the information. "That doesn't make any sense. She would never go there. Not on purpose."

"There is more…"

Fane holds his breath as Grigori leans back in his chair. He stares hard at Fane, no doubt weighing how much this information might cost him. "She's in bad shape. My informant said she arrived at his door looking like a cat dragged backward through a meat grinder.

He pause, rubbing his hand down his arm. Fane can tell his news bothers him. "There was a guy with her too."

A tremor begins to build in Fane's chest. "Malachi?"

Grigori nods. "We've been chasing him for years. He's a slippery one, always managing to sneak away at the last moment. I'd like nothing more than to get my hands on him."

"There won't be much left of him after I catch him," Fane growls. His lips peel back as he bares his teeth.

"That's what I was hoping you'd say," Grigori smiles.

Fane starts to rise, conscious only of the need to get to Roseline, but Grigori holds up his hand. "There's more that you need to hear."

Fane sinks down, reluctant to waste any more time. "My informant says someone is looking for her. He's paying top dollar for anyone who finds her."

"Who?"

Grigori levels Fane with an even stare. "Lucien."

Fane flinches. His stomach twists as he shakes his head. "So it is true? I had hoped Sadie was wrong."

Grigori nods. "As did we, but it has been confirmed."

"It won't take Lucien long to track her down." Fane lurches to his feet, staggering as he begins to pace. "I have to go after her."

"She isn't the same girl you knew, Fane."

He looks up, his chest feeling empty of all but rage. "What do you mean?"

"She's changing. I don't know into what, but it's not pretty. My informant said it looks like she is starting to grow...scales."

"Oh, god." Fane leans to the side, clutching his stomach as it rolls violently. He feels faint and feverish at the same time. Color drains from his hands as he pushes himself back upright, wiping his mouth to try to ease the foul taste within.

"Is Lucien definitely behind the attacks?"

Grigori nods. "We believe so. My men are already searching for him. They think he is based out of London."

"How do you know that?"

The hunter grimaces as he drops his gaze. "Because there is no way Roseline could have survived a long trip."

Fane sucks in a deep breath, fighting for a calm he fears he will never feel again. "I'm going after her."

Grigori stands. "My men need to be here. I'm afraid I can't offer you any assistance."

"I understand. I appreciate you telling me this more than you know." He manages a weak smile. "I will take Nicolae with me."

"No." Grigori holds out his hand. "I think that would be unwise right now. In your absence it might be…difficult to keep everyone in line. Nicolae may be young, but the hunters respect his birthright. If both of you leave, I don't know what might happen here."

"Sadie is too vulnerable. I can't take her with me." Fane frowns, hearing the truth in the man's words. He straightens his shoulders, making a decision. "I will go on my own."

The hunter smiles as he rounds the table. It's a tight smile, but present none the less. When he holds out his hand, Fane hesitates. "Go on. It's not going to bite."

Fane smirks as he clasps Grigori's hand. "Never thought I'd see the day."

"Me either. Maybe Nicolae's idea of truce really isn't so crazy after all."

Nineteen

As William cowers behind him, Fane second guesses himself for the millionth time as to how Sadie managed to talk him into bringing her brother along. William is the last person who should be going into Torrent.

When he hears the clomping of heavy footfalls approaching the exterior door, he places a warning hand on William's arm. "Don't say a word."

William nods, swallowing loudly. Fane stifles another sigh. *This is going to be a disaster.*

The door swings open to reveal a hulking bouncer. The man's tattoos and bull nose ring are a dead giveaway. "Remember me?"

The immortal nods, unconsciously rubbing his nose ring, just in case Fane might decide to rough him up again. "You came for the girl?"

Fane hesitates for only a second before nodding. *How did Castor know why he was here? Is the bouncer the informant?*

"Follow me." Castor turns and heads back into the dark, leaving the door wide open. Fane's brow furrows at the blatant lapse in security. Even though the club won't be open for a couple more hours, Torrent is never left open to the public.

He casts a warning glance back over his shoulder at William and grabs his arm to lead him in. The door squeals on its hinges, slamming shut behind them. William yelps, shaking with nervousness.

"You'll be fine. I won't let anything happen to you."

Fane is not sure if his words reassure the boy, but William says nothing further. Fane isn't here to babysit. He's here for Roseline.

The darkness seems to stretch on for an eternity before they finally reach the glowing red light above the door. The familiar scent of stale blood and body odor greets him as he sweeps into the bar. William stumbles over the threshold, too busy trying to take it all in to notice the steps ahead of him.

The bouncer turns and rolls his eyes at William. Fane offers him a tight smile in understanding. "Where is she?"

"Up the stairs." The guy points behind the bar, but instead of showing them the way, he leans back against a high top table and lights up a cigarette. His hands visibly shake as he takes a puff. Fane's gaze narrows.

"Something the matter?"

"Go up and look for yourself. Never seen anything like it." His voice quakes as he takes another drag. He reaches out, shaking his finger at Fane. "I hope you're good for the money. My boss won't take kindly to paying for the damages."

Fane turns to look back over his shoulder at the bouncer. "You know who she is, right?"

"Yep, but rumor has it Vladimir is gone now. Seems to me the one to be worrying about is Lucien."

The man's bald head is slick with sweat and his eyes are dilated with fear. The only problem is, he isn't afraid of Fane. "Lucien's back from the dead, man. Haven't you heard? He's running things now, and that pretty little thing up there is his pet. No one is allowed to touch her." He eyes Fane with open suspicion. "Aren't you one of his guys?"

"No." Fane points at William. "Anything happens to him while I'm gone and I'll gut you myself. Nice and slow. Understand?"

"Course." The beefy immortal rubs the front of his shirt, obviously annoyed. "Wouldn't touch him, mate."

"Good." Fane moves back toward William and leans in close. "You get into any trouble, you shout for me."

"You're leaving me here?" William's voice sounds small and squeaky. His eyes are wide with unrestrained fright.

"Our friend here is going to watch over you for a bit. I'll be back in a few minutes."

Without waiting to hear William's protest, he turns and heads into the back room. He hardly notices the gaunt girls lying on the floor of rows of cages. Their scent does nothing for him.

When he reaches the bottom the stairs, he pauses to listen. There is no sound above him. This worries him.

Obviously the bouncer is worried about something. Despite the man's large size, he didn't get the job by chance. He knows how to hold his own against drunken immortals. Fane is sure he has seen his fair share of ugly scenes.

Whatever is at the top of the stairs must be horrible.

Fane climbs silently and quickly. He pauses just outside the door, pressing his ear against the wood. His hearing is excellent, a fact he usually brags about, but today it fails him. There is nothing but complete silence on the other side of the door.

"Roseline?"

His call is met by a small scuffling sound. His fingers curl around the door handle and he slowly turns it. Just as he begins to open the door, something big and solid slams against it. Fane rears back, startled. He reaches out for the banister to steady himself.

"It's me, Fane. Can I come in?"

A second bang against the door. This time it sounds less solid and more…wet.

Fane flings open the door and ducks as a mass of red meat flies across the room at him, smacking against the wall behind him. Fane's eyes widen with surprise when he turns to see part of a large intestine sliding down the wall.

"What the—"

Something cold and moist slams into his chest. He coughs, gagging on the putrid scent of rotting flesh. When he looks up, he finds Roseline crouching across the room, her crazed eyes narrowed on him.

She is covered in crimson. It looks as if she'd actually gone swimming in a pool of thick, oozing blood. Her hair is plastered to her scalp and her naked body is coated in flaking bits of dried blood.

"Oh god," he gasps, taking in the hunch of her shoulders as she leans over her prey.

The body is mangled beyond recognition. The face has been gnawed off completely. Severed limbs encircle Roseline, each cleanly cut away from the torso. Fane can see one hand on the sofa, a foot tossed against the window just above the sink.

Streaks of blood are splashed across the walls. It looks like a gusher left a wide stain on the ceiling overhead. The carpet has soaked up much of the blood from the body. There is a trail leading down the hall and around the corner. She obviously drug the body out here.

"What have you done?" He steps into the room, completely numb.

Roseline grunts at him and plunges her hands back into the meaty flesh. A squelching sound turns his stomach as she lifts something that looks disturbingly like a kidney. He raises his hands. "Now, I know what you're thinking and that's a bad idea."

He ducks just before the object soars over his head. Fane's right knee buckles as he rolls to the side, coming up just beside the sofa. Roseline stares at him through her matted hair, her gaze cold and unseeing.

"Do you know me?"

No sign of recognition. A low growl begins in her chest and rises to her throat as he moves along the length of the couch.

From there he can see something shiny wrapped around her left hand. It is long and thin, like fishing line or floss. He stops and watches Roseline as she wraps her fingers around the odd string and brings it down onto the corpse, using it to saw through another chunk of meat.

Fane's stomach lurches as he spies the missing hand. It is adorned by a single ring: a serpent with fiery red eyes.

"Malachi," he mutters, clutching the back of the couch to remain upright.

Roseline looks back over her shoulder at him. The curve her spine is pronounced, as if she has not eaten in weeks. Her cheeks are sallow and her arms, what little isn't buried under an inch of blood, appears skeletal. Her skin possesses the slightest hint of green.

"Oh god." He can feel the shaking in his legs and knows he is about to pass out. Judging by the wild look in her watchful eye, that would be unwise.

"Roseline? Can you hear me?"

Her snarl is followed quickly by the gnashing of her teeth. Fane frantically tries to think of a way to get her out of here safely and noiselessly, but he struggles to think. The wild beast before him hardly resembles the girl he knew and loved.

Anger boils deep in his chest at the thought of what it took for a transformation like this. He hadn't known it to be possible, but then again, there was still much of this world that he doesn't know or understand. What he does know is that Roseline is beginning to resemble one of the Eltat that attacked them outside the Hell Fire caves a couple weeks back.

His gaze sweeps the room for a weapon or anything can be used to subdue her. Judging by the streaks of fresh blood glistening from her chin, she has fed recently which means she will be strong, very strong. Fane scolds himself for not bringing along another immortal to help him.

He's going to have to take her down on his own, and that will not be an easy task.

Then his gaze falls on something on the kitchen floor, just beyond where Roseline is sitting. Fane leans up onto his toes. Just beneath the broken table he spies Malachi's head. Small patches of hair have been ripped free.

Frowning, he looks back to Roseline at work. She grunts softly as she lowers the string to the body and begins slicing again. His eyes widen as he realizes what she's holding. *Angel hair.*

"Of course," he whispers, finally putting together the pieces to Malachi's identity.

She must have known what Malachi was. Only angel hair would be strong enough to sever bone. Fane swallows roughly against the bile rising in his throat. Roseline dismembered Malachi with his own hair.

He closes his eyes for the briefest of moments, silently hoping that the man had been dead before she began cutting into him.

Pure, innocent, lovely Roseline has become the monster she always feared.

A plan begins to form in his mind, insane enough that it just might work. He will only have one shot to take her down and restrain her with the angel hair. There's no way he can make it past her to the kitchen before she attacks so he only has one chance…take the hair she has wrapped around her fingers.

Fane bends his knees and braces. Terror spirals through his veins, chilling him. Never in his three centuries of life has he felt so afraid. His fingers curl against the stained fabric of the couch as he prepares to push off.

One. Two. Three.

Blood trails from the Torrent bouncer's nose, the cartilage hanging in two torn pieces. The large immortal cowers on the ground, his hands raised to protect his face. "I swear I don't know nothing."

"Now we both know that is a lie, now don't we, Castor." Lucien's lip curls into a vicious snarl as he leans over, dragging his claws through the flesh of the bouncer's hands. Four gashes open up, nearly deep enough to see his tendons.

"Let's try this again. Where did Fane take her?"

Lucien's tongue flickers out of his mouth, tasting the air for the man's fear. It is genuine, but then again, he expected no less. Castor knows who he is. The name Lucien Enescue should strike fear into any living soul, immortal or not.

"I…I dunno. He left a few hours ago. Didn't say where to."

"Liar!" Lucien's scream echoes down the narrow alley, unusually deserted for this time of night. It is after midnight, and even though the weekend pub hops should be well under way, no one has dared to come down this street tonight. London is still reeling from the discovery of Ordin's body in the Thames earlier today.

Castor cowers low, his chin almost pressing against the uneven stone path. Years of grime clings to the stones. The smell of refuse and feces lingers even after a good street cleaning. Lucien grins as he stomps down onto the bouncer's head, grinding his face into the muck.

"I want a name and a place. If you tell me those two things then perhaps I shall consider letting you keep your gut intact. Are we clear?"

"Yes," Castor grunts from beneath Lucien's clawed feet. He can no longer wears shoes, unable to bear the constraining feel of them since his transformation.

Lucien rolls his neck, enjoying the stretch of his muscles. His strength is growing and his senses are improving. Even though he didn't plan to be affected by Roseline's blood, this new transformation has turned out to be quite a bonus.

"Fane said something about taking her back to somewhere safe. That's all he said."

Applying more pressure, he can hear Castor's teeth beginning to shatter. He continues to stomp on his face, ignoring the bouncer's pitiful wailing pleas. "Anything else?"

"I don't know," Castor splutters. A spray of blood stains the ground.

Lucien lifts his foot. He leans over and buries his claws into Castor's side. Blood seeps around his nails as Castor screams, flailing about on the ground. "I need a name."

"Chicago!"

Lucien wipes his claws on Castor's shirt. "See. That wasn't so hard."

"So you'll let me live?" Castor whimpers.

"I only agreed to leave your gut intact." With a mighty stomp, Lucien crushes Castor's head in. Blood seeps from the remains of his eye socket. Lucien shakes off his foot, scraping off slimy residue onto the curb. He turns and leaves the immortal on the side of the road.

Someone will come across the body in the morning and London will be gripped again with fear, wondering if this most recent attack was meant to be a part of the string of murders, or something else entirely.

Once they begin the autopsy on Castor's body they will discover that his anatomy isn't quite human and yet mysterious enough to attract attention. How many more immortal remains will show up in the coming days?

He can only hope many, many more.

And what will the humans think of Torrent? He is almost giddy at the thought. Kidnapped girls discovered. Vats of blood confiscated. There's no way he could make up such a brilliant newspaper headline, even if he tried.

Puckering his lips, Lucien whistles a cheerful tune as he begins to plan his trip to America. Fane was a fool to take Roseline somewhere so obvious, but this could go in Lucien's favor. Perhaps it is time to take his killing spree across the pond.

Twenty

 T he hallway feels narrow to Gabriel as he hurries forward. It's probably just him. None of the hunters seem to notice the tight space as he passes, but that may be because he has Elias right over his shoulder. The angel has to stop low to keep from bashing his head against the ceiling.

Elias' wings are tucked behind his back but still wide enough to brush against either side of the hallway. His broad chest and bare skin look deep bronze in the dim lights that hang from the ceiling at random intervals. Gabriel can't help but wonder what Seneh would have looked like here with his ebony skin.

The thought of his fallen guardian is too painful to think about; Gabriel pushes through a set of double doors at the end of the hall and slams right into William. He catches his friend just before William tumbles forward.

"Nice moves," William mutters, rubbing his arm as Gabriel releases him. Red marks slowly begin to appear on the human's pale skin.

Gabriel winces. "Sorry about that.

"Guess you're still adjusting too."

"Too?" Gabriel frowns, looking around the room. His gaze falls on Fane and a few black clad men that he doesn't recognize. They must be some of the hunters that Nicolae brought with him. Gabriel is amazed that a truce could have been formed between the volatile enemies, but so far, the only encounter he'd heard rumor of ended with a bloody nose and two black eyes.

As his careful gaze completes its sweep of the room, he finally notices Sadie. She's not the Sadie he remembered, and the difference is as remarkable as it is blatantly obvious. She casts a smirk back over her shoulder at him before turning to listen to what Fane is saying.

"What happened to her?" Gabriel asks.

"After you took off, she tried to stop Malachi from taking Roseline. He gutted her." William's voice cracks with emotion. Gabriel can tell there is a hint of accusation in his voice. "It was bad, Gabe. He split her open like a prize pig. I've never seen anything like it before. And I tell you what...Hollywood has been lying to us, man. That crap is gross!"

"Tell me about it." Gabriel says, closing his eyes at the memory of Seneh's body slipping beneath the surface of the red pool, caught in the current. "So what happened?"

"Fane saved her."

This surprises him. "But Nicolae..."

"Way ahead of you dude." William tugs on his arm and pulls him back toward the wall so they can speak without interrupting Fane's battle plans. "Nicolae was a wreck. Guy went off his rocker for a bit. He was sure Sadie wasn't going to make it."

Gabriel looks toward Nicolae, noticing the tension between him and Sadie. "They look pretty intense right now."

William nods. "He almost lost his place among the hunters. It was really touch and go for a bit. They thought he'd betrayed them for turning her. Thought she'd just become another monster."

When Gabriel stiffens, William slaps his forehead with the palm of his hand. "Sorry."

"Nah. It's cool. I'm still trying to get used to it myself." Hearing the slip affects Gabriel far more than he lets on. His transition into the paranormal world hasn't been an easy ride. People have been hunting him, killing his friends and trying to use him for their own evil purposes. How the heck is he supposed to have any chance to process the normal stuff when he kept getting shoved into battles?

"So she's ok? I mean, she handling it all well?"

William shrugs and leans back against the wall. He crosses one foot over the other as he tucks his hands deep into his pockets. "She doesn't really like to talk about it much. I think she's afraid I won't get it or freak out again."

"Again?" Gabriel smirks.

William offers him a sheepish grin. "Yeah, I guess all of this stuff is just a lot to take in."

Gabriel nods in complete understanding. "Yeah, it really is."

Elias shifts beside him and William casts a guarded look in his direction. Then he leans in toward Gabriel, far closer than normal. "Do I stink to you?"

Gabriel laughs. "I saw a few showers when I came in. If you've got a problem…"

"No, not that," William waves him off. "I mean my blood. Sadie says I stink and Fane does nothing more than grunt a reply."

Finally understanding his friend's meaning, Gabriel clasps William on the shoulder. "You smell good enough to eat."

William beams, pumping his fists in the air. "I knew it!"

Fane glares over his shoulder at the outburst, but quickly returns to his meeting. The black clad hunters, shrouded in the shadows of the far side of the room, smirk knowingly. Obviously they have spent enough time around William to know what he is like.

Elias' feathers rustle as he laughs, slipping in behind Gabriel from the hall. "You humans are strange beings."

William stops jumping around to stare wide-eyed at Elias. The angel's deep voice and overpowering presence subdues him quickly as his gaze falls on the crown of feathers rising over Elias' shoulder. He casts a worried glance at Gabriel.

"Holy crap," he mutters, backing away.

"Don't worry, Will. He's with me."

"Good to know. I'll just…I'm just gonna go check on your room." William slips behind Elias and out the door with only the rusting of his parka to announce his escape. Obviously adding an angel to the eclectic mix of supernatural beings is a bit too much for him.

Once William is out of the room, Gabriel falls silent, listening to the hushed tones of the battle plans being drawn up at the far end of the room. He hears the tightness in Fane's voice as he speak of someone's death, a guy name Castor. Gabriel's ears perk up on the details about Lucien.

Craning his head, he tries to hear snippets of the conversation about trailing Lucien to America, but he finally gives up. Their hushed voices are too low for him to hear from this distance. Instead, he is forced to occupy himself with surveying the room around him.

It is not particularly long or wide, but the walls were created to conceal sound and are reinforced to keep intruders out. The world outside could have vanished completely and he would never know.

The walls are off white, much like the outside of the base. The exterior was designed to help distinguish it from the snowy tundra outside. The ceilings are unnaturally high for such a squat building. He glances at Elias from the corner of his eye and realizes that he hardly has to duck his head at all in here. Did the Senthe somehow know an angel would fight alongside them?

Large maps line the far walls, although he can't see any tactical reason for them. The terrain all around is mostly flat with a wide expanse of trees to the west and south. A large lake lies buried in forest to the north, within a two-hour walk from the base. This location is as remote as could be.

If he rises up onto his toes, he can almost see a map laid out on the large table in front of Fane. Several men surround it, giving him only glimpses through the small amount of spacing between them. Sadie glances back at him from time to time. He can tell she is anxious to come speak to him, but her gaze flickers back toward Fane and she returns her attention on him.

Gabriel frowns. Since when did Sadie care what Fane thought?

"He is her mentor now," Elias whispers into his ear. His breath is warm, reminding Gabriel of how his feathered wings blaze like the sun when stretched out.

"You mean lap dog," he mutters under his breath. Sadie's lip curls into a smirk as Fane's shoulders stiffen as Gabriel's voice carries easily to the immortals in the room.

So much for an easy reunion, he thinks.

"Fane," Gabriel calls, interrupting the immortal's discussion. "We need to talk."

Fane nods curtly, motioning for Gabriel to wait in the hall. Gabriel grits his teeth at the obvious delay but silently obeys. He is anxious to see Rose. Elias said she would be here, but he's confused as to why she didn't come to greet him. In the pit of his stomach, he knows Fane is delaying for a reason, and it has nothing to do with babysitting the hunters.

Something feels wrong in the air. He can't quite place it, but there is a heaviness that seems to have little to do with the coming battle.

He follows Elias' lead back out of the room and closes the door with more force than is necessary. Elias stares at him, his eyebrows rising, but he doesn't question Gabriel's act of frustration.

Leaning back against the wall to wait, Gabriel begins to fidget after only a few minutes. First, he stuffs his hands in and out of his armpits. Next, he picks at his fingernails, as if trying to remove invisible dirt. Then he moves on to pacing the four-foot span of the hallway.

Elias watches him but remains silent. Several hunters squeeze past, entering and leaving the room. It is obviously the hub of this organization, and Gabriel is on the outskirts of it all.

"Patience. Your time will come," his mentor says, his gaze focused unseeingly on the wall across from him.

Gabriel knows Seneh's has taken its toll on Elias. Seneh was his companion for over a millennia and although Elias doesn't speak of his death, Gabriel knows Elias has questions about how and why Seneh died. Gabriel's just not sure that he's ready to explain yet.

The door beside them opens and Sadie steps out, quickly closing the door behind her. With little hesitation, she throws her arms around Gabriel's neck, squeezing him hard enough to pop the vertebrae in his neck. "Good to see you too, Sadie."

She steps back, her smile firmly plastered on her face. "Good to see you alive. Last time I saw you, you looked about as messed up as an alley cat in heat at the pound."

Gabriel laughs, not sure if he should take that as a compliment or not. "You've certainly changed."

With a small twirl, Sadie gives him the full view. "What can I say? Immortality looks good on me."

"I bet Nicolae agrees with you."

Red instantly stains her cheeks as she glances at the door. Nicolae and Fane have remained behind. "Yeah. That's not…it's just…" she sighs, running her hands through her short, cropped hair. "Yeah, I guess he's cool with it."

"Someday you'll have to tell me the story." Her smile falters. Gabriel doesn't miss a single nervous tic as she shifts her weight, inching slightly away from him. "Where's Rose?"

Now she openly turns away. "Fane has all of the details you will need about—"

He grabs her hand and yanks her back. "Sadie, please. I'm dying to see her. Can't you tell me anything?"

She grimaces, obviously torn. Darting a glance back at the closed door, she tugs on his arm and they move further down the hall. She peeks down the adjoining hallway to make sure they are alone. "It's not pretty. I've only been allowed to see her once and that only lasted about a minute. Fane yanked me out just in time."

He blanches at the tremor in her voice. "In time for what? What has happened to her?"

Sadie chews on her lip. She crosses and uncrosses her arms with obvious discomfort. "I don't really know. I heard Fane and Nicolae talking about Lucien and some place called Torrent, but that didn't make any sense to me. I mean, the guy's dead, right?"

"Lucien?" He turns to look at Elias. "How is that even possible?"

His guardian's brow is deeply furrowed, but his gaze is clear, certain. "You knew, didn't you? That's why you left for so long." Gabriel accuses.

Elias nods slowly. "You didn't need to know in order to complete your second task. It was better this way."

"And Rose? Was she just a causality in some stupid 'bigger plan' too?"

His anger rises right alongside his blood pressure. A thumping begins between his ears, masking the rapid beating of his heart. Elias doesn't look away from his direct gaze. "I have never lied to you, Gabriel. I told you she had a path to follow. This was her path."

Sadie releases a cry of outrage, turning to face off with the giant angel. "You let this happen to her, didn't you? You could have stopped him from hurting her. She is in agony because of you!"

Gabriel cringes at the pain in Sadie's voice. Obviously, whatever Roseline has endured during his absence is beyond forgivable. He can see that fact clearly written in Sadie's enraged features.

"I am sorry that you feel that way," Elias says to Sadie, "but without Roseline's transformation, Lucien would never have been weakened. Without her, he could not be killed."

"What do you mean?" Gabriel turns on his mentor. His hands shake at his side. He clenches them, struggling not to throttle the angel himself. Knowing Elias, he would probably let him do it too.

"Roseline's blood is special, just like yours. Both of you were chosen and your destinies were entwined long before you were born. You could not succeed without her and likewise for her. Nothing happens by chance, Gabriel."

"So Rose had to endure horrible pain to save me?" He spits out the words, disgusted by the way they feel on his tongue.

"To save us all," Elias amends.

The door at the end of the hall opens to reveal Fane. His direct gaze instantly takes in the tension in the hallway. He approaches with no hint of urgency, but Gabriel doubts that it does not exist. Fane's love for Rose has always been clear. The pain she has endured must have cut him just as deeply as it does Gabriel, probably deeper since he has seen the state she is in.

"You have obviously heard the news." Fane's words are clipped as he turns a disapproving glare onto Sadie. She rolls her eyes. Fane sighs heavily but nods for Nicolae to take her aside. She goes with him peacefully, but not without a few snide comments for Fane's benefit.

Fane turns on his heel and heads back the way Gabriel and Elias first entered. Apart from a cursory glance at the angel, Fane gives no hint of recognition or curiosity. Perhaps Rose is far worse off than Gabriel initially feared.

When they reach the exterior door, Fane shoves it open and steps out into the blustery cold. The winds claw fiercely against Gabriel's clothes, whipping his hair into a tangled frenzy. His exposed skin burns as they trudge away from the camp and toward the far tree line.

"Where are we going?" Gabriel shouts against the wind.

"She had to be contained, for everyone's safety." Fane motions over his shoulder to follow him. The three men burrow into the heart of the blizzard for nearly ten minutes before Gabriel spies the approaching forest. Once they cross over the threshold, the wind dies down enough for him to lower his hand and take a look around.

Tall pines tower overhead, shielding them from the brunt of the storm. Snow cyclones whip in and around the base of the trees, altering the landscape. The howling of the wind is muffled within the forest, almost eerie in the twilight.

Fane hikes on for another twenty minutes before he comes to a halt at the top of a slight ridge. Gabriel cranes his head back, searching the darkening sky. The sun hangs low in the sky. "Are we here?"

"Yes." That one word feels loaded with so many emotions that Gabriel feels buried under the weight of them. What will he find on the other side of that crest? How bad is Rose?

Fane turns and looks at Elias, who nods his head in return. Elias steps back, spreading his wings to provide warm golden light in the receding daylight.

"Beyond that rise you will find an ice block shelter. The walls are made of stone, steel and ice. Thick enough to prevent her escape, even if she were lucid enough to try to break free. Roseline will be waiting for you."

Gabriel takes a step forward but hesitates. Now that he is finally here, only a few steps away, he fears going to her. Will she forgive him for leaving her? For not saving her from Malachi or Lucien?

He can only imagine the horrors that she has endured in his absence. Hanging his head with shame, he knows this is his fault. He could have saved her that night at Bran Castle. She would still be whole, healthy and as lovely as ever if he had, but fate had chosen another path for him.

I will make it up to her, he silently vows.

"Will she know who I am?" he asks, staring at the top of the ridge in the glow of Elias' wings. He doesn't look at Fane. Instead, he keeps his focus straight ahead, toward Roseline.

"No," Fane whispers. Pain is etched deeply into each word. "But she will still want you."

Lucien never liked America. It is too bold, too outspoken, and far too brash for his liking.

He misses the Old World.

Chicago was a waste of time. He spent an entire day sniffing out airports, bus terminals and train stations to discover that Fane and Roseline had never stepped foot in any of them. He should have known that idiot bouncer would lead him astray, but he hadn't taken the man to be so noble. Lucien gnashes his teeth at his own mistake.

At least I am making the most of it, he chuckles silently, pleased with his impromptu plan change. If he can't find Fane on his own, Lucien will give him a reason to come to him.

Standing beneath the St. Louis Arch, Lucien struggles to see beyond the tall glass buildings that shield the rest of the city. The river below him is brown and dingy. The glittering lights of the casino across the water are glaringly obnoxious.

In the shadow of the arch, Lucien goes to work arranging the bodies. He knows he has to ramp up the horror if he wants to continue to gain the notice of the world. This should keep reporters talking for a while.

Thirty women sprawl across the Arch grounds. The inner five-point star, made of bodies, converges on an outer circle, creating a pentacle of death. Not a single drop of blood can be found on the iced ground. Each victim was drained of blood through tiny teeth marks all along their arms and legs and then cleaned meticulously before being placed here.

Lucien steps back to admire his work, hardly showing any sign of exertion. Killing this many women in a single night is no small task, but he couldn't risk unleashing his Eltat on the city. Americans are far too trigger happy for that.

Wiping his hands on his dark cloak, Lucien turns at the sound of approaching footsteps. Sneakers slap against the concrete path. Blond hair appears over the slight elevation of the hill.

Lucien licks his lips with his forked tongue. "Perhaps there is room for one more."

Twenty-One

 T he door creaks on its hinges as Gabriel steps through into the pitch black room. There are no windows in the building and much of it has been built into the sloping ground. He can't help but wonder if this was done to conceal the building or to help naturally soundproof it.

The floor is slick beneath him, and cold vapors rise to tickle his legs. He inches his fingertips along the ice block wall, searching for the light Fane told him would be there. Twenty steps into the darkness his leg slams into the corner of a metal table.

Gabriel grunts, reaching out reflexively when he hears a metal lantern topple. He grasps the cold handle, righting it on the tabletop. Upon further investigation, he discovers a box of matches and lights one up.

He squints as he tries to adjust to the sudden light. A dented red lantern appears before him and he quickly sets to work lighting it. Three matches and a few singed fingers later, the lantern flares to life.

The warm light, spilling over the table and onto the floor, reveals little detail of the room. It is small and square, void of anything but the table and a single chair. An unopened book rests atop the table, its binding still unbroken. Whoever sat here never even touched it.

Fane, he thinks, wondering how many countless hours he waited here. But what would he be waiting for? Surely if Roseline were able to improve on her own, she would have done it by now.

Do immortals need medicine? No. He rubs his forehead, remembering how blood is used to heal all wounds. Then why not just take some blood from William or Nicolae? Surely, they would have offered if it meant helping their friend.

Gabriel sighs, knowing William probably would have put up a fight about that. His acceptance of all things fangy seems to be fragile at the moment, but Nicolae would have. Gabriel had been told when he first arrived how distraught Nicolae was over Roseline's state. Surely, that must stem from a friendship formed during his absence. So much has happened while he was gone.

Raising the lantern, he searches for a door. Fane told him there is only one. This building is used for one purpose: to hold a prisoner. He is sure Fane never dreamed it would be used for Roseline.

According to Fane, the entire compound had been deeply disturbed when they brought Roseline here. They spoke of the evil foreboding it represented, but Fane chose not to see it that way. He couldn't let himself, and Gabriel understands why. If Lucien is capable of taking down Roseline, their most fierce and talented warrior, what more could he do to them?

The Senthe are battle-hardened after years on the front lines, fighting to protect the immortal world from the mortal one, but Roseline was to be their leader. Even Fane said he would submit to her. No other immortal has been trained so viciously.

Roseline's name was spoken in awed whispers when he passed through the base, but no one had told him what to expect within these ice block walls.

His boots crunch on the floor as he moves toward the back of the room. It appears to be a solid block of ice and yet he knows she must be just beyond. He can feel her, even though he can't explain how. He always has and he prays that he always will.

"Rose?" He runs his fingers along the wall, searching for any sign of a door. He begins at the far left wall and slowly and meticulously working his way right. He is nearly to the end of the wall when his finger catches on a sliver of space.

Backing up, he raises the lantern and struggles to see the entire doorframe. It is there but nearly impossible to see. No doubt a human, or even an immortal casting a cursory glance, would never notice the door's presence.

He sets the lantern on the floor and runs his finger along the wall until it slips into a tiny opening. He digs in, grunting with effort as the heavy door slowly slides toward him. The space beyond is in total darkness.

Nervous tension courses through his hands, causing them to quake as he lifts the lantern and steps into the room. The light spills over onto the floor, as icy and barren as the outer room. Two metal legs appear as he raises the lantern higher to reveal a drape of white.

"Rose?"

He steps forward, unsure if he should be cautious with his approach. His instincts scream that he is in danger, but his mind wars with that feeling. This is Rose, his Rose. She would never hurt him.

A low growl stops him in his place. It sounds deep and animalistic, unlike anything he has ever heard before. For a second, he fears that he has somehow stumbled onto a grizzly bear, but when he raises the lantern toward the far corner, he realizes he is in far more danger than he imagined.

Roseline crouches against the wall, her nails digging deep into the ice, suspending her nearly four feet off the floor. Her hair is twisted and matted and her face is contorted with rage. Her skin is sickly green and strangely luminescent.

Her once warm and inviting eyes hold a reddish tint now, narrowed and deadly. Her nostrils flare as she cocks her head, bobbing back and forth like a venomous snake.

"Rose," he gasps. The sight of her makes Gabriel's blood freeze in his veins. Now he understands Sadie's anger and Fane's hopeless tone on the ridge. His Rose is gone. All that remains is a mindless beast.

Dried blood clings to her arms and neck. Her lips peel back to reveal teeth that are decidedly more jagged than normal and utterly lethal.

"What has he done to you?" Gabriel's legs threaten to buckle beneath him. Never in his wildest nightmares could he have summoned up such a hideous face for his beloved. He doesn't know how Lucien survived his beheading, or how he managed to poison Rose, but Gabriel will make sure his father pays for this.

He steps closer and Roseline snarls at him, gnashing her teeth. If she had truly been a snake, she would have been coiled and ready to strike. Gabriel shifts another foot forward, more cautious this time. His mind whips through countless scenarios and none of them turn out in his favor. If she attacks him, he won't be able to harm her. His life would be in her savage hands.

"Do you know me? It's Gabriel?"

His words seem to fall on deaf ears as she glares back at him. The weight of the lantern in his hand seems to grow heavier by the second, reminding him not only of his dependence on its light, but also how cumbersome it would be if she were to attack.

"You saved my life once, in Sorin's dungeon. I never got the chance to thank you for that." He inches his right boot closer, raising the light high enough to hopefully shadow his movements. "You could have let me die, probably should have, but you didn't."

His progress is infuriatingly slow toward the center of the room. "Do you remember how I almost hit you in the face with that football at school?" He chuckles softly. "Now I know that there was no way possible that I would have hit you. You probably could have ground that ball into dust right before my very eyes."

Another tiny step. The slight swing of the lantern makes Roseline curl inward, ready to spring off the wall. Gabriel pauses for a moment.

"I never got to tell you how amazing you looked at my party either. When I opened the door and saw you, I thought I'd trip over my own feet just trying to get next to you. And then you slipped on that darn floor," he laughs, cautiously. "I knew the instant I had you in my arms that I'd do anything to keep you there."

Roseline cranes her neck, the low growl subsiding fractionally. Gabriel takes that as a good sign as he prepares to take another step. "The music was loud and my so called friends were all drunk, but you made it all worth it. I knew when I looked at you that I could trust you. I knew you would appreciate my art studio. Do you remember it, Rose? It had orange roses on the table by the window. You said they were your favorite."

A slight flicker in her eye is the only hint that he might be getting through to her. Gabriel inches forward again. He is now only two feet from the metal table in the center of the room. A twisted white blanket lies atop it, dangling off one side. Four leather straps are piled beneath the table, each snapped cleanly off.

Red bruises mar her wrists and ankles. Gabriel grits his teeth at the knowledge of Fane restraining her. But staring at the woman before him, Gabriel can't help but understand the need for such actions, even if he is loath to admit it.

"When you ran off, I used to sit up there and draw you. Sometimes it was just your face, or your profile, or even just the way your hair would fall over your shoulder when you were chatting with Sadie in the lunchroom. I clung to those images, sure that I'd lost you forever, but I hadn't. I found you."

She shifts, uncurling her fingernails out of the ice slowly. The screech of her nails sends shivers down her spine as he surveys her position and frowns. He has no clue how she is up there. There is nothing to sit on and she's not holding onto anything. It's almost like watching a scene right out of a Spider Man movie.

"I promised you I would come back, but that was wrong. I never should have left you in the first place. I promise I will never let anything take me away from you again."

Roseline's eyes widen, not fully open but far better than when narrowed. They look less like slits now. Gabriel smiles up at her. "I have loved you since the first day I bumped into you. I never really got the chance to tell you that."

She sways, but he can't tell if that's a good thing or a bad thing, so he decides to continue. "When all of this is over, I swear we will be together again, like we were meant to be. I never used to believe in destiny. I thought it was a bunch of crap, but then I met you and all of that changed."

He slowly takes the final step up to the table and presses his fingers into the hard surface. It is cold. She obviously hasn't laid there in a while.

"I love you, Rose."

Her ragged breath catches for a split second, but it's enough. Gabriel smiles, knowing that she heard him. She is slowly beginning to return to him, no longer the beast but his beloved Rose.

"I'm going to set this lantern down now. Is that ok?"

He leans over, letting his right arm stretch toward the floor. The instant he breaks eye contact with her, she attacks.

Sharp claws curl into his flesh, digging nearly deep enough to touch bone. Gabriel cries out as the lantern crashes wildly to the floor and the flame flickers out. He is plunged into complete darkness.

Rose screams like a wild animal as she claws her way around to his back, digging her nails into muscle and sinew as she goes. Gabriel grabs for her arms, missing each time by a split second. She is lightning fast.

"Rose, stop!"

She growls and kicks him in the kidneys, nearly toppling them over. He lurches back, throwing them against the wall. The crunch reverberates in his ears as she snarls, wriggling between his back and the wall.

He fights to pin her there, desperate to keep her from doing any more damage to herself or him. "Listen to me. I'm here to help you!"

Roseline swipes her claws across his face, drawing blood. As his scent fills the air, Rose thrashes into a frenzy. Her snarls rise to deafening proportions as she bucks against him, desperate to be free.

Her teeth gnash beside his ear. He reaches back over his shoulder and slams her head back into the wall, stunning her just long enough for him to reposition. "I'm so sorry," he grunts.

He whips around and latches his hands onto her arms, pressing his knee into her waist to keep her pinned against the wall. "I want to help you~"

"You can't," she hisses. "It's too late."

"Never." His grip tightens against her struggles as he desperately tries to figure out a plan. He can't let her go but he can't keep her here. Fane doesn't know what to do with her and if the hunters ever find out just how bad she is, they will want her put down like a rabid dog. He can't let that happen.

You will face three trials, Gabriel. Elias' earlier words spoken during their flight to Canada slip through his mind. *The first was self-denial. You chose to leave Roseline behind and fulfill your destiny. The second is the sacrifice of flesh. Your journey to Eden to retrieve the Taral fire sword fulfilled this task. The third will be your hardest challenge of all. Redemption.*

At the time, Gabriel didn't have a clue what Elias had meant, but now, staring into the glowing red irises of Roseline's eyes, he understands.

Roseline bucks wildly against Gabriel's grip in the pitch dark. His fingers dig into her forearms as she snarls and spits in his face, wild like a rabid animal. He takes a deep breath, praying for some sign of the girl he fell in love with only a few short weeks ago, but he can't find a single one. His heart aches with the realization that Roseline is gone.

"I promise I'm going to save you." He lowers his head and brings one arm up to meet his lips. Roseline's fingers curl into claws, swiping blindly at him as he sinks his teeth deep into the flesh of his wrist. His nostrils flare as the potent scent of his blood rises around him.

Roseline falls eerily still.

The sound of his blood pattering against the icy floor sounds distant as he offers her his wounded arm. Strong hands latch around his bicep, nearly yanking his arm from its socket.

He can feel hear her licking her lips in the dark as she is consumed by need.

"My life blood for yours," he whispers as her teeth bury deep into his flesh.

Fane paces atop the ridge, eyeing the angel at his side with a mixture of emotions. Suspicion is the obvious first choice. Although he hasn't sensed any reason to fear the giant, he hasn't felt at home around the guy either. The second emotion is awe.

The angel stands nearly a foot over Fane's head, and with his wings fully expanded, he is an awesome sight. Fane crosses his arms over his chest, only to let them fall free to hang by his side again. "He's been in there a long time."

Elias nods in silent agreement. Fane kicks at the base of a tree, feeling only a sight sense of satisfaction when the heavy boughs dump their load of snow.

"Do you think we should go check on him?"

The angel shakes his head.

Fane frowns. "I think I'm starting to see why the kid gets annoyed with you."

Elias laughs. "It does happen from time to time."

"Ah, he can talk!" Fane tilts his chin to look up at his companion. "May I speak frankly?"

"You may."

Fane leans his back against one of the towering pines, letting the bark sink deep against his back. "I think you know more than you're letting on."

"Perhaps." The angel dips his head in agreement. "But the same could be said for you."

Fane's heavy sigh brings a smile to Elias' lips. "You don't like Gabriel much, do you?"

"I have nothing against him," Fane says.

"A very vague response for a very exact answer."

"Meaning?" Fane presses.

Elias points toward the building ahead of them. It lies deep in the shadow of night. "It burns you that you aren't the one in there with her."

"So?"

"It is not your place, Fane. It never has been."

The angel's words don't sit well with him. Fane has never been a big believer in fate or destiny. He likes to think things happen for a reason but that he still has control over what he chooses when he is presented with two options. Roseline was the best thing that ever happened to him. Even though he knows their time together is over, he can't help but wish for those times back.

Elias rustles his feathers as he tucks them against his back. They continue to glow but the light in the small clearing is greatly diminished. "I know this is not easy for you. Your love for Roseline is a evident, but eventually all things pass. Are you willing to step aside and let Gabriel fulfill his destiny, even if that means hurting Roseline?"

Fane's jaw clenches tightly enough to pop his jaw. His fingernails carve into the sensitive flesh of his palms. "What do you mean 'hurt Roseline'?"

Elias turns to stare into the dark. Fane can't help but wonder if the angel is somehow able to pierce through the steel and ice to be able to see what is happening within the confines of that small building. "Sometimes pain isn't a bad thing."

As Fane mulls over his words, Elias lowers himself to the ground, shifting until his legs are crossed and sinks into a meditative pose. "I didn't think angels were into all of that stuff," Fane mutters.

"We aren't, but I have a feeling we may be here a while."

Twenty-Two

The pain in Gabriel's head is debilitating as he struggles to rise on his feet. His knees threaten to give out on him as he grasps onto the edge of the table and pulls himself upright.

The darkness is confining. He can hear Roseline's steady breathing but nothing else. He can't even be sure if she's fallen asleep or finally passed out. All he knows is that she's not moving.

Wincing at the stinging pain from the gash in his wrist, Gabriel wills his legs to hold firm as he rises to his full height. It takes far more effort than it should. His head swims, threatening to tumble him back to the ground.

Everything hurts.

A fire has begun along his skin, slowly burning deep to his bones. Gabriel stumbles forward, arms outstretched before him as he searches for the wall. He has lost all sense of direction, unable to tell if he is heading toward the door or away.

His fingertips crumple against the rigidity of the ice wall when he reaches the far wall. Sweat beads on his brow, slowly sliding down from his hairline into his eyes.

"Fane!" His cry sounds croaky as it fades off into rasping coughs. He pounds his fists against the wall of ice, ignoring each stab of pain.

He is desperate to escape so he can find help for Roseline. In the dark he can't tell if she is healing, but at least her screams have ceased. That was the worst part. Worse than feeling her drain the life from him or the searing pain that followed when their blood mingled.

Gabriel can feel the poison that turned her into this mindless monster. It is a part of him now.

Will I become a thing too? This thought makes his breath catch, but he quickly stuffs it back down. It doesn't matter. Saving Roseline is all he cares about. If that means he will suffer her fate, then so be it.

"Fane!" His voice is hoarse, but slightly stronger than before. He opens his clenched fists and slaps his palms against the wall. The cold stings his hands, but he doesn't care. He fears he will go insane if he is trapped much longer.

He kicks and beats against the ice until he is panting with effort. Sweat slips down his neck and into the collar of his shirt. He turns and leans his back against the wall, too worn out to yell anymore. Sliding down the ice, he decides that he is finally being punished for leaving Roseline.

When he closes his eyes, he feels exhaustion setting in. His limbs feel heavy and his chest squeezed. *Is this how Roseline felt?*

A faint scraping sound catches his attention. He lifts his head and turns his ear to the wall. He is sure he heard something.

"Hello?"

The sound comes again, faint but definitely there. Gabriel pushes up on his hands and knees and rises just as a sliver of light spills in through a crack in the wall. He can hear deep voices on the other side.

"Help us," Gabriel croaks as he falls to his knees. The light is intense when the door opens wide, and he raises his hand to shield his eyes. He sways in place, sure that he's about to face plant when strong hands grasp his arms and pull him to his feet.

"You are safe, young one."

"Elias," Gabriel mutters as he closes his eyes. The warmth of the angel's skin is nearly unbearable, but he clings to the giant, desperate to be free of this room. "Rose..."

"I'll take her," he hears Fane say as he brushes past. His gasp follows almost immediately. Gabriel feels rather than sees Fane turn to stare at him. "What did you do?"

Gabriel clutches his stomach as a series of coughs wrack his weakened frame. "What I must."

San Francisco is a bustling place. With its red trolley cars and colorful row houses, it reminds Lucien of a circus. His travels across America went far smoother than he would have imagined. In Romania he is feared, in Europe he is avoided but in America, he seems to be a bit of a novelty.

Despite the humans blindness to his true nature, they seem attracted to his eccentric style of dress and speech. The woman at the train station nearly fell over herself when he approached the window. His slow smile broadened when she leaned forward and unconsciously bared her neck to him. She tasted delicious.

Americans are a curious breed. Perhaps they are not as bad as he originally thought.

Standing just short of the lapping water, Lucien stares up at the Golden Gate Bridge. Each steel cable is illuminated against the dark sky, making him think of cages and chains. He smiles and lets his gaze drift lower.

The steady stream of traffic has died down greatly since the evening rush hour passed several hours ago. The party crowd came and went, leaving only those poor souls forced into working the night shift at the docks below.

Lucien folds his arms over his chest, looking beyond the support beams to the ropes dangling down. There are fifteen of them in total, each weighted with a local or tourist he found walking the streets earlier in the evening. Killing them had been fun, but the tricky part was tying them up with no one seeing him. It's a good thing he's an expert of hiding in the shadows.

Tomorrow morning, the world will know he has been here, and Fane won't be able to ignore him any longer. Time is running out for Roseline, and he wants to be there when she turns.

Everything smells wrong. Roseline scrunches up her nose as she opens her eyes. She instantly squints at the brightness of the room. The walls are white and shiny but in a very unusual way. She steels herself to take another look, this time keeping her eyes narrowed.

Rolling her head to the side, she realizes why the texture of the walls seems so foreign to her. It's made of large blocks of ice, almost like an igloo, but square instead of domed. No human could walk across such a surface without ending up on their face or backside.

Four lanterns illuminate the corners of the room, their handles dangling from metal hooks drilled into the ceiling.

She stiffens at the sound of footsteps just beyond her room. No voices or other sounds reach her. It is disturbing to be locked into such a confined space with no memory of how she got there. "Hello?"

Who is beyond this room? Did Malachi move her when she was unconscious? She frowns, struggling to remember. Her memories are a wash, blurred and irretrievable. "Is anyone out there?"

Footsteps rush toward the door from different directions, but they pause just on the other side of the door. She can hear a muffled argument now and strains to hear the words. Human shadows appear on the other side of the door but are too distorted to reveal their identity.

One of the shadows apparently wins the argument and a shoulder slams against the wall of ice, revealing a thick door, a seamless entry and exit point that only the designers of the building would know about. Although it looks vaguely familiar to her, she can't focus on that right now.

Roseline holds her breath, curling her fingers tightly around the edge of the table she lies upon as the door opens. Her mouth drops open in shock as she catches her first glimpse of Gabriel's beautiful smile. She flies off the table and throws herself into his waiting arms.

"You came for me," she cries into his ear, breathing his familiar scent deeply. She closes her eyes, praying that she never wakes from whatever dream this is. "I knew you would."

Strong arms curl around her back, holding her aloft. Her toes stretch down toward the floor, rubbing the tops of his feet. A small grunt alerts her to his distress and she releases him, sinking back to the floor.

"Are you really here?" she asks, grasping his arms, feeling the raw strength of his muscles.

"I am," he grins, pulling her back into his arms. As she nestles into his neck, she vows to never let him go again.

"What took you so long?"

He laughs and places a kiss on her temple. "You know me. Saving the world, one damsel at a time."

Roseline clings to him as tears stream down her cheeks. "I missed you so much."

Her words choke off as he pulls back, his gaze gentle and filled with warmth as he smiles down at her. "Not as much as I've missed you. Wait until you meet Elias. He'll tell you what a pain I've been."

"What happened to me? How are you here? Where is Malachi?"

He brushes strands of hair back from her forehead. "You've been through a lot the past week."

"Past week?" She frowns, trying once again to sift through her failing memories. "Where am I?"

"Canada."

Her breath hisses past her teeth. "The Senthe base?"

Gabriel's eyes brighten with surprise. "You know about it?"

"Of course." She swings her legs down to sit on the edge of the table. "I helped design it with Fane. Well, the idea of it at least. I was never allowed to see the actual construction."

"Why not?" Gabriel shifts to lean against the wall. Even though he tries to hide it, she can tell he is tired. The skin beneath his eyes betrays the slightest hint of purple, and his steps seem slightly labored.

"I was married to the enemy. I'd be the last person they would tell." She watches him closely, still unsure if he is really here. "Something is wrong."

Gabriel blinks. She can't tell if he's shocked by the change in topic or her tone. "What do you mean?"

"You're not telling me something. I feel good. Better than good. That shouldn't be possible. And you," she pokes her finger toward him. "You look like you're hung over. What happened?"

He shifts, shoving his hands deep into the pockets of his jeans. She can't help but see the boy she first met in the hallway of Rosewood Prep not so long ago. He has changed so much, and yet in some ways, not at all.

"You won't be sick again. Elias says the poison is gone."

"Gone?" The word comes out in a whisper, mingled with awe and confusion. The fact that she has no clue who this Elias is pales in comparison to the reality that she feels healthy. "How?"

Gabriel shoots her a lopsided grin. "I've got skills."

"No!" Her fingers dig into his forearms as she stares at the fine lines around his eyes. "What did you do?"

Reaching out his hand, he gently runs his hands through her hair, pausing to cup her cheek in his hands. "I saved you, just like I was always supposed to do."

"But the poison! It'll kill you!" She clings to him, terrified of what he has done. She can't stop to see how selfless this act is as her fear masks all other emotion.

His touch is soothing as he wraps her in his arms. "I'm fine. A little weak but I'm good to go. Don't worry."

"But you could have died," she protests, staring up at him. How could she have lived with herself if she found out she was the reason for his death?

The first time he sacrificed himself for her, back in Sorin's dungeon, it nearly broke her heart. Now, she can't bear to think of doing anything different. "I can't lose you."

"You won't. I'm not going anywhere." He rests his head atop hers and begins to rock ever so slightly, but it is enough to calm her. He is here, holding her. Perhaps Gabriel is right. Maybe this time they can face the future together, side by side.

Twining her fingers through his, she vows that no matter what happens in the coming days, she won't leave his side. Lucien is sure to lash back once he discovers she is gone. No doubt, that has already happened.

If Fane brought her to the Senthe base, that means things are far worse than she thought. It's time to get caught up to speed. "Take me to Fane."

Twenty-Three

Fane glances up from the TV when the door opens and quickly sighs with frustration. What is taking them so long? Roseline woke up over an hour ago. They should have been back by now.

He taps his fingers against the metal table, trying to force himself to stop obsessing. He has no right to her anymore. His place is here, helping to finalize the battle plans, and yet his heart and mind are off in the woods.

"It sucks, doesn't it?"

He blinks, realizing Sadie has leaned over to speak to him. "I don't know what you mean."

"Course you do. I can see straight through your pathetic attempt to appear calm." She wags a finger at him. "You're dying to go to her, aren't you?"

Fane shifts his body away, annoyed. "She's not mine anymore."

Sadie's laugh is tinged with a bitterness that Fane is all too familiar with. "So you think it's just that easy, huh? Man, you really are an idiot."

He stiffly turns in his chair, his jaw clamped down tightly. "I suggest letting this drop before I give you another lesson in manners."

"Oh, I'm quivering in my boots." She slouches back into her chair, her arm slung carelessly over the back.

Fane is sorely tempted to lash out and whack the back of her head, like a frustrated mother scolding her child, but instead he smiles and sits up a little straighter. "Hey, Nicolae? Isn't it time for another training session? Sadie seems to have some pent up emotion she needs to release."

Nicolae blinks as he raises up from the map table. His face is emotionless, but Fane can see easily see his poorly concealed pain. Nicolae nods curtly and marches toward the door.

Fane closes his eyes, instantly sorry for using the boy against Sadie. When her punch lands soundly on his bicep he doesn't complain.

"That was cruel and you know it," she hisses as she rises to her feet. "What kind of man are you anyway?"

His gaze drops to the floor. "You are forgetting that I haven't been a man for a very long time."

She starts to speak, taking a step toward him, but changes her mind. He watches as her feet move away, refusing to look up until the door closes soundly behind her.

Fane groans and leans back in his chair, his hands covering his face.

"Don't tell me you've taken up torturing Sadie and Nicolae in my absence."

With his breath caught in his throat, Fane lowers his hands and blinks, sure that the vision before him will fade at any moment. Roseline smirks and plants her hands on her hips, shaking her head in amusement. "I expected more from you, Fane Dalca."

He rises unsteadily to his feet, gripping the edge of the table for support. "Is that really you?"

"In the flesh."

He crushes her in his grasp, twirling her about so that her feet leave the ground. Her laughter sounds like the peals of church bells on a beautiful autumn morning, reminding him of a better time, when the world was his, and so was she.

"I can't believe he did it," he mutters into the silky strands of her hair.

Fane's arms stiffen as he smells *his* scent lingering on her. He slows to a halt and releases her, remembering his place as he steps back.

"It's good to see you," he responds stiffly.

"It's good to be back." Roseline's smile brightens her entire face. His chest aches at the sight of her and yet he can't bear to look away. "I think it's time for you to fill me in on what's been going on. Why are we here? You know the Senthe base was only for emergencies."

Fane nods and motions for her to sit. Over the next half hour he fills her in on Sadie's transformation, all of the murders, the uprisings happening around the globe as fear begins to grip the humans and how Nicolae convinced the hunters to join in their fight.

The more he speaks, the more grave she becomes. She hardly moves, hardly breathes as she soaks it all in. "And now we are all here, in one place, exactly where Lucien would want us."

"Yes, but we are one step ahead of him." Fane shifts his attention to the TV that flashes through random shots of Lucien's more recent killing spree. "We sent him on a wild goose chase to America while William and I brought you back here."

Roseline's lips thin as she turns to look at him, surprised. "You unleashed him on an unsuspecting country just to keep him from finding me?"

Fane swallows roughly. "We had no other choice."

"There is always a choice!" she shouts, rising to her feet. Her cheeks flush with anger as she pounds on the table. "I am not worth those human lives!"

She stabs her finger at the TV. He winces at the sight of the empty ropes still swinging from the bottom of the Golden Gate Bridge. Luckily, the new isn't showing the actual footage of when the bodies were first discovered.

"We have already begun to leave breadcrumbs for him to follow us here. Once he reaches Canada there will be fewer casualties."

Roseline rolls her eyes as she raises her hands to rub her temples. "I know you're not that stupid, Fane. Bloodshed will follow him from San Francisco all the way north to us. What's really going on here?"

He looks away, unable to meet her intense gaze. "It had to be done."

"Why?" She rounds the edge of the table and stops before him. His hands tremble with the overwhelming desire to take her into his arms, hold her and never let go again, but he forces himself to focus.

"It doesn't matter anymore."

"It does to me," she whispers. He flinches as she reaches down and gently pulls his chin up. He clamps his eyes closed, his heart hammering in his chest, as she squats down before him. "Fane."

He exhales, silently berating himself for being weak, for making it so obvious to her. Of course she can hear his pulse thumping wildly and smell the sweat that clings to his brow. "I couldn't leave you behind. I searched..." his voice chokes off. He shakes his head, refusing to look at her.

"You did this for *me*?"

All he can manage is a stiff nod. When she releases his chin, he hangs his head with shame. "I've tried to let you go. I swear it, but when he took you..."

"I know," she whispers, settling down before his legs. She places her hands on his knees and waits for him to look at her. When he does, his breath catches at the sight of tears in her eyes.

"I'm so sorry, Fane. I never meant to hurt you."

He wipes at his eyes, angry with himself. "I don't blame you."

"And Gabriel?" She presses gently.

He hesitates, unsure of how he really feels about the boy: remorse to be sure, sadness no doubt, but no malice. "You know I could never hate him, not when you love him so much."

A tender smile tugs at her lips as she rises up to eye level. "Can I?"

His muscles lock down as she winds her arms around his neck. She leans in and rests her head upon his shoulder, holding him. Tears dampen his shoulder and his resistance shatters completely.

Fane takes her into his arms, holding her as tightly as she clings to him. She trembles in his arms, and in that moment he realizes just how terrified she had been. He buries his nose into her shoulder and gives her the only thing he can...support.

"Does Gabriel know what happened to you?" he finally asks as she leans back. She will give him the details when she is ready. Her fear is enough to tell him how unbearable her abduction must have been.

She shakes her head, swiping away her tears with the back of her hand. "No, and I don't want him to."

Fane releases his grip on her shoulders, sliding his hands down along her arms until he reaches her hands. He clasps them in his, resisting the urge to twine his fingers with hers. Instead, he cups her hand, squeezing it tightly. "I don't know what Lucien did to you, but I know you would never have hurt Malachi on your own."

Roseline falls eerily still. "What did you just say?"

"Malachi. You…" He frowns, seeing the genuine confusion on her face. "You don't remember, do you?"

She pulls back from his grasp, sinking to the floor. Her eyebrows furrow as she stares unseeingly at the far wall, trying to draw up the memory. After a couple minutes, she shakes her head and looks back at him. "There's nothing. It's just…gone."

Fane releases the breath he has been holding and smiles. "It doesn't matter. It wasn't you."

"Tell me," she says, surging up to her knees. "What happened?"

Reaching into his pocket, he closes his fist around something cold and metal. He extends his hand and slowly uncurls his fingers. Color drains from her face as she stares down at the red-eyed serpent ring Malachi always wore.

A single tear slips down her cheek as she reaches for it. "He saved me…in the end."

Fane nods. "I figured that was what happened."

Roseline closes her eyes and clutches the ring to her chest. He may have helped her, but he skinned the old monk alive and killed Enael. What little sorrow she feels for his horrible death is marred but this knowledge.

Fane watches as she draws her hand away and opens her fingers. The ring looks large in her hand, nearly stretching the length of her palm. With quivering fingers, she lifts the ring and places it on her forefinger. A look of defiance sharpens her gaze as she looks up at him.

"Lucien has many sins to pay for."

For the first time since she entered the room, Fane sees the old Roseline, the fiery girl he knew existed all along. "Then let's make sure that he does."

Sadie follows behind Nicolae down the darkened hall, not the least bit excited about being forced into close proximity with him. This is all Fane's fault.

A tiny sliver of guilt manages to wiggle in as she realizes she could have been a bit nicer to Fane. He is obviously hurting. Poking fun at him probably wasn't the brightest thing she's ever done.

"Where do you want to go?" Nicolae asks over his shoulder.

"Oh, now you're speaking to me?"

His shoulders rise and fall with an exaggerated sigh. "I'm not going to do this with you, Sadie. We are here to work, not bicker."

She stops and crosses her arms over her chest. When Nicolae finally notices she's not behind him, he turns and walks back. "What? You really want to do this here?"

"Sure. Why not? You afraid people might hear what you have to say?" She lashes back, knowing exactly how much he would prefer not to speak about their relationship around his hunters.

"You want to talk now? Fine!" He stomps up to her, allowing his height and bulk to intimidate her. She steps back but doesn't let her glare fade. "You want to hear how seeing you ever day but not being able to be near you drives me crazy? Or how torn I feel between my duty to the hunters and my love for you?"

She gasps, stepping back a step. "You love me?"

"Of course I do," he shouts, reaching out to pull her close to him. She stumbles forward, placing her hand on his chest.

"I'm a mess without you, Sadie. I can't think. I can't eat. I can't fight."

Her mouth gapes open, but he continues before she can speak. "Do you have any idea what kind of pressure I'm under? If I choose you, my men might turn on us and hunt us for betraying them. I can't risk that, not if it means risking your life. So yes, I pushed you away, but only because I can't stand the thought of losing you for good."

His grip tightens on her arms as her knees threaten to give out on her. She blinks rapidly, trying to process everything he said. She can't seem to get past the *I love you* part.

"You really love me?"

Nicolae's gaze softens as he raises his hand to gently brush along her cheek. "I have since the first time you rejected me. And every time after that."

She flushes, thinking of how mean she's been to him. "You were just so…"

"Nerdy?"

"I was gonna say you were as annoying as a bad rash, but yeah, that works too." She cracks a grin.

He pulls her close, leaving only a few inches between them. Sadie's lips part, mesmerized by the way he is staring at her. She can feel the importance of this moment. She could turn him down and walk away, forever regretting that decision, or she can embrace his love and risk losing everything.

"Just kiss her already," a gruff voice shouts from down the hall.

Sadie looks over Nicolae's shoulder, instantly flushing when she realizes the hallway beyond is filled with hunters. Nicolae blinks, obviously shocked by the smiling faces around him. "Seriously?"

Grigori laughs as he steps out from behind his men. "Look, we may not like the way things turned out, but Sadie hasn't ripped your throat out yet, and believe me, some of us wished she would have over the past few days."

A chuckle of agreement rumbles through the hunters. Sadie flushes as Nicolae's fingers slide down her arm to grasp her hand. "So what are you saying?"

Grigori looks to Costel and Bodgan. Sadie knows these two men are the ones Nicolae is most worried about. When they each crack a hardened smile, she breathes a sigh of relief. "We will stand by you, even if that means she is by your side too."

Tears sting her eyes as the men begin to hoot, pumping their fists into the air. She laughs, embarrassed and overwhelmed at the same time.

"Thank you," she says, clinging to Nicolae's arm. He turns to look at her, his gaze filled with tenderness.

"Will you have me?"

"Of course, you big oaf." Reaching up behind his head, she yanks him close, crushing her lips upon his. Roars of laughter and clapping fill the hall, but she hardly hears any of it as she sinks into his embrace, knowing that she is finally where she is meant to be.

Lucien breathes deeply, savoring the metallic aroma that clings to the snow covered ground. Crimson streams out around him in wide rivers of cooling blood. The scent is heady, mouthwatering with its intensity.

Lifting the edge of his cloak, Lucien tiptoes out of his masterpiece, careful not to disturb any of the bodies he has so elegantly arranged. The human cross spanning the middle of a clearing just on the outskirts of Anchorage, Alaska is twenty bodies long and fifteen bodies across, his largest feat yet.

Each have been stripped of their exterior clothing, leaving their flesh open to the elements. Lucien looks to the sky above, noticing the churning gray clouds pregnant with snow.

"That won't do." He leans down to retrieve a red canister, sloshing with gasoline. Throaty laughter rises into the night as he walks the line, dousing each man and woman. He pauses at the base of the cross and tosses aside the canister.

"This should get their attention."

With a flick of his wrist, Lucien tosses a lighter onto the foot of the man closest to him. The blue flames spread like wildfire, bubbling flesh and burning hair. The scent brings a wide grin to Lucien's face, and he digs out his cell phone to place the emergency call that will bring reporters swarming to the area.

He cuts off the call and momentarily closes his eyes. He is getting closer to Roseline. He can feel it.

"I'll see you soon," he whispers to the north sky as he turns and heads back to town. He has business to attend to.

Twenty-Four

Roseline slips from the conference room, curious to find out what all of the racket is. Hooting and hollering echoes from the north end of the building. She silently winds down one corridor after another, her steps silent. These passages are as familiar to her as the halls of Bran Castle.

"Hey, gorgeous."

Gabriel appears in the doorway of the room that he shares with his angel guardian. Peeking past him, she is amazed to even consider that the two of them have any space to move in the closet sized room, especially with Elias' wingspan.

"You all moved in?" She asks, offering an awkward wave to Elias. Their first meeting in the forest beyond the ice cage had been strained. This one isn't gearing up to be any better.

When Elias dips his head, his wings rise over the planes of his shoulder. Her smile falters at the imposing sight. Although Gabriel has told her that he trusts Elias completely, she still isn't sure that she does, not after her time spent with Malachi.

Elias may not be among the Fallen Ones, but that doesn't mean he is as good as he claims to be. She vows to keep a close eye on the angel. If he so much as dares to look at Gabriel the wrong way, she will take him down.

"Home sweet home." Gabriel grins, closing the door behind him. "I assume you weren't just passing my way for a stroll. On your way to be nosy, aren't you?"

"Am I that obvious?" She laughs as she takes his hand.

It feels like it has been a lifetime ago since they began their hunt for information on the mysterious cross that is tattooed onto his forearms. Now, she hardly even thinks of it. The markings have become a part of him, forever etched into his flesh as evidence of who and what he is.

At first, she had feared that their forbidden bond would bring pain to him, and she had been right, but not in the way she had thought. She never could have dreamed that it would have been Sorin that tortured him instead of her husband Vladimir. But now, both are gone and there is nothing to stand in their way from being together once they deal with Lucien.

She smiles as she squeezes his hand, knowing with all her heart that this is right. *He* is right. Their bond has never been stronger.

They walk side by side down the darkened hallway, following the swelling sound by instinct. Although the compound is not overly large, it has many twists and turns to slow down any attacker that might stumble across it.

She allows Gabriel to take the lead, wanting to measure how much his senses have been dulled by Lucien's poison, but he never falters, never attempts to go in the wrong direction. She breathes a sigh of relief.

Perhaps the poison didn't affect him near as much as I thought, she muses silently.

"There they are," Gabriel whispers as they round the corner and come face to face with a human pile up.

The hunters near the back sense their presence and fall silent, turning with their backs to the wall to allow them room to pass. As soon as they do, the hunters fill in behind Gabriel who takes up his position at her back.

Roseline steps forward, smiling at each hunter in turn as they move aside. She recognizes many of them from their attack on Vladimir; others are new to her, but seem no less interested in her. She holds out her hand in greeting to Grigori, grateful to see that he has come to join in their fight. "How's the nose?"

He laughs. "It's been better."

"Still fit for battle, I assume."

His chest puffs up. "Of course. Nothing could keep me from it."

"I thought you might say that." She grins and waits for him to move aside. When he does, Roseline squeals with delight at the sight of Nicolae bending Sadie over in a long, slow kiss. She had no idea he was so limber.

"Sadie! You're alive!" She wants to rush forward and embrace her friend. but Gabriel tightens his grip on her hand, holding her back.

Sadie breaks off the kiss and pokes her head out around Nicolae. "Rose!"

Beating against his arms, Sadie fights to be free from Nicolae's grasp. He blinks, disoriented for a second. When he looks up and sees Roseline, he releases Sadie. Once fully upright again, Sadie throws herself at Roseline, crushing her in a huge bear hug.

"It's so good to see you," Sadie gushes, squeezing Roseline tightly.

"Easy, Sadie. You can hurt me now," she chuckles as she pries herself out of her friend's grasp.

"What happened to you? You were all…" Sadie sticks her fingers in the sides of her lips and pulls, growling in imitation of a very silly looking monster. "I was so worried about you. I tried to come see you, but Fane was tossing his weight around again."

"For good cause, I'm sure," Roseline laughs, stepping back just far enough to get a good look. "Wow. You look amazing, Sadie."

A hint of a blush rises along her neck as she ducks her head, uncharacteristically silent. "Oh, don't let her fool you. She's loving it," Nicolae smirks, reaching out to take Sadie's hand in his again.

Roseline tries to smother her own grin. "And I'm sure you're not complaining too much either."

"Heck no," he crows, yanking Sadie back into his arms. He lifts her chin and plants a kiss on her lips.

Grigori chuckles, drawing Roseline's attention. She arches an eyebrow. "You're ok with this?"

He shrugs. "It's better than listening to him mope all the time. I think I would have slit his throat myself if he hadn't finally gone and kissed her."

Gabriel's laugh vibrates in his chest as he draws Roseline into his arms. "It's about time. The way you were staring at him on our way to Romania made me want to gag, Sadie."

Nicolae's eyes widen in surprise. "Really? You did that? I never noticed."

Sadie shoots an evil glare in Gabriel's direction. "It wasn't *exactly* like that."

"Oh, yeah it was. You were practically drooling over him," Gabriel laughs. He cries out as Roseline pinches his side, shushing him.

Sadie flushes several shades of red when Nicolae pulls her close, dipping his head to whisper in her ear. There is a definitive increase in the heat staining her cheeks. Roseline smiles, thrilled that her friends have found happiness.

"Is William here too?" She glances around but finds him oddly absent. He should be here, ready to do his brotherly duty in the event Nicolae decides to get a bit too handsy.

Sadie's grin widens. "Oh, he's probably off hunting for Claudia. She loves hiding in dark corners and leaping out to scare the crap out of him."

"Claudia Voss? How did that happen?" Roseline turns an arched eyebrow toward Gabriel.

He laughs and shakes his head. "Once he stopped panting after Daelyn, he finally realized how great Claudia is. Now the guy is smitten. Fane tried to warn him against falling for her, but you know Will. He's too hard-headed to listen to reason."

Roseline chews on her lower lip, unsure if this new turn of events is a good thing or not. She looks back over her shoulder at the group of hunters, still in shock over their acceptance of Nicolae and Sadie. When she turns back, Nicolae catches her eye and winks.

"Is this the part where you say I told you so?" Roseline smirks.

He shrugs. "Only if you want me to."

"Don't hold your breath," Gabriel chuckles, pulling Roseline into his embrace. He wraps his arms around her waist and rests his head against the top of hers.

"Alright. Show's over," Grigori calls, turning his back on the two couples. "We have drills to run, gentlemen. Let's get those done before dark, shall we?"

Most of the men linger long enough to pat Nicolae on the back before heading to retrieve their winter gear. A few linger to cast worried glances at the new couple. Bogdan and Costel are among them but are quickly sent on their way by Grigori.

Roseline leans back into Gabriel, loving the feel of being in his arms, safe and secure. But how long will it last?

"Fane mentioned to me earlier that we are going to try to lure Lucien here so we can avoid any more human deaths. What do you have planned, Nicolae?"

Nicolae releases Sadie's hand and shoves his own deep into his pocket. When he removes it, he holds up a small black device, not all that unlike a normal smartphone. "This is a satellite phone. Once the rest of our men arrive tomorrow, you're going to make a call and entice him here. I'm sure once he hears your voice he will send his entire army here to retrieve you."

Gabriel's arms stiffen around her. "You're using her as bait?"

Nicolae nods. "For now, but there's no way Lucien's going to get close to her. I promise you that, Gabriel."

Roseline's lips peel back as anger floods through her. "On the contrary. I'm planning on getting *very* close to him."

Roseline pins her hair back from around her face, expertly weaving her long tresses into a braid that hangs over her shoulder. The wind in the Arctic Circle is fierce, easily blowing strong enough to knock a human over on a nice day, which today isn't.

Her hands are still shaky from her healing the night before. Her memories are vague, hardly more than a whirlwind of images, most of which she would rather not think upon.

She remembers Gabriel's face. His hair is longer now and his jaw is lined with stubble. His beauty has only increased in their time apart, but that is not what she remembers now. It is his eyes.

There is a depth to them that she has never seen before, an awareness or perhaps an awakening. He seems so sure of himself now, as if he knows exactly who he is and why he is here. She envies that strength.

When did he become the confident man she saw leaning over her bed last night. His touch had been gentle as he leaned over her bedside last night to place a gentle kiss on her forehead. It was so achingly sweet she nearly cried. She longed to ask him to stay, knowing that he would, but she knew how much her healing had cost him. He needed rest.

Closing her eyes now, she remembers the call of Gabriel's blood, the frenzied thoughts that tore through her mind as he drew close to her in the dark. She had wanted to bite him and drain him just like she'd done to Malachi.

And then what? Would she have torn him limb from limb too? Resting her head against the mirror, tears sting her eyes as she realizes she honestly doesn't know.

But she can't dwell on the what-if's of yesterday. She leans back and wipes away her tears for the second time. There are battle plans to draw up and nothing will keep her from helping out.

This morning dawned bright and frigid. Frost clung to the windows and pipes. Roseline smirks at William's muttered swearing from the men's bathroom other side of the wall as he attempts to coax warm water for a shower.

"It's not going to work, you know." Roseline calls, her voice still shaky from her unshed tears.

"A guy can still hope," he growls. More swearing follow after a loud metal clank. She can hear William hopping about on one foot, no doubt nursing the other.

Roseline shakes her head, laughing despite herself. She stops short, her smile faltering as she catches her reflection in the mirror. The deep purple rings around her eyes have faded. Color has returned to her cheeks, but there is still a haunted gleam in her eye.

Will she ever be able to forgive herself for killing Malachi?

She closes her eyes, willing the images to flee. It wasn't her, not really. She would never have hurt him if she'd been in her right mind, but she hadn't been. Her dreams bring back the memories. Now, she can't escape them.

Gripping the edge of the sink, Roseline expels the contents of her stomach. Dry heaves follow, but still she can't stop.

"Rose? Are you ok?" Gabriel raps on the bathroom door.

She grabs a towel and wipes her face clean. Tossing it aside, she quickly brushes her teeth again and leans back against the wall before calling him in. He approaches slowly, unsure of what he is walking into.

"I keep seeing him, Gabriel. Every time I close my eyes or try to sleep."

He sighs and moves further into the room, letting the door shut behind him. He reaches out for her, gently pulling her into his arms. She nestles her cheek into the hollow of his neck, desperate for his touch. "It's going to take time."

Tears silently slip from her eyes, running the length of her cheek before dripping softly onto his shirt. Small wet stains spread across the white fabric, forming one large damp patch. With one hand, he holds her close and with the other, he softly combs her hair.

"It wasn't you, Rose. You know that." She nods, pulling away to wipe at her nose. Tear streaks glisten on her cheeks, he moves his hands to cup her face. "Malachi was not a good person. Maybe at the end he chose to do the right thing, but he had many sins to pay for."

"But not with his life. Not like that."

"No." He stops her from pulling away. "Not like that, but he wasn't innocent. Not like Ordin or Enael or countless others. He was a Fallen One. There is no redemption for them."

"And me?" She looks up into his eyes through her tears.

His gaze softens as he leans in close, fitting his nose into the natural curve of her own. His breath washes over her face and she closes her eyes, inhaling his familiar scent. It is stronger than before and more pronounced than when he was a human. She doesn't think it is possible to be more attracted to him than she is in this very moment.

"I saved you. Our love did that. There is nothing left to redeem," he whispers, placing soft kisses on her eyes, nose and cheeks.

Her chest rises and falls with each caress. She leans into him, desperate for his words to be true. Does he have that sort of power? It's true that he took her poison upon himself, removing Lucien's vile blood from her own, but can he save her from her deeds?

His lips press warmly against the corner of her mouth and she moans, wrapping her arms tightly around his back, sealing them together. Gabriel pulls back just enough to look down at her. She pouts, tugging him close again, but he resists.

His smile is warm as he bares his heart. "You are the most beautiful thing I have ever laid eyes on."

A blush rises into her cheeks as she smiles. "That's a terrible line."

Roseline savors the taste of his lips as he silences her. He presses her back against the wall, molding his body around hers. She claws at his back, begging for him to be closer.

As she parts her lips, she vows that she will never let anyone separate them again.

Lucien paces only a few steps in front of the blistering heat of the fire, penance for letting his anger get the better of him. He knew the phone call was only a matter of time. Fane couldn't let his rampage continue. *The sorry sap cares far too much for the humans.*

What Lucien hadn't expected was to hear Roseline's voice on the other end of the line.

It was her tone that threw him into a fit of rage. She was normal. Completely normal.

His claws clack against the wooden floor as he turns and heads back the way he came. *Something happened up there. Something major.*

Lucien has been stewing over Roseline's words all morning. *It's time.*

Two simple words, but he has no doubt about their meaning. She wants revenge and he will be more than happy to bring it to her. There is one final kink in his plan that he must sort out first.

He should have gone to Russia himself. The Eltat can be trusted for their loyalty but not their brilliance. By the time he discovered Gabriel's location, the boy was already long gone. But Lucien did manage to collect something of value.

Lucien turns and leers down at the blonde haired girl that sits propped in the corner. An ugly purple bruise mars her cheek. Her lower lip is split open, but the bleeding has stopped. Lucien can tell that she can no longer see clearly out of her right eye, but the left is wide and glaring openly at him.

"You have my spirit, Katia. I like that," he says in fluent Russian as he turns to walk toward her. "Too bad about your mother though. She might have lived if she'd been half the fighter you are."

Katia's lip cracks open with fresh blood as she spits at his boots. "My mother was a great woman."

Lucien laughs as he sinks down before her. "How would you know? She died giving birth to you."

She leans forward, straining against her manacles. They cuff at her wrists and ankles, chained to the floor between her legs. "Because I am nothing like you."

Lucien's lips peel back into a gruesome grin. Blood stains the cracks between his pointed teeth, evidence of a recent feeding. He watches as she reacts to the putrid scent wafting from his mouth.

"With that look in your eye, I'd say you wouldn't hesitate to rip out my throat if you had half a chance. That makes you a murderer."

Katia's eyes narrow. "Killer. There's a difference."

"No." He shakes his head and laughs. "You would enjoy it. That makes it murder."

He crosses the room in five long strides and pauses at the door. "Don't do anything stupid. I'd hate to kill you before the big event."

With the flip of his finger, he plunges her into near darkness. Only the light of the flickering fire in the hearth is left to keep her company as he seals the door behind him.

<u>Twenty-Five</u>

Roseline looks up from her blade, the sharpening stone in her hand falling still as she watches Gabriel pace back and forth before her. He has made the same trek countless times throughout the evening. He never speaks and never pauses, but his growing weariness is becoming more obvious with each pass.

"You need to save your strength," she says, resuming her work. The blade glistens in her hand. It will soon be sharpened enough to slice cleanly through an immortal's sternum.

It feels good to have her swords in hand again. She feels grounded for the first time since the attack on Bran Castle.

It's hard for her to really comprehend that her time spent in the pit was only a couple of weeks rather than years. In the three lifetimes she has been alive, never has such a small amount of time stretched on like eternity.

She will have to thank Lucien personally when she sees him again.

"You can't expect to survive this war if you're hardly able to walk." She runs the stone along the edge of her blade, savoring the familiar grating sound. Fane used to chide her about using such archaic methods, but she refuses to change. This feels right. It is who she is. The world may change around her, but that doesn't mean she has to like it.

Gabriel lifts his head to stare at her, blinking rapidly, as if trying to process her words. "I'm not scared, if that's what you're thinking," he says defensively.

"Who said I was thinking anything at all?" Another swipe with the stone. This time the glide is slightly smoother. If she were to run her finger along the blade now, it would certainly leave a mark.

Gabriel latches onto the back of a chair. The muscle along his jaw flinches as he grinds his back teeth. She can tell he is frustrated, angry even, but she remains silent. He will speak when he is ready.

He sighs and sinks down onto the seat across from her. He leans forward to place his face in his hands, his elbows propped up against his knees. The seat looks far from comfortable, but then again, the Senthe base was designed for functionality.

"I can't help feeling like all of this is my fault," he mutters into his hands.

"Your fault?" Roseline frowns and sets her blade on the table. She pushes back, crossing her arms over her chest as she stares at the crown of his head. "I think there is plenty of guilt to go around."

She should have known this would happen. Although Gabriel is obviously far more than just a human, he was raised as one and must be struggling to deal with the transition. Roseline has had over three hundred years to adjust. He has had just a few weeks. She can only imagine what must be jumbled up in his mind.

"No matter how I look at it, I'm at the center of everything that has happened. Good or bad, I'm involved." When he looks up, his gaze is hollow, vacant and lifeless. "Why is this happening to me, Rose?"

The right half of the *Arotas* cross, etched deep into Roseline's silver blade, burns bright blue as Gabriel absently runs his finger across the cold surface. His own tattoos begin to pulsate with brilliant waves of blue.

"Don't even think about changing the subject. It's a sword. Nothing more." She leans forward in her seat. The leather thongs that crisscross the length of her black pants stretch taut as she bends to meet him eye to eye. "None of this is your fault. Seneh. This war. My capture. It all happened for a reason, but you are wrong about one thing. This isn't just about you."

"Then what is it about?" The skin around his eyes is notably darker than earlier in the day. His skin is almost pasty in complexion. His hair has lost much of its blond sheen. Instead, his strands look thin and stringy, oily to the point of appearing unkempt. He looks more human than immortal at the moment and that terrifies her.

What if Lucien's poison has somehow reversed his transformation? Can immortality be reversed?

She shudders at the thought. He would be like a lamb sent to the slaughter tomorrow.

Roseline struggles to shove aside her doubts as she stares him down, determined not to give away any hint to her mounting fear. "This is about survival. Seneh believed in you. He gave his life to ensure that you would survive and to fulfill your mission. I may not know much about this prophecy, but I know that people are dying because of it and that means whatever your role is in all of this, it's major. I have a feeling your actions tomorrow will be far more pivotal than any of us realize."

Gabriel's brow furrows. "No pressure then, huh?"

She leans forward and grasps his hand. "This war is no longer just about good and evil, Gabriel. It's about our survival. Humans know about us now. We can't go back to living among them, hoping that stories and legends will keep them at bay. They are getting braver. Some are starting to fight back. You have heard the reports coming out of Africa and China. Immortals are dying. My friends, who are as innocent as you and I, deserve this. If we don't stop this madness here and now, I fear what might happen."

"An old time manhunt?"

She nods. "It's already happening. Lucien has whipped the entire world into a frenzy, and I don't think life for us will ever be the same."

"So what do we do?"

Roseline offers him a half-hearted smile as she squeezes his hand. "We take one day at a time. First, we take down Lucien and then figure the rest out after."

"And what about you?"

His fingers flinch in hers and she twists her wrist slightly to allow her fingers to twine through his. "You saved my life."

"I did, didn't I?" Gabriel grins. He rises from his chair and skirts the edge of the rectangular meeting table without breaking his hold on her hand. Sinking into the chair beside her, he tugs gently, pulling her forward.

Unable to resist his charm, she allows herself to be drawn to him, swinging her leg out so that she easily sinks into his lap. Removing her hand free from his, she wraps her arms around his neck.

"I guess we're even now," he mutters, his gaze lowering to focus on her lips.

She can feel the urgency in his fingers as they knead at her lower back, begging to sneak beneath the lace sewn onto her leather corset. She laughs at the pout that tugs at his lips when she places a hand on his chest to stop him from stealing a kiss. "I'm trying to be serious right now."

"Me too." When she shoots him a stern look, he laughs and leans back but doesn't move his hands away. "Fine. I'll behave. For now…"

Roseline gently cups his face in her hands and leans close to lightly brush her lips against his. "It's not that I'm not interested."

"But…"

"But right now you need to be focused. You've never been in a battle like this before." Her grip on his cheeks tightens. "I can't lose you."

"You won't. I've trained."

A cascade of loose bronze curls falls over her bare shoulders as she shakes her head. "This is different. You've never taken a life before."

"I almost did—" she places her finger on his lips to still his indignant protest.

"Fighting to retrieve that fire sword isn't the same thing as looking in someone's eyes as you bury your dagger in their heart. You've never had to hear the final beats of life or watch the light fade from their eyes." She leans back, letting her hands fall to his chest, directly over his heart. "You feel their death, Gabriel. Enemy or not, your first death will forever haunt you."

"Did yours?"

She nods, sighing heavily. "I don't want to talk about it."

He reaches out and pulls back the curtain of hair that has fallen over her left eye. "Will you tell me someday?"

"Someday," she whispers, knowing that she will avoid that conversation for as long as she can. The memory of her first death is tied intricately with her honeymoon with Vladimir and that is a memory she would rather never share with Gabriel.

He leans in close, so close she feels dizzy with the heady aroma of his scent. No matter how many times she is with him, it never ceases to overwhelm her. "Promise me something."

The sharp edge of his words puts her on alert. What could he possibly want? His eyes search her face as he places his hand over hers, holding them tightly to his chest. "Promise me you won't do anything stupid tomorrow."

Roseline laughs. "And here I thought you were gonna try to be all macho and tell me to stay behind."

"Like that would ever happen!" He grins, leaning forward to plant a kiss fully on her lips.

She melts into his embrace as his arms wind around her back, pulling her close. She considers pulling away to finish their conversation, but as his mouth parts and his tongue darts across her lower lip, she can't remember why they haven't just been doing this the entire time.

Fane glares up at William from across the room, his annoyance mounting. He was fine with the first few wooden stake wisecracks, but now the boy is taking it too far. William may diffuse his fear with humor, but Fane has his limits too. He rises from his seat and weaves through the swarm of hunters that fills the conference room. They arrived last night under the cloak of dark and there is little room to maneuver now.

Immortals from all areas of the globe have been filtering in throughout the day. They now stand three hundred strong with nearly two hundred hunters alongside. Fane has no idea what sort of an army Lucien will bring with him, but after Roseline's call, he has no doubt Lucien will pull every servant, gutter rat and immortal into this fight.

On the eve of battle, everyone tries to enjoy one last night with their friends and brothers.

Enoch and Theus arm wrestle at a table to Fane's right. A cheering group of hunters hold up wads of cash into the air as bets are made. Ambrose and Daelyn whisper in the corner, eyeing a young hunter, whose baby blue eyes and blond curls caught their attention when he first arrived. Julian rolls his eyes and turns away, filing his nails into perfect half circles.

Fane places his hand on Grigori's shoulder as he passes, pleased to have the man fighting on their side. His new sense of appreciation for the man's skill on the battlefield and as a leader has come as a surprise to Fane. Who would have thought that he could begin to form a friendship with his enemy?

But then again, maybe the hunters aren't his enemy any more. The lines are shifting and new bonds are forming. Perhaps peace can be an option.

"I was watching you last night," he says to Grigori as he passes. "Remind me to stay out of range of your broad sword."

Grigori grunts with pleasure and Fane returns his focus on William. The boy stands near the wall, a heavy sword held aloft over his head.

"By the power of Gray Skull." He raises the sword higher. It wavers in the air, threatening to fall as he sucks in a great breath to prepare for a loud bellow. "I have the power!"

Sadie giggles as she rocks back into Nicolae, who sits just behind her. Gabriel chuckles, shaking his head in amusement. His blond hair falls over his eyes. Fane looks to Roseline, who shrugs back, obviously as confused as she is. Claudia is all smiles beside Roseline, but he can tell she's just as lost as they are.

"Seriously? Prince Adam of Eternia? Cringer the mighty battle cat? Skeletor?" William gapes in shock. "Are you telling me you don't know who He-Man is?"

He drops the sword to his side, narrowly avoiding cleaving his leg in two as it clatters to the ground. Once his hands are free, he clutches his chest and staggers back in shock. "I'm appalled at how uneducated you are in 80's pop culture."

Roseline shrugs. "We never really watched TV."

"Return of the Jedi? Mad Max? Aliens? Top Gun? Robo Cop? Tron? First Blood?" With each movie title William announces, his voice rises higher and higher. His face begins to turn red as he rushes through each name. "Breakfast Club? Terminator? Rocky? Indiana Jones? Die Hard? These are all classics!"

He stares at the blank faces surrounding him and shakes his head. "I'm so disappointed in all of you. These movies helped shape my childhood."

Without Fane having to say anything to him, William turns and walks away, dejected. Sadie rises to follow, but Claudia waves her off. Her hair whips behind her as she rushes to grab the door and follow him out into the hallway.

"What's wrong with him?" Gabriel asks. "I thought he was just joking."

Sadie shakes her head as she draws her legs up into her chest. "You know how uncomfortable he is being the only 'normal' one here."

"Yeah, but those are just movies," Gabriel protests.

Sadie sighs and leans back in Nicolae. "Not to him. To William, they represent everything you and I aren't anymore, Gabriel…human."

The silence is broken as the hunters return to their discussions. Most talk about what weapons they will select for the battle. Others tell wild stories about their last night in Amsterdam or exaggerate details of their time spent hunting wild game in the jungles of the Amazon.

Fane sinks down into a chair behind Roseline and her friends. He tries not to let Gabriel's arm slung over her shoulders bother him, but it does. He fears that it always will.

"He can't go with us," he says softly.

The group turns and stares at him. Roseline's gaze narrows, but it is Sadie who speaks first, casting a worried glance at Nicolae. "Who can't?"

"William. He's a liability."

Roseline stiffens at Sadie's cry of outrage. "Just because he's not an immortal or some uber hunter with spy gear doesn't mean he can't be useful."

"You know that's not what I'm—" Fane begins but Roseline cuts him off.

"A battle is no place for your brother, Sadie. You know that." She reaches out and places a hand on her friend's arm. "He will be safe here."

Sadie's brow furrows with indecision. Nicolae leans forward, resting his chin on her shoulder. "They're right. You'd never forgive yourself if he got hurt."

"Or worse," Fane adds.

She glares up at him but he doesn't flinch. She needs to face the truth, even if it hurts. "He'll be alone here. You know he'll be mad about that."

Her protests are pathetically weak, and she knows it. "Couldn't Claudia stay behind with him?" Gabriel suggests, offering Sadie a sympathetic smile.

"No," Fane shakes his head. "She's one of our best fighters. We're going to need every sword we can find."

Roseline sighs, scrunching her nose as she thinks it over. "I have to agree with Fane. We need her. Sorry, Sadie."

Fane watches as Sadie curls her legs inward and presses her face to her knees. He feels some remorse for upsetting her, but it had to be done. He turns and walks away from the group, feeling like more of an outsider than ever before.

Roseline raps her knuckles on the doorframe of Gabriel's room. She steps back and waits, tugging nervously at the hem of her shirt. When the door opens, Elias's tall frame fills the entire doorway. "Gabriel isn't here right now," he informs her in his deep voice.

"I know. I actually came to speak with you, if that's ok."

"Of course." He steps back to allow her to enter. As she passes by, she can't help but brush up against his wings. The feathers are softer than they appear and warm to the touch. She moves quickly toward the opposite wall to allow him to close the door behind her.

When he does, he turns and crosses his arms over his chest. She finds it rather disconcerting that he's never wears a shirt. His muscles remind her of a bull, strong and well developed.

She clears her throat and forces her hands down by her side. "I came to speak to you about Gabriel."

"No," he shakes his head as he lowers himself onto the bottom bunk. Even while leaning forward, the tops of his shoulders are wedged by the top bunk. "You came to speak about his fate."

She nods and slowly sinks down onto the only chair in the room. Elias stares at her with wide, seeing eyes. "You fear for his safety tomorrow, but it is not for you to decide his fate."

"But it's ok for you to mess around with it?" She shoots back. She instantly bites her lips, scolding herself for her sudden outburst of anger. She knew this conversation would be an emotional one, but she needs to keep her anger in check.

"I understand why you would see it that way, but I am truly nothing more than a guide. I do not know his fate any more than you do. Gabriel must decide that on his own."

"And Lucien? How does he play into all of this?"

Elias shifts, lowering his elbows onto his knees. "Lucien was a surprise to me. I'll admit that. All of my sources led me to believe that Vladimir was the one we would be fighting, but you took care of that for us." His chuckle is low and rumbling, like thunder rolling across a humid summer sky. "That was quite an impressive show, young one."

"When we got word that Malachi had taken you, I knew something was wrong, so I got Gabriel to safety then went looking for myself. I had my suspicions that it had something to do with family blood. Only that can heal all wounds. Unfortunately, I was right. Gabriel unknowingly saved his own father that night in Sorin's dungeon."

"And you knew Lucien took me and you still let me stay there?" The pitch of her voice rises as the panic of her imprisonment washes over her again. The fear of her transformation mingles with the image of Enael's death.

"I am very sorry about what happened to you, Roseline, but it was not my place to interfere."

"Interfere?" She leaps to her feet, seething. "Do you have any idea what he did to me?"

"Yes." He nods solemnly. "In fact, I know the details quite well."

She hesitates, confused by his words. "How?"

"Because Malachi was reporting to me on your progress."

That was the last thing she expected him to say. Goosebumps crawl along her skin. "He...he was?"

"Think what you like about him, but his actions in the end proved that he was trying to pay back for all of the wrongs he committed."

Roseline rubs her hands along her arms, feeling chilled. "And did he?"

Elias slowly shakes his head. "That was not the way to do it, but at least he tried. He saved your life and because of that, he also saved Gabriel's. I am grateful to him for his sacrifice."

"Sacrifice?" The word feels wrong rolling around on her tongue. "He didn't die a noble death."

"On the contrary, Roseline. He died saving you, the only girl who ever showed him that there was an ounce of good in him. Do you know of anything more noble?"

She sucks in a breath, fighting for a calm that she doesn't feel. Elias smiles sympathetically. "Without his blood, you would be lost by now. I know you didn't mean to kill him, but the fact is, if you had not, this war would have been over long before it even began."

Her legs begin to shake as she sinks back onto the chair. Clasping her hands between her thighs, she rocks slightly, overcome with conflicting emotions. "And Gabriel? Will he have to pay for his sacrifice too?"

When she looks up at the hulking angel, she notices the hint of a tear in his eye before he turns away. "I don't know. I pray not, but his fate is out of my hands."

Twenty-Six

A snowflake falls from the heavens, landing gently atop Roseline's arm. She looks down, confused by the odd texture. It isn't cold or wet but it is soft and warm, caressing her arm just before it catches on a gust of wind and sails away.

She looks up at the overcast sky. More white flakes have begun to fall. A few here and there. Glancing around her, she realizes that she's not the only one who has noticed them.

Fane lifts his hand to catch one. He rubs his finger across the rise of the object, his eyes widening in wonder. "It's a feather."

"But that's impossible. There aren't enough birds in the area." Roseline blinks, staring in wonder at the silent fall of thousands of feathers. Most are white, while others are brilliant gold, silver and red.

She turns at the hitch in Gabriel's breathing. A wide smile brightens his pale face as he stares back at her. "Angels."

Looking to the heavens, she can't see anything above but the low hanging clouds. Surely, if there were angels above, she should be able to see them just as easily as she can see Elias.

The tall, golden winged angel smiles down from above. He plucks a feather from the sky and holds it close to his own wing. Although crimson in color, it is an identical match. "They have come."

A murmur quickly spreads through the ranks. Immortal and hunter alike search the skies but to no avail. "Why don't they land?" she asks.

Elias releases the feather, watching as it slowly drifts to the white ground. "They will fight from above."

Staring out across the blustery plain, she knows Lucien is out there somewhere. She can hear the distant clacking of Eltat claws against the ice and the hiss of their flickering tongues, but they are not alone. The whisper of a thousand feet and the clattering of sheathed swords drifts on the wind.

Never before has there been a battle of this magnitude among her kind. She has seen men rise up against each other and fall to their graves but never her brethren. Not like this.

She tightens her grip against her blades, drawing reassurance from their even weight. The battle axes strapped to her back sit comfortably along her spine. Metal tipped darts line her belt, waiting to be plunged deep into Lucien's heart. He will pay for his treachery. She will make sure of it.

Behind her, Nicolae shifts. She glances over her shoulder to see immortal and hunter standing side by side, ready to fight together, in one accord. She never would have dared to dream it, but Nicolae did. Perhaps he is far wiser than she gave him credit for.

She dips her head in acknowledgement of Grigori's authority. His nose still carries the wounds from their previous encounter, before her truce with Nicolae, but it is not anger that stares back at her now, but respect.

Perhaps there really can be peace.

A hand slips into hers. She looks up and smiles back at Gabriel as he squeezes her hand. "Are you ready for this?"

"I was born ready."

"So was I." He doesn't release her hand as they turn together to face the coming hoard.

They appear from the north, a mass of snarling beasts held back only by their master's command. Roseline scans the crowd, meeting eye to eye with many of her brethren, men and women she knew and loathed for their love of depravity.

She spies out Mastus the Greek first. The violent winds tear at his ridiculous white toga. Beside him is Alamesia. The red-haired gypsy sways her colorful skirts back and forth. Roseline can hear the tinkling of the bells at her ankles.

Leif, a blue-eyed Scandinavian stands just beyond them, clutching a silver hammer as if he were Thor himself. Two rows back she spies out the broad, almond-skinned Keli, whose victims are typically passed off as shark attacks along the warm coasts of Hawaii.

Milap and Hakan, twins from the Cherokee nation stand side by side with a black braid draped over each of their right shoulders. Kuma and Aiko look completely out of place in their full-length crimson kimono robes. A samurai *katana* hangs from each of their waists, hidden just under the sashes that hold their robes closed.

Mateo is further back in the ranks. His insatiable appetite for blood created the myth of the Chupacabra in the Americas. With the hulking frame of a small bear and long spikes imbedded in his back, he didn't have any trouble convincing the locals that he was a beast. He began draining farm animals first, but quickly moved on to wilder game like coyotes and mountain lions.

Roseline shudders and looks away. This fight will be bloody. Too many lives will be lost for one man's greed.

The grip on her hand suddenly increases and she whips her head to the side to stare at Gabriel. His jaw is clenched, gaze riveted across the tundra. She follows his gaze, realizing his intense focus is on Alexi, a small Russian whose skill with a blade is renowned. A girl stands beside him, her arm trapped within his grasp. She is white with terror and she hasn't stopped looking at Gabriel since she arrived.

"Someone you know?" A tiny sliver of jealousy nags at her.

He nods stiffly. "She's my sister, Katia."

"Sister?" Her words hiss between her teeth. "But you never told me..."

"I thought she was safe." Roseline winces at the force of his grip but does not try to pull away. Despite the pain, she finds his righteous anger comforting. She has no doubt Alexi will be among the first to fall.

"You have to go after her." His jaw tightens as he shakes his head. "You must. She's your family."

The hoard across from them appears to ripple outward. Roseline stiffens, standing her ground as the crowd parts and a single man appears. Loud hissing rises from the Eltat along with the cries of approval from the immortals.

Sadie gasps beside Roseline, obviously shocked by Lucien's true nature. Roseline catches Nicolae's frown from the corner of her eye, but she does not acknowledge it. He needn't know Lucien's real face to know he needs to die.

The hunters grow restless behind them. She can hear their grips tighten on cross bow and sword hilt. Many hunters will die here today, but their deaths will be honorable. She will see to it that their families hear about it.

"Thank you," she whispers to Grigori, turning just enough that he knows to whom she speaks. He bows his head, his lips pressed into a tight line. "If we survive this day, I will owe you a pint when we return home."

A shadow of a smile lights his face before he refocuses, calling out a gruff command to one of the younger hunters. Roseline follows his gaze, noting the boy isn't that much older than Enael was. She prays that he dies well and swiftly.

When she turns back, she notices William's absence at Sadie's side. She breathes a sigh of relief, thankful that he actually obeyed Fane. To be fair, William's protests had been weak at best. The battlefield really was no place for him.

Fane steps up from behind and places a hand on her shoulder. She reaches back and squeezes it, grateful to have him fighting beside her once more. His presence is reassuring as she stares across the frozen lake at Lucien.

"You can do this," he whispers in her ear before he steps back.

Gabriel turns, casting a glance back at Fane. It is neither combative nor possessive. Roseline is surprised to realize that, in his own way, he is thanking Fane for his help.

"Do we just let him walk all the way out here to chat?" Sadie asks as Lucien heads their way.

"No," Roseline hears Nicolae reply. She braces, waiting for him to give the order to attack. Holding her breath, she knows this is the calm before the storm and possibly the last breaths she will ever take.

Twining her fingers through Gabriel's, she knows that this is the only place she wants to be.

Lucien's eagerness is threating to bubble over as he approaches the small rise that separates his vast army from the pathetic one that has gathered around Roseline. He can see her, achingly beautiful to a normal eye, but glaringly hideous to his. His eagerness ebbs as he narrows his eyes, noting how vibrant she looks.

Curse you, Malachi, he hisses silently to himself. He doesn't know how the angel did it, but her transformation has been ruined. He grinds his teeth together, blunting the razor sharp incisors he planned to sink into the flesh of her throat after he wiped out her army. This will not do. She is meant to be his.

"Greetings," he calls out with false affection.

A murmur carries on the wind from his enemies' side. His eyes widen with genuine surprise when he spies out numerous black-clad hunters mingled in with immortals.

What is this? Have my enemies gone soft? He chuckles to himself, rubbing his hands together as his excitement begins to build. *This battle will be one to remember.*

"I have no desire to fight any of you," he calls, pausing to let his words travel the distance. "I only came for Roseline Enescue. Hand her over to me and I will let you live. If you do not…" he allows his words to tumble into silence as he shrugs indifferently.

He waits, searching through the crowd for any sign of weakness that he can play on. He growls, realizing that the hunters stand firm in their decision to fight alongside Roseline.

"So be it."

He raises his hand and flicks his wrist in the air. The sky begins to darken, churning with crimson and ash. The winds rise, whipping at Lucien's black cloak. He raises his hands to cover his face as crystals of ice lash against his skin.

A terrible roar pierces the low cloud cover before two clawed feet appear, followed by armor plated scaly legs and the underbelly of a monstrous beast. Roseline's army backs away, mouths hanging open at the sight of the onyx talons that dig deep into the frozen earth.

Fiery eyes lock onto Lucien as fire puffs between gaping jaws, each tooth sharp and reeking of death. Two horns protrude from the dragon's head, and spikes run along the curve of its back, trailing down to its coiled tail.

Lucien grins as he returns his gaze to Roseline. He can see her fear, but also her determination. The dragon was a surprise, no doubt. The legend was that the last of their kind died out thousands of years ago. Of course, he was the one who started those tales.

"What is that beast?" Katia's voice carries from behind him.

Lucien grins, answering for her. "Maelstrom the Wanderer. My pet."

He stretches out a hand and runs it along the rigid plates that cover its nose. Humid air hangs before its great nostrils, melting the snow with each exhaled breath. "He is a fine specimen. The best to ever come from my hatchery."

Staring across the clearing, he grins, enjoying the unease that ripples through Roseline's forces. Fighting immortals, Fallen Ones and Eltat was something they were prepared for. The thought of fighting a dragon has given him the advantage.

He waves his hand before his face, annoyed with the feathery snow that steadily falls from the sky. "You have no chance of survival," he shouts. His gaze sweeps across the clearing once more and lands on his son. Lucien's lips peel back over his sharpened teeth as he notices the boy's elevated breathing and the faint sheen along his brow.

So, that's how she was healed. His grin widens as his mind spins through countless outcomes, each one leading to Gabriel's inevitable death. He continues to rant about the miracle of his dragon to the fearful army assembled before him, all while silently plotting his next move.

He turns toward Maelstrom and shouts a command. The great beast's wings unfurl as it launches into the air, hovering just over his head. "The time has come for you to choose. Return to me what is mine and you will live to fight another day."

His gaze narrows on Roseline as she flushes with anger. Gabriel tries to grab her arm, but she blurs out of sight as she yanks a cross bow from the hand of green-eyed hunter beside her and releases the arrow directly at her brother-in-law.

Lucien leaps to the side as the arrow spikes high into the air. "You missed," he laughs staring up at the arrow as it plummets to the earth five feet away from him.

His laugh cuts off as a second arrow slams into his shoulder, narrowly missing his heart. He lifts his gaze to stare into the blackened hatred of Roseline Enescue.

"I never miss," she growls. Tightening her grip on her swords, she leaps into battle.

Twenty-Seven

W hen the battle first broke out, Gabriel had clear sight of Katia. She was just over Lucien's shoulder, terrified but trying to appear brave. After Roseline sent off her first arrow, he knew exactly where he was going. The problem is…all hell broke loose.

Of the light of his fire sword makes it easier to see in the smoke that rises around him. It penetrates the dark, slices through his enemy with ease, but still he can't find her.

Roseline is off to his left, grunting and twirling, downing immortals with finesse. Under different circumstances, he would love to stop and watch her and admire her skill, but he has to find Katia. She isn't trained for battle and hardly knows how to protect herself against the supernatural.

"Katia!" he shouts over the din of clashing swords and screams of the dying. He steps on the chest of a dead hunter, whispering his apologies as he rises onto his toes to see. Just through a break in the haze he catches a glimpse of her racing toward the trees. A group of Eltat chase after her, barely five feet behind.

The stark terror on her face is enough to get him moving again. He dips and dives, rolling over Claudia's back. "Thanks," he shouts as he races toward the tree line.

Low hanging branches tear at his face and arms as he runs at a full sprint. He clutches the hilt of his sword tightly in his hands as he leaps over a fallen log and slashes down at the slowest of the group.

It squeals like a pig as its chest opens, the wound instantly cauterized by the sword. He leaps over the writhing Eltat and races on. The next two go down as easily as the first, but the final two turn and fight, each flying at him from different directions.

Their whips are made of angel hair, unbreakable and deadly. Near the tips, bits of glass and sharpened metal have been wound, creating a vicious weapon that tears into his flesh each time he moves a fraction of a second too slow.

Blood seeps from his arms and legs. His back stings as the glass burrows into his flesh and is yanked free. He stumbles, falling to his knees as a second whiplash tears into his side. Warm blood paints his shirt to his side.

With a mighty roar, he rises, swinging his sword with two hands. He narrowly misses one of the pig-snouted creatures and stumbles off balance. When he goes down, he knows he's in trouble. One leaps on top of him, pelting him with punches to his ribs and kidneys. He cries out, more furious than in pain.

They are strong and fast. Each time he reaches around to grasp their scaly legs or tail, they shift away, always remaining just out of reach. "Hold still," he grunts as he lifts up suddenly, flipping the creature off his back.

Red eyes gleam from behind a tree then disappear. A scream rises from behind him and he turns to find Katia in Lucien's grasp. His father's face is heavily scaled and his nose is slotted like a snakes. His eyes are a deep scarlet and his fingers are elongated and curved with heavy claws.

"Looking for something?" Lucien hisses.

Gabriel breathes heavily, his hands clenching into fists beside his sheath as he straightens his shoulders. The fiery pain in his back lances straight through his shoulder, but he refuses to show any weakness. "This is between you and me. Leave her alone."

Lucien's tongue flickers through his lips as he grins. "On the contrary. This is a family matter, son."

His fingers curl, digging his talons deeper into Katia's flesh. She cries out, fighting against his grasp but Lucien only laughs. "So frail, isn't she? Too bad she was never turned, like you. I'm sure she would have made an interesting immortal."

He traces a claw down her cheek, his smile widening as blood trails after. She whimpers, her eyes wide and pleading with Gabriel. His anger seethes just below the surface, but he keeps it reigned in tightly.

"Let her go, Lucien. She's nothing to you."

"True," his father's nods. "But she does seem to mean a great deal to you."

With a twist of his wrist, he snaps Katia's upper arm. Gabriel cries out as his sister's mouth drops in a silent scream. Color drains from her face as her knees buckle, and she falls slack in Lucien's grasp.

"Monster!" Gabriel screams as he dives for his sword and rolls to his feet, ready to strike, but Lucien is gone.

Gabriel whirls around, searching the trees for his father, but Lucien has vanished. He growls, spinning around to check for any sign of his retreat but all he can see are the Eltat racing back toward the battle. He tucks his sword into its sheath, squelching its flame for the time being.

"It's ok." He bends down beside Katia. "I've got you."

"You come," she whispers, her head lolling against his arm as he lifts her up. She feels as light as a feather in his arms, much too fragile to be in a place like this. She needs to be taken somewhere safe.

"Hold on. I'll get you out of here." He begins to jog, holding out his arms to keep her aloft, desperately trying not to jostle her too much. She clamps down on her lip, fighting to still her cries of pain.

By the time he arrives on the edge of the battlefield, Katia has passed out. He searches for Fane or Roseline but can't find any trace of them. Grigori and Claudia fight side by side against one of the hulking monsters Lucien no doubt kept hidden from the world. It is as wide as a car and covered in a sickly green fur. Horns and multiple eyes seem to be its main defense, apart from the large wooden club it swings at Claudia's head.

The beating of wings draws his attention and he breathes a sigh of relief as Elias lands beside him. His chest boasts several burn marks and his feathers are still smoking from the aerial battle above. "Can you take her back to William? He can watch over her."

Elias nods, following Gabriel's gaze toward the hideous beast. Claudia ducks, narrowly avoiding a low cut toward her head. "It's a troll. Nothing more." He waits for Gabriel to turn and look at him. "Its weakness is in the center of its forehead. That's its most sensitive spot. One clean shot and it will go down."

"Good to know." Gabriel grins as he hands his sister over to his guardian. "Take care of her for me."

"Be careful." With a rush of air, Elias rises into the sky, spiraling in a golden glow. Gabriel watches until Elias disappears and then rushes to aid his friends.

Blood and gray matter splatters against Fane's face as he slams his spiked mace into another Eltat's head. The fighting is intense and the earth is covered in slickened gore. All around him smoke rises from the ground. Bodies lay singed as the fires smolder deep into the flesh of the dying.

The screams of pain are horrific. Hands reach out and clutch his legs, begging for mercy, but he doesn't have time to kill them all. He lunges and slams his mace into the back of a deformed fallen one, its face shrunken and nearly every inch covered in oozing boils.

Its breath reeks as its death shrieks rise and stutter off into hiccupping gasps. He stomps down on its back, wrenching his mace free.

A battle wages from above. Blood and feathers fall from the sky, shielding much of the fighting from view. The dragon roars in pain as it blasts fire into the sky, its beating wings contorting the clouds.

The bodies of scorched angels fall from the sky, their feathers charred and blackened. Trails of smoke filter through the air as they plummet to earth, never to move again.

Fane ducks as an angel smashes into a group of Eltat, too stupid to look up. He leaps, easily clearing one angel just to lurch to the side to avoid another falling from the sky.

He blinks against the haze of smoke, searching for his friends. Gabriel took off as soon as Roseline struck Lucien. Fane lost sight of him as he leapt into the enemy line, his fire sword slicing cleanly through dozens of enemies at a time.

Roseline was right behind him, rushing headfirst into danger. He tried to follow but was quickly swallowed by the hoard.

"Fane!" He ducks instinctively as a flash of silver cuts through the air just in front of him. Pain races across his chest as a thin line of blood appears. "Alamesia," he growls, charging after her as her colorful skirts dance away.

The tinkling of bells is lost to the sounds of battle as she hops over piles of bodies. Some are clad in black while others wear nothing more than soiled scraps of cloth. Both sides are taking huge losses, but who is winning?

As Alamesia prepares to leap, Fane swings his mace and buries it into her side. She shrieks and falls to the ground, curling in on herself as she clutches the mace. Fane yanks on the handle, grinning at her fierce cry.

"Stop, please!" Her pitiful pleas are lost on him as he raises his boot and stomps down on the mace.

He can feel her ribs cracking and shattering as his foot lowers. She claws at the crowd, desperate to get away.

"Not this time," he crows as he slams down on the mace a final time, forcing the spikes straight through her heart.

Her scream dies off as her head lolls to the side, her vacant eyes staring up at the fire rolling overhead. Fane wipes blood from his face and tugs his mace free.

"Good shot," Nicolae shouts as he slams into Fane's back, his crossbow firing at a group of Eltat crawling toward them. "Just like old times, huh?"

Fane nods, gritting his teeth as they attack together. Their enemy's death comes swift under their skilled hands. Nicolae growls as he twists the neck of the final Eltat and lets it drop with hardly a thought.

"Where's Sadie?" Fane shouts. Spotting a Fallen One trying to crawl away, he reaches behind him and retrieves a small dagger, hurling it at the creature. It howls, bucking wildly as the blade buries into the base of its neck. It falls to the ground, twitching.

"Over there. She's with Roseline."

"You left her?" Fane growls as he grabs a handful of Nicolae's shirt and yanks him toward the direction he pointed to.

"You needed help," Nicolae protests.

"No," Fane shouts as he shoves his way toward Sadie. "You never leave your girl behind. Ever."

He frantically searches through the bodies, praying he doesn't find her, find Roseline. Panic begins to heighten his senses as his grip on Nicolae's shirt tightens.

"Fane. Chill out, man. She's right there!"

He looks up, relieved to see Sadie swinging a battle ax at the back of fallen one with ease. Her footing is good, her stance wide and weighted properly. He breathes a sigh of relief and releases Nicolae. "Sorry," he mutters and stumbles away.

"Fane, where are you going?"

He ignores Nicolae's cry as he plunges over a pile of bodies, rolling to the other side. Sadie is safe for now, but he can't see Roseline. Where is she?

A hand grabs his leg with such force that it topples him to the ground. His hands sink into the entrails of a hunter. His face is splattered with blood from a sliced artery. Fane turns to see Ambrose clutching his leg, the lower half of her body missing.

Her chestnut hair is matted with blood and her violet eyes are glazed with pain and terror. "Please," she gurgles as blood bubbles from her mouth.

Fane nods and rises to his feet. Ambrose lowers her face to the ground as he swings his mace, bringing it down squarely over her heart. She doesn't scream or thrash. She just falls silent, at peace.

He stumbles backward, horrified by her death. How many others have they lost?

Turning around, he stares across the battlefield and spies Daelyn's flaming red hair, her head nearly five feet from her body. Julian Le Roi's tall frame has been cut in half. His only remaining eye stares up at Fane, accusingly.

Fane's stomach lurches as he falls back, landing beside the stricken face of his friend, Enoch. The immortal's black hair has been used to choke him while his stomach has been sliced cleanly open.

Enoch's chest rises and falls unsteadily. Fane rushes to his side and grabs the hunter's body, ignoring the fact that Bodgan Ardelean would be the last hunter to want to save an immortal with his own blood. "Drink, friend. There is still time."

A sword surges up through Enoch's chest, sending Fane sprawling backward. Bodgan's body flops to the ground as Kuma withdraws his samurai sword from Enoch's chest. Kuma yells in a foreign tongue and leaps straight for Fane.

Fane rolls to the side, narrowly missing the slashing sword. Kuma's brother, Aiko, attacks from the opposite side, forcing Fane back into a pile of bodies. Blood clings to him, coating every inch of bare skin and making it harder to move.

Fane leaps to his feet, his mace already swirling overhead, as a scream rises behind him, high and definitively feminine. "I'm here," Roseline shouts, pressing her back against his.

The clash of steel is sudden and evenly matched. Fane has never fought Kuma or Aiko in battle before, but the tales of their deadly skill is proving to be highly accurate.

Sweat forms along Fane's brow as he fights off Kuma. He is desperate to keep track of Roseline, but her movements are steady and sure as she presses Aiko back.

"Watch out," she shouts as she shoves him to the side, narrowly missing being pummeled by a falling angel. Its enormous body slams to the ground, sending Fane sprawling. Roseline regains her footing first and slices at Aiko. Blood gushes from his arm as he retreats, leaping backward over the angel.

Roseline immediately follows, remaining on the attack. Fane kicks out his foot, taking Kuma unaware. With a slash of his mace, he buries the spikes into the samurai's back, downing him with one blow. Kuma's grip on his *katana* slips as he falls face first into the crimson muck.

"Behind you!" Fane shouts as Roseline lunges toward Aiko. She screams as a metal tipped dart slams into her shoulder. Her sword falls from her right hand and she goes down, momentarily disorientated.

Mastus leaps at Fane, his white toga stained with the blood of his friends and family. The Greek screams as Fane locks his hands around Mastus' head and pulls. Fane can feel the flesh of Mastus' neck protesting, then slowly giving way as he yanks the head free.

He tosses it aside as Mastus' body slumps to the ground. Fane turns and feels his heart stop as Mateo crawls atop a pile of bodies and turns, spikes first, and leaps backward toward Roseline. Locked into a fierce battle with Aiko, she can't see the coming attack.

Without thinking, he shoves her aside and grunts as the impact slams him to the ground, crushing him under the weight of the bear-like immortal.

He blinks, fighting to see as suffocating pain debilitates him. The spikes have buried through his back from tailbone to skull. He can't move, can't breathe. All he can do is scream.

Twenty-Eight

Roseline's mind shuts down as she watches Mateo slam into Fane. Her friend's cry of pain wrenches at her heart as she stumbles to her feet. Sounds fade around her until all she can focus on is Fane's muffled cries. They rise higher and higher each time Mateo rocks to free himself.

"You're not going anywhere." She shoves her sword down through his thigh, staking him to the ground. Mateo's wild red eyes meet hers as she grabs her other sword and stakes him through his arm. He growls and snarls like a wild animal but his thrashing eases as rivulets of blood seeps streams down his leg.

She drops to the ground, reaching under Mateo for Fane's hand. His grasp is weak as his eyes clamp tight against the pain. She can hear fluid filling his lungs as he struggles to speak.

"I'm...sorry," he croaks, wincing at the effort it takes for those two words.

"No." Her heart is wedged in her throat as she snuffs back her tears. "I'm sorry. I should have seen him coming."

"Not...your...fault." Fane gasps for breath, wheezing. His eyes are glossed over when he looks at her. He cries out as Mateo lurches to the side. When Mateo falls back, the spikes burrow deeper into Fane's chest.

Tears fall freely down Roseline's cheeks as she grasps his hand in hers. "I'm going to pull him off and then get you some blood."

"No," Fane says hoarsely. "Too...late."

Mateo wrenches again and Roseline rises up to punch him in the face. He growls at her, spittle flying from his mouth as he tries to bite her. This time she makes sure to take a few teeth with her. He subsides, but not without several threats of dismemberment.

She lowers back down and sucks in a breath at how pale Fane is. "Hold on. I'll save you."

Biting into her wrist, she goes deep, making sure to sever an artery. Blood flows freely from her arm as she presses against the ground, inching her arm toward him. "Drink!"

His eyes flicker toward her arm and then shift away. "Kill...me."

"No!" She struggles to lift Mateo's weight so she can get closer to his mouth. The hulking immortal feels unbearably heavy as he flails, beating at her with his sharp nails. She slams her fist into his face and he falls still. When she drops to her knee and tries to reach Fane, he doesn't try to reach for her. She can see sadness in his eyes and realizes that he's saying goodbye, giving her a chance for survival. A healing now would greatly weaken her, but she doesn't care. "I'm not going to lose you!"

"Sword...kill...Mat..." his eyelids flutter closed as blood seeps from the corner of his mouth.

Roseline chokes back her tears as she struggles to reach him. "Fane, please! Answer me!"

He lies still, barely breathing, but he never answers her again. She sobs as she wiggles out from under Mateo. Rage mingles with loss as she rises to her feet. Mateo follows her movements as she shifts to stand between his feet, her hands gripping the hilts of her swords.

Mateo giggles like a mad man, salivating. Roseline's expression grows cold as she wrenches both of her swords from his leg and arm and holds them together over her head. "Goodbye, my dear friend."

She clamps her eyes shut as she slams her swords into Mateo's chest, skewering his heart. She pushes with all her strength until she feels the blades piercing through his back and into Fane. Her hands tremble as she falls back, stumbling to the ground.

She lifts her face to the sky and screams, one long shriek of remorse for Fane.

When Nicolae and Sadie find her, surround by blood and death, her chest rises and falls rapidly. Rage burrows deep into her soul, incinerating what little mercy she might have shown to her enemy.

"Rose?" Sadie whispers, stretching out her hand to touch her friend.

"Don't," Nicolae warns, drawing back her hand. "Let her be."

"But she's nearly catatonic," she protests.

Nicolae pulls her away as Roseline rises. Her aqua eyes are dark and her expression is tight, void of emotion. She slowly shifts her fiery gaze toward Nicolae. "I'm going to need a new weapon."

Roseline spins the battle-ax in her hand, getting the feel of its weight. It is sturdy, forged from Romanian steel. Although it is not as finely crafted as the Brules dagger Nicolae loaned her as a backup, it will certainly do the trick. "Stay here. I don't want either of you getting in my way."

"No way," Sadie protests, pulling against Nicolae's grip. "I'm not letting you go out on a death march with no one watching over you."

"Sadie," Nicolae hisses through his teeth, tugging on her arm.

"It's insane," she continues. "She's completely out of her mind."

"Sadie!" Nicolae shouts.

She turns, her face reddened by blood and gore. It clings to her cheeks, matting down her hair. "What?"

"This is what she is best at. Trust me." Nicolae says, offering Roseline an encouraging smile. "She's going to tear this place apart to get to Lucien."

Roseline doesn't grin nor does she acknowledge his words in the slightest. She just turns and walks away, winding a path through the carnage.

Bodies litter the ground. Some are still moving and moaning while others lie still. Fingers, toes and other various assortments of limbs scatter the ground before her. She doesn't try to step over them. She just stomps forward, her gaze ever alert for Lucien.

The haze has begun to lighten and the sounds of the dying dragon have faded away. *When did it fall?* she wonders but quickly dismisses the thought. It doesn't matter when or how. All that matters is that it won't be throwing any more fireballs at her.

Through the shifting smoke, she can see small battles still raging. The battle is not over, but as far as she can tell, neither side has won. Hundreds lay slain, possibly more. Too many good men and immortals were lost today.

A creature with slimy skin and oil slick black eyes deeply set in its head slithers out and wraps its fingers around her arm. She reacts with hardly a thought, slicing cleanly through its arm. It squeals and retreats back into the smoke to lick its wounds.

A shout from several feet ahead causes her to break into a run. Her feet slosh through the melted snow as she stomps through the inch of blood that coats the ground.

"Get back here," a masculine grunt greets her as she emerges from the smoke to find Grigori locked in fierce battle with Keli. The immortal's pointed teeth have shredded through much of Grigori's right arm, tearing his muscles nearly down to the bone. It hangs by his side, completely useless.

"Grigori, no!"

Her cry comes too late as Keli whips out of Grigori's grasp and tears out his throat in a single bite. Blood sprays in all directions as Keli pulls back with the hunter's flesh dangling from his teeth.

Roseline snarls as she leaps forward and buries her ax deep into Keli's back. With both hands, she wrenches it to the right, severing his spinal cord. She shoves him off her blade and kicks him onto his back.

His eyes are wide and bright with rage. His arms and legs fall to the side, unusable.

"Go on," he croaks, blood seeping from his toothy grin. "Kill me."

She bends now, kneeling with her weight against the butt of the ax. "For the sake of my friend that you just murdered, I'm going to let you live."

Roseline rises, ignoring his pitiful wails as she works to move all bodies away from him. Death would be too easy for him. Now he will suffer, lying paralyzed in the middle of the arctic tundra with no hope of ever getting the blood he needs to regenerate. Revenge is sweet.

Searching through the remains of the two armies, Roseline grows fearful as she reaches the edge of the battlefield. Lucien is nowhere to be seen and neither is Gabriel.

"Lucien," she screams at the top of her lungs, cupping her hands around her mouth. Let him find her. She's itching for a fight.

"Roseline!"

She turns at the sound of the cry. Narrowing her eyes, she sees Claudia sprint through the smoke. The instant she spots Roseline, she swerves and races to her side.

Claudia shows little sign of exhaustion when she comes to a stop before Roseline. Her fair skin is stained red and her clothes are badly shredded. Small wounds line her arms and neck, slowly seeping blood, but for the most part she seems to be fine.

"Have you seen Gabriel?"

"No," Claudia shakes her head. "The main part of Lucien's army has fled to the trees. Theus has followed them, as have the remaining hunters. I believe Costel is leading that group."

"And who remains on the battlefield?" Roseline turns and looks to the horizon. The twilight sun has begun to poke through the layer of cloud. A single plume of smoke rises from the east where Maelstrom is taking his last breath. A wide river of blood flows out before her as far as she can see.

"Where is Fane?"

Roseline turns her face away, shaking her head. Claudia's sigh is heavy, weighted under the unconceivable loss. "I'm sorry," she whispers

Wiping away her tears, Roseline nods. "Where is everyone?"

"Your friends are alive. They are working to round up the survivors as we speak. Our kind will be fine, but I worry about the hunters. We are not prepared to care for so many wounds. Many of them may still die."

Roseline gives Claudia a hard look. "We will not turn any that do not wish it."

"Of course, I just thought…"

"No," Roseline cuts her off. "We owe it to them to give them a choice. Immortality is not something to be chosen lightly."

Claudia's pained smile makes her think of her own transformation. Roseline places a hand on her friend's shoulder. "We weren't given a choice. They deserve better."

"I agree," Claudia nods. "I'll let Nicolae know."

As Claudia jogs back up and over the small rise, Roseline turns her gaze to the trees. There is no sign of movement and no hint of her prey, yet she feels drawn to the forest. Looking back over her shoulder, she knows that she is needed here, but she can't shake the feeling that Gabriel is somewhere out there.

She tightens her grip on her ax and sprints toward the trees, terrified and exhilarated at the same time. With each step she takes, the surer she is that Gabriel waits for her.

Gabriel stops and sniffs the air, checking to make sure he is on the right track. He caught his father's scent not long after he took down the troll. It was faint, but definitely there. He instantly turned and ran back into the woods, away from the battle, away from his friends.

With each slap of his foot against the ice, he knows that he might never see Roseline again. Is she still alive? Does she search for him?

He grits his teeth, increasing his speed as he burrows deeper into the woods. He promised never to leave her side, but loyalty to his sister and desire for revenge drove him to break that oath. Guilt riddles him as he presses on, knowing that if he survives this day and she does not, he will never be able to live with his decision.

Take care of her, he silently whispers in prayer.

He has no idea if there is anyone listening, but if angels and dragons can be real, then why can't God?

A glint of steel flickers before his gaze a split second before he feels blood seeping down his chest. He winces in pain as he turns and stares at his father.

Lucien tsks, shaking his head in mock disappointment. "I would have thought Elias had trained you to expect a trap." He moves forward, surprisingly light on his clawed feet.

Gabriel realizes that his father's arms and legs have doubled in size since he last saw him. Lucien's long hair has begun to fall out of his scalp in large clumps. His lips have smoothed out into long lines and his ears have shrunken back into his head, giving him a more reptilian appearance.

"But then, I wonder if perhaps you were merely thinking about something else. Perhaps a certain someone?" His words come out as a soft hiss as he sways in the tiny clearing. His tail swishes back and forth against the ground, unearthing twigs and fallen pine needles from the snow.

"Leave Roseline out of this," Gabriel roars, reaching for his sheath. He withdraws his sword, its blade igniting the instant it touches the air.

"She was never yours to have. She was meant for me." Lucien's toothy grin stretches wide across his face. Gabriel can hear the scales around his mouth shifting to allow this expression. "I planned this hundreds of years before you were born, and I don't appreciate you messing with my plans."

Gabriel lunges. His sword creates a fiery arc through the air, but Lucien easily sidesteps his advance. "I expected better from you, though. You left her to fend for herself today. That's poor manners, son. Who knows what could have happened to her?"

Gabriel fights back his growing fear. *Does Lucien know something I don't? Is Roseline really gone?*

With a mighty roar, he spins and attacks. Lucien's blade parries with ease, shifting to toss him off balance. He tsks and twirls again, beginning the beautiful dance of dueling swords. For every attack Gabriel makes, Lucien blocks and slips away.

"Stand still and fight me like a man," Gabriel growls.

"Ah," his father raises a finger as he moves around to face Gabriel. "But I am not a man. I never have been."

"Then what are you?"

Gabriel braces for some sort of snide comment, but Lucien surprises him by lowering his sword. "I am the first among the Fallen Ones. The one who was first cast out. Haven't you figured that out by now?"

"Sorry, didn't really care to spend much time thinking about you."

Lucien growls and launches himself at Gabriel. When their blades clang together, tongues of fire drop from Gabriel's sword. "Insolent boy. You are nothing to me. Do you honestly think your foolish little sword can defeat me?"

Gabriel grins. "Actually, I do."

With a mighty shove, he pushes Lucien back and cuts his sword across Lucien's stomach. His father's haughty grin contorts into a grimace as the fire begins to spread. Like a match set to gasoline, it quickly eats away at his clothes.

Lucien stumbles backward, clawing at his chest as the flames rise higher. His screams turn to shrieks as he stares wildly at Gabriel. "What magic is this?"

Gabriel holds his sword aloft. "Only a Holy sword could take down something so wretched."

Lucien wails as he sinks to his knees. The flames lick at his fingers, rising up his arms and around to his shoulders. Gabriel lowers his sword, breathing heavily with the weight of it. Sweat clings to his brow as he watches his father burn. Lucien plummets to the ground, curling into a fetal position. His pulse is frantic as he beats at the spreading flames.

"Gabriel!"

He turns at Roseline's call. "I'm here."

She sprints toward him with a bloodied ax clutched in her hand. She is painted with blood and her leather corset torn in several places. Scrapes and cuts line her bare skin, but she is intact.

"I was so worried." He ignores his father's shrieks as he rushes to meet her, consumed with relief. "I should never have left you."

She races into his arms, crushing her lips against his. Her fingers curl around his shoulders as she molds her body to his. "I never want to let you go again," she breathes.

"Me either." He wraps his arms tightly around her. Gabriel breathes deeply, overlooking the scent of the foul blood that clings to her pores to find the one scent unique only to her. He smiles, pressing his lips to her bare shoulder and Lucien's cries fade away.

She is safe, he repeats over and over again in his mind.

As he pulls back to cup her face, he fears that he might not be able to be the man she needs. She is so strong and independent, but as she rests her head on his chest, he knows that she still wants him, even if she doesn't need him to protect her.

"We did it," he whispers, pressing his lips against her hair.

Exhaustion tugs at him as the weight of what they have endured falls over him. How many of his friends made it? How many of their enemy still live to fight another day?

Roseline leans back to look up into his face, her smile tender and filled with loving promise. She rests her hand over his heart. "I love you."

"No more than I love you." Her smile tugs at his heart. He looks away, staring deep into the forest, lost in thought. Lucien's cries have faded. The scent of burnt flesh stings his nose and throat.

"Are you ok?"

When Gabriel looks back at her, he knows the timing is right. He places his hands on her waist as he smiles down at her. "I know this isn't the most ideal time, and certainly not the best place, but I can't wait any longer. I want you in my life,

Rose. Not just today or tomorrow, but for all of eternity. With Vladimir gone, there is nothing to stop us."

He lifts his hand to cup the back of her neck gently, holding her close. "I pledge my heart, my life, my soul to you on this day and all the days to come. My life, bonded to yours, if you will have me."

Tears escape from her eyes as she nods. "My life, bonded to yours," she repeats.

Rising up onto her tiptoes, Roseline leans in to kiss him. Gabriel pulls her close, encircling her in his embrace. The kiss is gentle and achingly tender. Her tears taste salty against his lips as he pulls away.

"You are so beautiful," he whispers, tucking a strand of hair behind her ear.

"You don't look so bad yourself." She rests her head against his chest as he places a kiss on the crown of his head, praying this moment could last forever.

"There's something I've been meaning to tell you..." he smiles as she lifts her head and steps back. The warmth of her hand against his chest gives him the courage. "From the moment we first met, I—"

His fingers flinch against her waist at a sudden stabbing pain in his chest.

"No!" Roseline's eyes widen in horror as a sword pierces up through the palm of her hand.

Gabriel tries to breathe, to think around the pain, but all he can focus on is Roseline's face twisted with horror. Lucien's peeling face appears over his shoulder. Gabriel can feel the heat of the flames licking at his back. "Next time, make sure I'm dead first," Lucien rasps.

Her shriek fills his mind as his legs give out on him. He tumbles face first to the ground, unable to stop himself. Snow fills his nose and mouth, blocking his airway. He tries to lift his head, but the pain in his chest is excruciating.

"Gabriel!" Roseline's scream sounds far away. A strange cold drapes over his body, chilling him to the bone.

Frantic fingers claw at his arm, wrestling him onto his side. He cries out as the blade shifts in his chest. Roseline swears as she clings to him. Her image is blurry.

"Hold on. I have to pull this out," she says, cupping his face in her hand. "I think he missed your heart."

He tries to brace himself, knowing the pain is about to increase tenfold. He can feel her fingers wind around the hilt. He clamps his eyes shut.

Agony rips through his chest just before a heavy weight crushes him. He can't breathe, can't think as Roseline and Lucien fight for control over the sword. He hears her muffled cry but can't tell if it's in pain or outrage. All he can focus on is the pain as the sword shifts, slicing deeper into his chest.

"Stop. Please!" The pain in unbearable, but not knowing what is happening to Roseline is worse.

They roll off of him and he gasps for breath. His lungs expand but only partially. The need to breathe, to focus on something simple, becomes his only goal as Roseline rolls on top of Lucien, beating at the flames that lick her clothes and hair.

Gabriel blinks and focuses on his father. His scaly exterior has almost burned completely away, leaving bubbling human skin beneath. The scent of charred flesh is nauseating.

"Roseline," he croaks, reaching out his hand. "My sword."

She whirls around, floundering along the ground in search of his sword. The instant her fingers grip the hilt it ignites. Lucien's wild roar is cut off as she spins and shoves the blade deep into his chest.

Roseline spits in his face. "Survive that!"

Gabriel's eyes widen as Lucien erupts into blue flames. His hands claw at the air as his skin begins to melt off his bones. Roseline backs away, dropping the sword to the ground as she rushes to Gabriel's side.

Roseline throws herself over his chest, trying to shield him from the flames as Lucien incinerates. Ash floats into the air as the last of the flame dies out, landing gently atop her hair. Gabriel blinks, staring up into the gray snow. It looks almost beautiful as the cold begins to sweep him away. He falls limp in her arms.

"Gabriel?" Roseline rocks him as his eyes slowly close as the pain begins to spread through his chest. "Gabriel!"

Twenty-Nine

Tears cling to Roseline's lashes, making it hard to see Gabriel clearly as he lies on the ground before her. His skin is pale and cooling to the touch. His lips are painted red with the blood that bubbles from between his lips. The wound in his chest seeps continually around the pressure of her hand.

He stares up at her, his gaze unfocused as he grimaces in pain. Roseline's lower lip trembles as she clings to his wound, desperate to stop the bleeding. She can hear the erratic beating of his heart and knows the sword severed his main arteries. She hangs her head as great sobs wrack her body, shaking her from head to toe.

"I can't lose you," she whimpers, clutching his right hand tightly. She hardly feels the stinging in her own hand as she leans toward him. His grasp is growing weak, far too weak.

"I'm going to save you," she whispers into his ear as she draws her wrist to her mouth. The wound from her earlier bite has already begun to heal. It only takes a small amount of effort to pierce the new flesh.

Holding out her hand to Gabriel's lips, she realizes that he is too weak to drink. It terrifies her to release his hand, but she has no choice. Now that the pressure is off his wound, the blood begins to flow freely from his chest.

She wrings her left hand around her right wrist, squeezing as much blood from her wound as she can. She cries out as it splatters against his nose and cheeks, only managing to get a small portion of it into his mouth.

Roseline holds her wrist only a few inches above his mouth and tries again. Her blood patters against his tongue, sliding down his throat, but he doesn't move.

"No!"

She throws herself upon him, clinging to his shoulders as she presses her ear to his wound, desperate to hear his beating heart. She gasps when she hears something, sure that there is still hope, but she quickly realizes the sound is not coming from him.

Leaning back, she stares blankly into the sky above her as Elias slowly descends. His great form seems to push the forest aside as he lands softly on the crimson snow. Roseline stares at his bronze feet, lit by the golden glow of his wings.

Her stomach rolls with disgust when she realizes Lucien's blood has mingled with Gabriel's on the ground. She starts frantically beating at the snow, desperate to keep Lucien's filth away from him.

"Roseline, it's too late," Elias whispers as he drops to one knee beside her. His hands are warm, nearly scorching against her bare skin.

Tears roll down her cheeks as she stares blurrily up at him. "It should have been me. Not him."

"No, young one. These things came to pass as they were meant to happen."

"But why?" A cry escapes her throat as she clamps her hands over her mouth, only partially aware of how much blood coats her hands. Her own blood mixes with Gabriel's and Lucien's. She feels numb. Grief roots her in place as she stares down at his...at Gabriel. She can't bring herself to say *body*.

"I never saw it coming. Lucien was in flames. He should have been dead. I should have checked, should have made sure..." she trails off as she draws her knees into her chest, beginning to rock.

Elias turns his face to stare at Lucien's remains. Blood and ash pool where the body had been. There is no chance of Lucien returning from the dead this time. He places a comforting hand on Roseline's shoulder. "This is not your fault."

She lifts her face to look at the giant, looking past the blood, sweat and burns to see the grief shining in his eyes. This man loved Gabriel too and intimately understands her loss.

"How can I go on without him? Fane is gone. Grigori fell. And now Gabriel..." she chokes up. Her hair falls in tangled waves about her face as she bows low over Gabriel's body. She places her hand over the wound that took him from her.

Blood seeps from her wrist and onto his chest as she clings to him. Her fingers dig into his sides as she rests her head on his shoulder, wishing that she could feel his arms surround her one last time, to feel his lips pressed against hers or hear him laugh when William cracks another corny joke.

She would give anything to see life in his blue eyes as he swings her around and around and to feel safe and secure in his arms…but that will never happen.

With a cry of outrage, she lurches to her feet and stumbles to a nearby tree. She clenches her hand into fist and slams it into the towering pine. The top of it shakes, swaying wildly as she repeatedly lands blows.

The skin over her knuckles tears and bleeds but still she continues. Her screams send birds flocking to the air and a loud groan echoes through the forest as a large crack forms in the tree, splintering upward. The ground rumbles as the tree rocks and threatens to fall, its roots unearthing beneath her.

"Roseline, stop." Elias grips her shoulders, raising her to her feet. She is limp in his arms, spent of energy and emotion. She watches the tree as it sways precariously, but it doesn't fall.

Her brow furrows and she shakes her head. She yanks out of Elias' grasp and slams her boot into the trunk. That final blow sends the tree crashing to the ground with a resounding thud. Roseline feels a tiny amount of satisfaction as Elias picks her up into her arms and unfolds his wings.

They stretch behind him, dazzling in their brilliance. As they sweep back, Elias crouches and leaps into the sky. Roseline's head rolls on his arm, staring down at Gabriel's body as she rises higher and higher.

He seems so small from up here. She feels completely numb as her eyes roll back into her head and blissful oblivion takes her.

Roseline stares down at the closed casket, knowing that she would like nothing more than to crawl inside with Gabriel. Numbness and bitterness were her companion on the long trip back to Romania. Sadie and William did their best to cheer her up, but she couldn't even bring herself to fake a smile.

Elias has remained by her side the entire time. She finds his presence both comforting and painful. She can feel his guilt and finds comfort in knowing she isn't alone in that sense.

The casket before her is beautiful pewter. It has been hand crafted and inlaid with silver, white gold and platinum. He deserved the best. It was the least she could do.

She lifts her gaze to the stone mausoleum before her, feeling the weight of the aged stone bear down upon her, as if it is slowly crushing her into the ground. Panic seizes her as the instinct to flee threatens to override her will to remain.

As if sensing her rising anxiety, Elias draws her hand into his own, engulfing her in radiant heat. She looks up through her tears to see him offering her a comforting smile. "You can do this."

"I still can't believe he's gone," she whispers, using the back of her hand to wipe her cheek clean. She thinks back to the last words he spoke, so tender and filled with a promise for a future together.

"He pledged himself to me right before he died. Did I tell you that?"

Elias' fingers clamp down around hers. "What did you just say?"

"A pledge. It wasn't anything formal of course, no rings or a lavish ceremony, but he meant it when he said he was bonding his life to mine. I like to think that it was meant for something more than just that one kiss."

His grip lessens but his eyes darken, his face shrouded. She glances up at him, surprised by his silence. "Is everything ok?"

Elias hesitates before nodding. As an afterthought, he plasters on a smile for her benefit and pats the back of her hand. "Yes, everything is just fine."

She frowns at the unusual tremor in his voice but drops her gaze, noticing Sadie standing on the other side of the casket. Her wounds have healed much faster than Nicolae's. He leans heavily upon a crutch, his ankle wrapped tightly in a black cast. The corner of Roseline's lip curls into a hint of a smirk at the thought of Nicolae being foolish enough to take on a full sized troll on his own.

Beside them, William stands with his hands crossed before him, his head bowed in respect. Claudia's hand is wrapped around his arm, a black mourning veil draped over her face.

Many caskets stretch out beyond Gabriel's, memorials of those who were lost. Daelyn, Enoch, Julian, Grigori…the list seems endless right now and the loss far too great to endure.

She turns her head and stares hard at the gold and bronze casket that holds Fane's body. Tears form along her eyelashes as her pain deepens. How can she live after having lost so much? Fane was her first reason to live. Gabriel her final.

Elias releases her hand and sets his arm down upon her shoulder. The tight grip of his hand reminds her that he also lost a dear friend. Although she never met Seneh, Gabriel spoke highly of his guardian angel. Perhaps, together they can figure out a way to carry on.

One by one, her friends say their farewells. Sadie's mascara streaks down her cheeks as she places her hand atop the casket and whispers goodbye. Nicolae gently pulls her away, pausing a moment to look back. William and Claudia follow behind them a short time later.

The hunters linger near the end of the line of coffins, paying their respects to their fallen commander. Roseline closes her eyes against her tears, deeply sorry that Grigori fell. He was a good man, gruff but honorable. He didn't deserve to die.

None of the hunters did.

She steps out of Elias' grasp, raising a rose to her lips. Tears slip down her cheeks and onto her black dress as she kisses the delicate petals. Stretching out her gloved hand, Roseline carefully places the rose atop Gabriel's casket.

"I brought you an orange rose," she smiles, rubbing her hand along the smooth surface. "It's our favorite."

Her shoulders shake as she tries to keep her emotions locked down, desperately fighting to bury them so deep that the numbness will return. She looks up as Costel Petran limps toward her, his arm in a sling and his left leg encased in a brace. Bandages wrap around his head, concealing one ear. His split lip curls into a smile as he approaches.

"I have never been much for apologies or admitting that I am wrong, but there is always a first for everything." His one good hand stretches out to grasp hers.

"I didn't know Gabriel, but I'm smart enough to know that he saved us all." He pauses to look down at the orange rose. "When you are ready, I'd like to call a meeting to draw up the official peace treaty."

Roseline blinks back her tears as she gives him a firm handshake. "I'd like that very much."

He nods and limps away, leaning heavily on the arm of Marcus Talbot, who managed to survive much of the war miraculously unscathed. Roseline watches as a large group of hunters follows behind, many of them dipping their heads with respect as they pass.

"I don't believe it," she whispers. She turns to look at Gabriel's casket and allows herself a small smile. "You did it."

"No," Elias says, pulling her along with him as he heads back up toward the castle. Stars have already begun to twinkle in the sky. The torches that line the path to Bran Castle create a pleasant glow on the ornamental gardens as they pass. "We all did."

THE END

Epilogue

The subtle rustle of feathers is the only betrayal of Elias' discomfort. He has sat, perched atop the opulent mausoleum, for many hours. Mists cling to the ground as pinpricks of dawn's first light appear on the horizon. The air is cool and damp, hinting at the coming arrival of spring.

His breath hangs in the air before him as he sighs. It is nearly time.

Pale pink and lavender begin to splash across the sky. Elias rises and stretches his arms wide as his wings unfurl. Their golden glow is subtle compared to the glorious sunrise before him.

Bending at the knee, Elias leaps off the roof. His sandals sink into the moist ground as he lands without a sound. Gravestones rise before him like crooked teeth, chipped with age. Moss and mud clings to the weathered stone. Impressions of footprints remain in the ground from the funeral several days before.

This cemetery rests on the opulent grounds of Bran Castle. From here, he can see soot from the fires that spread along the castle walls during the siege a couple weeks before. The entrance remains exposed to the public, but no one has been brave enough to cross its threshold.

Elias folds his wings behind his back as he turns to face the arched wooden door of the Enescue Mausoleum. The carving is intricate, scrolled by a master artist's hand. The walls are made of long, rectangular stones, each offset from the row below. Two white stone pillars frame the door, tapering slightly near the ceiling of the roof's awning.

Elias pushes open the door. It creaks on its hinges as it swings inward, the sound echoing in the narrow room beyond. It is only about twenty paces deep and ten across, small considering the amount of immortals who have fallen over the past few hundred years, but then again, only a few of their bodies remained intact for burial.

As he steps inside, his wings brush against the doorframe. Names have been etched onto the wall, some harder to read than others. Dates detail the lives of ancestors long since buried. The air is heavier within the stone tomb. Dust particles rise into the light, filtering through the small rectangular windows that encircle the room as Elias moves forward.

He passes through the center of the room and heads toward the back wall. Roseline's former husband, Vladimir is missing from the vault. Elias pauses to wonder what happened to his body as the angle traces his fingers across each name on the wall until he finds the one he is looking for. Drawing back his hand, he curls his fingers into a fist and slams through the wall.

Stone crumbles around his arm, pattering against the floor. He withdraws his hand and peers into the tomb's depths. He smiles as he spies a silver handle. Thrusting both hands through, he grasps onto the casket and yanks it from the wall.

Elias turns his face away from the explosion of stone. Small pebbles pelt against his bare chest before clattering to the floor. As the dust begins to settle, he reaches across the casket and grabs the metal handle, gently easing it to the floor.

The exterior is pewter in color, with silver hinges. The once smooth surface has been marred by Elias' plunder. He lowers his head, closing his eyes against the memory of Gabriel's death. He will never forgive himself for not being there to aid Gabriel in his battle with Lucien, but Elias has always known that Gabriel's fate was never in his hands.

Roseline's profession of their shared love bond had shocked him into silence at the funeral. He dared to hope as he pried into the details of that tender moment out of Roseline over the days following Gabriel's death. Elias has no doubt that his sudden departure after the funeral had caused her pain, but he had to make sure his suspicions were true. Dipping low, Elias raises the lid of the coffin.

"Only family blood can heal all wounds," he mutters as he smiles down at the boy he was charged to protect, certain that Roseline had no idea that her tender farewell had brought about Gabriel's salvation.

No hint of death clings to him now. His wounds are healed and his skin is flushed with color. The faint fluttering of a heartbeat rises from his chest.

Elias leans over and whispers into the boy's ear. "She is waiting for you."

Gabriel's eyes flutter open.

ABOUT THE AUTHOR

Amy Miles was born and raised in a military family but has now settled with her husband and son in South Carolina. She is also the author of Defiance Rising, Forbidden, Reckoning and Redemption. To learn more about her and her books, visit AmyMilesBooks.com or @AmyMilesBooks on Twitter.

ALSO BY AMY MILES
DEFIANCE RISING
An excerpt

<u>One</u>

I've been told that this world used to be a beautiful place, filled with twinkling electric lights and tables overflowing with food. A place where children played in parks and couples took leisurely strolls on Sunday. A time when humans weren't slaves to aliens or nature. Staring out over the concrete graveyard before me, I find that hard to imagine.

I have no idea what the name used to be for this place. It has been lost to the past, like so many things. Now, my friends and I call it what it is——the City.

All that remains of my parent's Earth are cracked sidewalks with grass and weeds growing up through the pavement. A maze of rusted cars and twisted lampposts scattered along each street create a web of devastation. Tarnished coins and glass shards form a glittering river winding through the City. In the distance, I spy broken skyscrapers rising from the ruins at jagged angles, symbols of a life long forgotten.

This is where the Caldonians live, where the Sky Ships land each night after scouring the woods for us. No one knows how many of them there are. I think my friends are too afraid to find out. If I were honest, I'd admit to being nervous as well.

My concern has swelled over the past couple weeks. That's when the tremors began. My friends say it's nothing, but I know whatever is causing the tremors is something important. I can feel it in my gut, and I'm hardly ever wrong.

After my mother died in a raid six months back, my friends and I were left in charge of the commune. There are a couple of the elders who remain but are too crippled to help maintain the rebellion. The children had to be protected, so we became the leaders.

Toren was the obvious choice as the head of our group and has risen as a natural leader. I can't say that I like taking orders from him, although I think he actually despises giving them more, knowing that I will disobey.

His girlfriend, Aminah, is my friend. Her sweet nature and mothering heart is a beacon of hope to the children of our group. She broke through my rough exterior when we were kids and, despite our many differences, still finds a way through my defenses.

Eamon is my closest friend and is notably the best hunter of our group, apart from me. Since the time I could hold a stick, we've been sparring. What once started as pretend stick sword fights led us to spear tossing, knife throwing and hand-to-hand combat. He is always at my side, watchful and quick to administer a reprimand if he sees fit. Eamon thinks I'm reckless, but I think adventurous suits me better.

Zahra is the last of our group and is as vain as she is obnoxious. We've been butting heads for as long as I can remember. It's not my fault Eamon is my best friend or that he hardly pays Zahra mind when I'm around.

Standing here, overlooking the City, I think of my friends, each one as dear to me as my own blood family. As a tremor ripples up through the soles of my boots, I know that I have to enter the City this time.

Clutching the strap of my canvas satchel against my chest, I rise from a crouch. "You can do this," I whisper, steeling myself.

I've been here several times over the past week, on this ledge, with fear wedged so tightly in my throat that I wonder if I'll be able to snatch my next breath. My fear is irrational but that never stops me from doubling over with crippling nausea.

It's not like I can't take care of myself. I'm stealthy enough to avoid Caldonian detection. I'm skilled enough to fight off any scavengers that might cross my path, but each time I come to this very spot, my pulse begins to thump out a cadence in my ears. My palms slicken with sweat and the pit of my stomach coils uncomfortably. The sense that I'm doing the right thing is evenly paralleled by trepidation.

"Don't chicken out this time." Pinpricks of pain shoot up my legs as I stretch up onto my toes, working out the kinks in my lower back. I've lingered too long on the ridge. Night will be upon me soon and I must seek shelter.

The Sky Ships come at dusk and dawn, like winged scavengers seeking yet another carcass to consume. Being caught out in the open is suicide.

When I was younger, the black ships would send me running for my mother's arms. I've never known a life without Caldonian oppression. My pathetic version of freedom has been paid for with gallons of spilled blood.

My parents chose to be part of the rebellion. I was born into it. Aminah and Zahra were never cut out for this life, so it was up to Toren, Eamon and I to learn how to hunt for food, set traps and scour the woods for salvageable ammo.

Eamon has an affinity for spears. He likes the feel of the smooth wood grain between his fingers just before he strikes. I'm the opposite. I prefer the rigidity of a blade—serrated and lethal.

I stomp my right foot and wait for feeling to fully return. I can't take any chances. I must be on top form when I enter these desolate streets.

The far horizon glows with beautiful shades of lavender and pale rose as I leap down the hill, riding the loose dirt like a surfer. A cloud of dust rises from the soil, clinging to my black shirt and pants. I dig the heels of my boots into the slope to slow my wild descent.

My arms pinwheel, compensating for the uneven terrain as I jump and land on a hard, unforgiving surface. Pain reverberates up through my legs and spine, but I ignore it as I stare wide-eyed around me. I can't believe I'm actually here.

I dip low and brush my fingertips across the rough ground and a word surfaces in my mind—sidewalk. I can't but wonder what the people here were like, when they didn't need to fear death or certain capture. Did someone fall in love in this spot? Did a little boy chase after a runaway dog? Did a mother soothe her crying baby on the rusted wrought iron bench nearby?

I close my eyes and smile at the uneven texture of the path, storing this detail for later consideration. It's so unlike the smooth stone of the caves where my friends and I live. I prefer this rough surface.

Debris litters the street before me. Brick rubble tumbles over from a squat one-story building on the corner. Crumpled plastic chairs and disfigured metals tables spill forth from various storefronts. Brittle autumn leaves spiral down the deserted sidewalk, a reminder as bitter as the harsh winds that whip against my face, chafing my cheeks.

I try not to think about how angry Toren will be when he finds out I've come here, or how disappointed Aminah will be when she discovers that I'm going to miss my surprise birthday party tonight. She should have known better than to entrust Zahra with that secret.

Eamon will take my coming here the hardest. There have never been secrets between us so this betrayal will cut deep. I didn't really have a choice, though. He would never have approved such a rash decision, but the tremors are increasing and I must know what is causing them.

I crouch low and race across the street, dropping down behind a partially melted car. Its shape is odd, as if the metal were heated then dripped over the side. It reminds me of a picture of a melted clock painting from one of the few books salvaged during the Assault. My mother's passion for art was one of the few things she and I shared. It never failed to draw me into her long forgotten world.

Peering over the hood of the car, I search the path ahead for any sign of life. Rumors claim that scavengers still dare to enter the City. Considering that I'm one tonight, I find this rumor to be dangerously plausible, but it's not *them* that I fear. Scavengers fight out of desperation, but the Caldonians fight on a completely different level.

The aliens look just like humans——two arms and legs, intelligent minds and oxygen rich lungs. They are beautiful in the most raw, elemental way possible. Their eyes are not confined to the limitations of blues, greens and browns like human eyes. They dip into rainbows of purples, oranges, reds and even some colors I struggle to place.

I squint up into the fading light as my fingers grip tightly around my pistol. It's loaded with a round in the chamber, ready for whatever might lurk in the shadows. My right pocket holds the spare magazine I managed to scavenge after the last raid, not enough to hold off a group of aliens but enough to create a diversion and run like heck back into the woods.

A pair of knives clings to my back, tucked into the braided rope around my waist. I like to keep them near just in case things get personal.

It is eerily silent as I push off from the car and skirt along a partially crumbled building. Some of the brick wall still stands. In parts, it rises well above my head. I can imagine there must have been another level above the ground floor but one glance through the window frame reveals only remnants of an upper floor. The back of the building is gone, blasted out during the Assault, the first and only day of the invasion.

I hold my handgun out before me as my boots crunch over an endless sea of glass shards. As far as I can see, only vacant windowpanes remain. I pull away from the wall to stare at a small reflective sliver, wedged into a twisted metal frame of what appears to have been a bookstore.

Rising onto my tiptoes, I peek through. Leaves and dirt clutter the floor. Small corners of yellowed paper flutter in the wind, the corners trapped under broken mahogany bookcases. Much of the interior of the building is stripped away. A large, charred circle near the center gives evidence to a fire, mostly likely from a scavenger holed up for the night.

Craning my neck, I peer up through the roofless building. Whoever lit that fire must've been desperate. A fire would've been easily spotted from above. Sinking back onto my heels, I can't help but wonder what happened to the former resident, but a reflection of myself tugs my curiosity in a new direction.

One violet eye blinks back at me, its lashes long and full. I pull back further to note the fullness of my lower lip and the small smattering of freckles that cross the bridge of my straight nose. Hunching over, I catch a glimpse of the wild mane of blonde hair whipping about my shoulders.

It has been a long time since I've seen myself. Our commune used to have a small hand mirror to share among everyone, but it was broken during a spat between Zahra and a younger girl who suffered from a serious case of "Eamonitis." Their ongoing feud to capture my best friend's heart started several years ago when he hit puberty and quickly topped the "most eligible guy" list.

Staring at myself now, I can see the subtle changes that have come with age. The image before me reveals a young woman instead of the adolescent girl I last saw. My pistol grazes my cheek as I push my unruly hair behind my ear and turn to observe my profile.

"You gonna stare at yourself all night, Princess?"

I whip around and take aim at the dark figure half a block behind me, leaning against the back end of a silver car. Judging by his height and build, I'd say he's about my age, give or take a few months. Two arms rise toward the sky. "I'm unarmed!"

With him in my sights, I approach slowly, waiting for a sound of ambush. I don't want to fire off a shot for fear of drawing attention to myself, but surely this guy isn't alone. "Who are you?"

"The name's Bastien."

"You got a last name, Bastien?" I creep closer. My pulse tap-dances in my ears as I pause less than ten feet from him. I clench my fingers around the gun as I try to ignore the sweat gathering along my neck. Adrenaline pumps through my veins, making me alert.

I take several deep breaths as I plot out my next move, as if this is a hunt and I'm staring down my dinner. What does he want? Is he a scavenger or one of the human traitors who collects women to sell to the Caldonians?

"Adair. It's Scottish." He cocks his head to the side. "Guess that little tidbit doesn't really matter when you've got a gun aimed at your head."

"Your heart, actually." My finger hovers over the trigger as I scan the guy standing before me.

Shoulder length raven-black hair tosses about in the wind, thrashing against his angular face. His chest and shoulders are broad, tapering down to a well-defined abdomen, although the exact contour is hard to determine hidden beneath a woolen sweater.

His raised hands are encased in threadbare gloves. Some of the wool fingers are missing, with frayed bits of yarn poking out. His jeans are stained and faded, patched with poorly stitched bits of random cloth. Light stubble clings to his chin and jawline, enhancing his rugged good looks with annoying perfection.

I notice all of this with a simple glance before meeting his curious gaze. Vivid blue eyes with pupils ringed in gold betray intelligence and, if I'm not mistaken, a hint of humor too.

"Something funny?" I ask through gritted teeth.

"Well, that depends." A ghost of a smile stretches across his face.

"On?" I adjust the gun in my hand. Although he doesn't move or show any signs of hostility, I find myself deeply unsettled by him.

"On whether you think your little toy pistol can beat my shotgun." He slides his arm down from the trunk of the silver car, revealing a sawed off shotgun. I silently berate myself for letting him get the better of me, although his concealed weapon doesn't come as a huge surprise. More of an annoyance. I don't like losing the upper hand.

"A bit old school, don't you think?" I smirk, not letting my gun drop a millimeter. "Now what do we do?"

Bastien's gaze rises to the sky. The final wisps of pastel blue and lavender begin to fade into black. "I'm going to invite you back to my place. I know it's a bit forward, but I'd rather carry on this delightful chat inside."

I drop my gaze to his hands, noting the sure steadiness of them. My mind screams for me to take my chances but my gut tells me that he's more than willing to pull that trigger. This won't end well for me.

"Fine." I dip my head in agreement, knowing that time is running short. Already I can hear the whirl of the Sky Ship's engines as it takes off. "Drop yours first."

The rising winds whip Bastien's hair about his face, obscuring his features, but his eyes remain locked on me. "You're insane! You really want to do this now?"

I twist my head just enough to hear the hum of an engine approaching from down the street. I chew on my lip, knowing I have two choices: trust this complete stranger or take on a Sky Ship with just a handful of bullets. It's not a hard choice.

"Lead the way." I lower my weapon but my finger remains on the trigger as he cocks the shotgun over his shoulder. Without another word, he turns and dashes across the street, weaving in and out of the abandoned cars.

I try to keep up with his fast pace, reminding myself to breathe as the winds funnel harder down the street. The Sky Ship is nearly on top of us.

"How far?" I glance back over my shoulder to find the tip of a black wing appearing over the edge of a building two blocks away. A hand grasps my forearm and pulls me through a dark opening in the wall. I stumble forward out of Bastien's grasp, fighting to remain upright as I falter down a steep set of stairs.

Metal clanging overhead alerts me to his location. I wait, gasping for breath as the walls rumble around me. The Sky Ship must be directly above us now. I press back against the wall, clutching my gun to my chest as I lift prayers for safety heavenward.

I jerk my pistol up to eye level as a light flares in the dark. Bastien shields his eyes with his arm and rears back. "Don't go shooting that thing in here! It'll kill us both!"

I drop the gun, squinting up into the light. It doesn't flicker like a fire. Its core is pure white instead of vivid blue or orange. Metal encases the cylindrical object, scratched and worn but showing little sign of rust. "What is that thing?"

"A flashlight."

I roll the word around on my tongue. "Never heard of it."

He shoots me a scathing look. "I wouldn't expect a tree hugger like you would have."

My brow furrows and I'm sure he's just insulted me in some way. Bastien slowly steps down the narrow staircase. As the light broadens around me, I begin to notice the dingy cement walls, lined with posters and advertisements. "Where are we?"

"It used to be a subway." He pauses beside me, waiting for some sign of recognition. This time I nod in understanding.

"My mother told me about these. Long, winding tunnels underground that would shuttle people from one end of the City to the next."

"That's the basic idea of it, yeah." Bastien waits for me before descending the final steps. "This is the safest place to be during a raid. I found this entrance a couple months back and haven't been bothered once." His arm brushes against mine as he squeezes past through the narrow doorway. I follow his lead deeper underground, passing silently by aged wooden benches and an empty enclosed booth with the picture of the subway on the side. The further we go, the quieter the hum of the Sky Ship becomes.

I stay close as we leap down onto the track and wind through the deserted tunnel. The air is thick down here, different from the caves. It feels weighty, filthy.

"This way." He flashes his light onto the track ahead and I see a glint of white and red.

"What is that thing?" I ask, as we approach the large metal object filling the tunnel.

"It's an old subway car." Bastien reaches up and cranks the metal handle on the door. I hesitate as he offers me a hand up. His smirk widens. "It's rude to refuse the aid of a gentleman, you know."

"Who said you were a gentleman?"

He stares pointedly at his hand, wiggling his fingers. "Don't leave me hanging here."

I swallow my trepidation and place my hand in his. The scratchy feel of his wool glove lingers long after he releases my hand.

Coming 2014
Netherworld
Book I of the Hallowed Realms Trilogy

The dead shadow my steps, beckoned by my call. It is my curse, my destiny.

I am a Banshee, a slave to the dying.

Aed, god of the Netherworld, has chosen me as his bride, but my heart belongs to another - a mortal whose eyes pierce the veil between our worlds. Our love is forbidden among the Hallowed Realms.

With Aed, I'd be free of my curse but bound to the Netherworld for all eternity. With Devlin, I'd risk his life if my betrothed discovered my betrayal. Can I accept my fate at Aed's side or risk everything for love?